ALMOST TRAGIC

WEST CREEK RANCH
BOOK 3

SAGE EVANS

Names: Evans, Sage, author. Title: Almost tragic / Sage Evans.

Description: Identifiers: Subjects:

[Colorado] : Everaye Press, [2023] | Series: West Creek Ranch ; book 3. ISBN: 979-8-9883281-7-9 (paperback) | 979-8-9883281-6-2 (ebook)

LCSH: Romance fiction, American. | Legacies--West (U.S.)--Fiction. | Revenge--West (U.S.)-- Fiction. | Vendetta--West (U.S.)--Fiction. | Ex-convicts--West (U.S.)--Fiction. | Family secrets-- West (U.S.)--Fiction. | Families--West (U.S.)--Fiction. | Ranches--West (U.S.)--Fiction. | Gold mines and mining--West (U.S.)--Fiction. | Fathers and daughters--Fiction. | Brothers--Fiction. | Cowboys--Fiction. | Western stories. | LCGFT: Romance fiction. | Western fiction.

Classification: LCC: PS3605.V3764 A46 2023 | DDC: 813/.6--dc23

To anyone who's ever thought they knew what was going on only to later realize they were mostly clueless. For every day that seems predictable but turns out completely different, and for last conversations that will never happen but you wish could.

Truly this book is in memory of my father-in-law, who passed away while I was working on it. He read my writing and teased me about the scenes that were too flowery for his taste, sending me hilarious memes and fun commentary. He lived modestly and loved with quiet assurance, letting you know he meant it.

There's a plaque on the wall in his ranch house of a John Gray quote: "Success lies in doing not what others consider to be great, but what you consider to be right." He lived what he believed. We miss him so much.

CHAPTER 1

MAX

I'M ABOUT to turn out of the courthouse parking lot when my brother Carter pulls in, coming toward us. He stops his white Ford beside mine and motions for me to roll the window down.

It's like he wants to argue publicly and get us both arrested.

A dull anger grows at the base of my skull and pounds furiously through my veins. I don't want to fight with him or upset Ellen beside me in the truck. His wife just walked on arson charges, and I'm not sure if Carter is involved, too, but what I do know is that my brother burned down Ellen's house 18 months ago, and I ran through it while it was on fire before finding her outside, injured in a ditch. The day is forever burned in my brain.

Carter raises his hand and makes a "C," curling his thumb and index finger, a code for me alone. It's been ours since childhood, a reminder that we're Corbetts and brothers on the same team. Neither of us has done it for a decade, yet he's trying to remind me of how close we once were, like he still remembers.

The expression on his face is a mixture of anger, confusion, and defeat—I feel sorry for him as much as I hate that I still feel anything for him at all.

I draw an enormous breath and turn to Ellen.

She makes a spinning motion with one hand, like rolling the window down. "If you don't talk to him, you'll spend all day wondering what he was going to say." Her tone is more light-hearted than the moment. Since we met, she's been this grounding force in my life, with her soft syllables and never-ending patience.

"Go on," she prods.

I jab a finger into the window switch, wait for the glass to slide down, and say, "What?"

"I'm trying to have a normal conversation, and you keep giving me these one-word answers," he says.

I match his tone, controlled and dangerous. "You want me to let you move back in at the ranch, retake your old position as farm foreman, and toss out the guy I've been trusting to do the job. Well, I'm not going to do it just because you paid someone off to get the case dismissed."

He snorts.

"Is that it?" I ask.

"That's not what happened."

"Regardless, the sheriff's incompetence doesn't change anything."

"So you're not going to listen to me."

"I'm listening."

"You're not." He scrapes a hand across the air between us. "What is the matter with you?"

"What's the matter with *you*?" I shoot back.

"Max, listen to me, okay? My wife didn't light anything on fire."

"I've listened."

"But my word doesn't change anything." Bitterness makes his voice come out as a low growl.

"After what you did to Ellen, I need facts."

"So that's it?"

"What else is there?"

"I guess that's it." He rolls up the window and continues past. His truck moves at a crawl.

I ease my grip on the steering wheel and breathe as I drive away from downtown toward side roads, skirting the highway.

Ellen needs to get back to her bakery, and I need to get to the ranch and move cows before the forecasted storm arrives, but I want to talk to her before her customers and employees surround us.

She reaches across the cab and rests her hand on my bicep.

I catch her gaze and attempt a smile.

A passing truck honks. One of the homesteaders my grandparents helped settle here. If it weren't for their homestead program, I wouldn't be in this mess with Carter, but I wouldn't have ever met Ellen either.

I lift two fingers from the wheel in acknowledgment and exhale deeply. *What do we do now?*

She came here as part of my grandparents' program, attempting to reset her life because she read their newspaper and believed their promises of this being a place to find a self-reliant lifestyle. She wanted to learn enough to return home and face her dad, and she had no idea the newspaper lying on his coffee table was there because he'd been attempting to ruin us, steal our land, and mine it for gold.

I drive the icy roads and finally turn to Ellen. "I'm so sorry, Flynn."

"It's not your fault." She smiles back at my use of her middle name, but it's bittersweet. She's pulled her dark-brown hair into a bun since we've been in the truck—her usual stressed-out habit —likely because of the trial or maybe because her dad collapsed at a board meeting yesterday. She hasn't called him to find out if he's actually sick or if it's just another speculator trying to drive his stock price down. There's so much going on that it's hard to focus.

All I want is the woman I love and some certainty that I'm doing the right thing by my brother.

He says his wife didn't start the fires, but Carter was apoplectic that our grandparents sold parcels of land to participants in their quirky homesteading program. He was furious that Nonna sold our ancestor's original homestead to Ellen, and to prove it he burned down the home Ellen had rightfully purchased. He didn't know her, but she wouldn't let him bully her into leaving. She might regret spraying him in the face with bear spray, but he shoved her into a ditch, and I didn't get there in time to stop my brother before he did it.

But what if Carter *is* innocent of setting these fires? If Christa didn't start them either? Her sunglasses being found near the scene of one of the fires seems circumstantial at best, but if her journal shows she'd been planning the arsons . . . I don't know. Writing in a journal is often freewheeling. I've written many things I never intended anyone else to see. But if she didn't start them, who did? Could they have hired someone to help?

This coil of thought has me twisted up inside.

Familiar ulcer pain blooms in my ribcage. I rub the heel of my hand where my chest aches.

Ellen presses her warm palm against my forearm. "You okay?"

"Yeah."

"Max." She raises her eyebrows.

I pull to the shoulder and throw the truck in park. "I'm fine. I don't want you to worry. I'll handle Carter, and we'll work it all out so you don't have to be afraid or uncomfortable."

She grabs my hand and gives me a sweet look.

The little things she does make me instantly lose track of the mess in my mind, letting the tension drop out of my neck and shoulders.

The first time we met, her hair was windswept and wild. She wore pale blue shorts and a Walt Whitman t-shirt and was on the side of the road with a flat tire on her Subaru in the middle of nowhere with no phone service. She was so determined to change it herself, so stubborn and fierce. It was almost hilarious, drawing an unrestrained desire to smile at her. I didn't know why she had come to Wyoming, but I knew we fundamentally understood each other.

But how long will she want to keep me around while I'm trying to give Carter a chance? Worry is barely perceptible under the surface of her expression, tightness around her pink lips, and a slightly wrinkled brow. She blinks at me, long lashes fluttering against her cheeks as she waits for me to come down from a stress high.

I wish this weren't our situation, but I can't have that less complicated history and still have Ellen. I relax into the quiet of the truck, the comfort of knowing she chose to start dating me despite knowing I'm conflicted about my brother.

"Can we work it out as a team?" she asks.

I exhale. "Sure, but I don't think this changes anything."

She sets her jaw and then tilts her head toward the window. "But you believe your grandmother's decision to cut Carter out of her will was because of the fires, particularly what Carter did to me. If there's no trial, how can you ever move forward?"

"I don't know. Nonna died before she knew Carter was going to be arrested. She didn't fully know what was going on, and I may not ever have enough information to know for sure either." I temper my words and tone because she doesn't deserve any of my angst. "But we can guess what happened and move forward. We're better off making the safe choice even if it's wrong."

"But he accepted the plea instead of forcing me to testify against him." She waits for me to counter that fact.

He spent four months in jail and is on probation for what he did to Ellen, but he initially lied about it. He might be lying again.

Carter has a temper that rivals mine, but he's a good dad to his son, and he's not a liar. Or . . . he didn't used to be, but he lied about what he did to Ellen until he couldn't get away with it anymore, and he lied to save me from going to jail all those years ago.

Old guilt tugs at me because everything seems to be blamed on Carter, even things I did in the past. Most people still blame him for putting the drunk driver who killed our parents in a wheelchair when I was 18 and he was 21. In reality, Carter took the blame for what I'd done back when we used to rely on each other.

All Carter has is the small parcel of land where he's been living with his wife and son. The ranch was supposed to be his as much as mine. I have 280,000 acres, and he has under 1,000. But he's been a prick to Ellen since the day they met. What he did was unforgivable, and yet Ellen wants to forgive him because it will take a little stress off my shoulders.

"No one believes Christa did this," she says adamantly, but Ellen doesn't know Carter's wife. They've never said a word to each other. Not that Christa is a bad person. I actually love my sister-in-law, maybe more than I love my brother as of late. She's a good mom to my seven-year-old nephew.

But that feeling isn't enough. This is what small-town gossip does. People become judge and jury on emotion alone.

"You don't think she did it either," Ellen says, poking me with the truth.

"Everyone thinks Carter is an arsonist," I manage to grit out despite the knot in my throat. So did I at first. After listening to his constant denials and seeing what he's let Christa suffer through, I'm unsure what to think.

"Can you let me have a say about what we do?" she asks, still giving me an intense look.

"Of course." I lean across the console and nuzzle her,

inhaling her amber-scented shampoo. She wraps her fingers into the hair at my neck, her touch sending little sparks of pleasure over me.

"I know this is hard for you but trust me to look out for what I want."

"Sure. Okay." It's more complicated than it sounds though. She's always offering to take things on, assuming some of my burden as if it's hers. I hold her closer because I have to prove she's still here and not some too-good-to-be-true fantasy I've been imagining.

She presses me away with both hands and readjusts in her seat. Seriousness straightens her brow and squares her shoulders.

She says, "It's the same thing you want me to do regarding your dealings with my father."

And he's such a pain in the ass, but I love her so goddamn much. She came here trying to get away from him. I don't mind that he's tormenting me, and I can try to forget how much he hates my family. I'd attempt to forget how to think at all if it meant making Ellen happy. Will I ever have my life together enough to give her the ring I bought?

I meet her hazel eyes. "You know how much I love you?"

Her voice carries all the humor of her sexiest smirk. "Definitely."

"Good, because you're seriously sexy when you look at me like that." I give her my best smile.

Her pink tongue darts out to lick her bottom lip as her attention slides over me, then her fingers leave mine and dip between the buttons on my shirt, landing on my undershirt and teasing the muscles below before settling on my belt buckle.

"Since we were in bed this morning, I've wanted to rub myself all over you . . . your abs . . ."

A gritty groan escapes my throat. I shift down in the driver's seat and give her all the permission in the world. If she's into it, I'll follow her to hell and back.

She's stopped moving and is staring out at the mostly deserted road with cars passing on occasion.

"You're not in favor of getting caught by a van full of your bakery customers?" I ask.

Her eyes sparkle. "And you don't mind that?"

I reach over and pull her in so I can drag my lips over her neck to her ear. "I was thinking how gorgeous you'd look when you're saying my name."

She draws back and smiles at me. "You are so cocky."

"Confidence comes with experience," I reply, smug.

"When you get home tonight, we'll see who's saying whose name first."

"Sounds like a reason to get home early," I admit.

Our eyes lock, and I swear she sees all my torments and mends them.

I wrap my hand into silky skin behind her neck, brushing the fine hairs that she hasn't quite tamed into a bun. She gives me a cute little grin just like the one she gave me while she was tousled and relaxed waking up this morning. Her eyes lit up as soon as she saw me. I move toward her, kissing her gently on the lips. She opens her wickedly sensual mouth as she brings her fingers to my jaw, drawing my tongue in with soft, teasing strokes.

My large hand cups her cheek. My calloused palm is warm against her soft skin.

It's the moment we break away, the trust in her eyes and her small breathless whisper, that sends my heart into my throat.

She's been trusting me to figure this out with my brother, and I need to get it done.

I pull back onto the road and hold her hand, never wanting to lose her. We finally arrive at her bakery. The warmth of ovens running since before dawn makes the space a haven—the only place I want to linger daily. I'd be here every morning if I didn't have so much other stuff to do at the ranch.

She gets to work behind the counter, setting up to help the

morning crowd: the guys from the bank next door, friends, my favorite librarian, mothers with kids, a few new faces, and the reverend from the Baptist church. Her employees take orders to move customers out the door. One of her dad's security staff sits at a back table in a navy-blue suit—a blond guy she's known for years. He showed up a couple of days ago. I tried to say hello, but he never talked. He doesn't even order anything. He sits at the same table, frowning while he stares at his phone. Spying, I guess.

I wish her dad would just let us be.

Of course, he won't do that though. Ellen's living here with me instead of returning to New York like he wants her to. I'm standing in the way of expanding the mines he operates on our property. He's hated our family for decades because of whatever Pops got mixed up with on an oil shale contract years ago. He harassed Nonna, trying to drive her into her grave with his attempts to bankrupt us. And here I am, living with his daughter.

My attempts to win him over worm through my mind. Trying to explain how much I love Ellen to a man who sees me as useless has been futile. Her father's words echo in my mind: "You'll wish you never met my daughter."

Good luck asking if it's okay to marry her.

Rubbing my neck, I avoid looking at the guy while trying to forget Ellen's dad and the mess he's forcing me into. Instead, I stare through the display glass at Ellen's coffee cakes, Danish rings, Bundt cakes, and croissants, perfect on matching lined pans.

Maybe all I want is her and some simplicity. To get married, flip them all the bird, stop caring about the mess, and live our lives. A smile builds inside me. Ellen's smiling back.

My coat and chinks are stiff as cardboard and combine to chafe the skin below my wool sweater, undershirt, and jeans. I'm ready to change out of my wet clothes and get into town so I can be inside with Ellen before the fluffy flakes turn into tiny icicles.

Unfortunately, one of the guys got his ATV stuck in a snow-covered ditch about four miles from anywhere. He's young, maybe 20, and hasn't yet gotten the hang of horses or ATVs apparently, but he works hard and hasn't complained about anything.

Listening to him pontificate about how he might convince a girl he met on a dating app to move out here from Florida has been a half-decent distraction from the melted snow threatening to freeze me solid.

"She'll get here and fall in love with me instead," says Crick Davis, the 17-year-old son of our farm foreman, from his seat on the other guy's ATV. He's thin with a lanky build, light blond hair, and a boyish mustache.

"Your ass," says Del, the beefy ranch hand he's tormenting. He gives the ATV's back end a hearty shove, but it doesn't budge.

I jump into the snowy ditch, taking the other side and helping him push. We rock the machine forward a couple of feet without freeing it.

Crick swivels to face us, talking, "She'll get here and decide I'm irresistible. A good Samaritan, responsible for keeping women away from cowboys who can't ride horses."

"Butthole," Del mutters.

Crick gives him a grin then turns to face forward and gooses the engine. The front end comes off the ground, almost sending him over on top of us along with the ATV.

We scramble up the ditch, and I grab the brush guard, lowering the tires back to the ground.

"Holy bucket," Del says, giving Crick a shove.

Finally fed up, I say, "You could have hurt any one of us."

Crick's shoulders slump. "Sorry."

"Get off," I say, pointing.

He moves to the side with his arms hanging loose. I take his place, ask them to push me in reverse, and give the ATV enough throttle to catch a grip. I ease the machine backward up the slope using the tracks Del made when he got stuck then drive it over a part of the ditch that's more forgiving, catching a bit of air.

Del and Crick whoop.

"Quit foolin' around," Davis yells from the other side of the pasture. He's finally moseying back, checking what we've done (I'm sure), as if I don't know what I'm doing or don't care enough to do it right.

"Yes, Daddy," Crick shouts back to his father.

"You're sure living the dream, workin' for your daddy," Del says.

Crick mutters, "My bosshole is an arrogant, condescending knob, but I'm suffering through the next eight months because I would obviously be no one without him. But you're not supposed to know that. Don't let on." His tone never changes, just this flat voice, a bit ironic and funny.

Crick and I remount and ride back together, with Davis behind and Del out front in case he gets stuck again. Gloved hands resting on the pommel, I settle into the ambling ride.

I remember being Crick's age, wanting nothing more than to escape from my tiny hometown and the sometimes-miserable work I was expected to do.

"Are you hoping to go away to school?" I ask him, a line of questioning I haven't pursued with him before despite all the hours we've worked together since Nonna died last July.

"I've been thinkin' of going to college on Broadway."

"For acting?"

"Yeah." He meets my eyes for a second then looks away.

"I guess there's a particular school you want to attend?"

"NYU."

"Wow, fantastic."

"Their musical theatre program is good."

Carter was in drama class. He loved everything Johnny Cash and used to try to get me to sing with him. Of course, being his younger brother, sometimes I did. He always made me sing the girl's parts in duets.

"What are you thinking about?" Crick asks.

For a moment, I'm not sure what to say. I finally ask, "You want to know what I was thinking?"

"Probably not, based on how you're frowning now that I've asked."

I suppress a laugh. "You know that Carter sings," I offer.

"Yeah, I know," Crick says. "He's pretty good."

"Yeah," I reply. He was good back then too.

Ahead of us and below, since we're on a bit of a rise, is a panorama of the ranch's finer aspects, the land and sky. Snow makes everything look a little softer. I came back after college, attempting to help Carter regain the status he'd had around the ranch before he went to jail for me. That decade-old history seems even more raw now that I own what I intended to help him acquire.

"What's your brother going to do?" I ask.

"Waylon's going to stay here forever, I reckon, but sometimes he talks about going over to work for Campbells at their place. You know, like, when he's not getting along with Daddy."

"Because he loves the land and this life."

"Waylon believes he's the center of the universe and God's gift to Wyoming. Daddy says Waylon is a lazy piece of shit."

I try not to smirk. "Do you have the grades to go to school?"

"Mostly."

"Keep them up, and if you need help getting there, let me know."

"Really?"

"Sure."

Davis comes up behind us, whistling until we turn around. He motions his chin toward Crick and says, "Go on. There's work to be done."

Crick moves out, kicking his gelding into a speedier gait.

I follow, keeping my pace, and Davis comes up beside me.

"Did we do alright, boss?" he drawls, in that certain tone, slow and condescending.

The truth is, he's a hell of a cowboy and a bit annoying.

"I think so," I say with forced enthusiasm.

"Can we put the horses up?" he asks.

"Sure. We'll put the horses up," I reply flatly. As soon as ownership of the ranch was transferred to me, he started acting like this. *Do you like what we're doing, boss?* But it's a little different than that. I guess it should be flattering, offering me a sort of deference, but it annoys me a bit. It's only been a few months since probate ended, and I need to give everyone a chance to adjust.

Davis is in a trusted position, placed there by Pops, and has served in the role since Dad died 17 years ago. Before that, Dad trusted him to fill in for him when he took time off to spend with Mom or us or went on a multi-day business trip.

Pops specifically wrote Davis into his will. Nonna did the same, paying him a hefty bonus to remain our farm foreman as part of her succession plan. She knew I'd be in shit over my boot tops and thought keeping him around was wise.

I've carried their approach forward, giving Davis a pay increase and the respect I'd want if I were in his position.

"I heard Christa's trial got canceled," he says.

"Yeah."

"Damned shame."

I don't want to think about the trial. I urge my mare forward, putting space between us and heading into the main cluster of buildings at the hub of the ranch.

The morning of the homestead arsons, Carter suggested that the homesteader whose house burned while his family was inside should be considered a suspect because he found an article about a man imprisoned in New Mexico for burning people's houses with them asleep inside. It's always seemed plausible that the article was about the father of the guy whose house burned, but I was there with Sam after the fire. I've never believed Sam burned his home or that he'd have burned his neighbors' properties, but maybe someone he knows is responsible. Someone who's not Carter, who has reason to dislike Sam, and who knows about that article and wants to frame him. Unfortunately, when I talked to Sam this morning, he got defensive. The conversation didn't go the way I'd planned. I've been trying to forget the stunned look of betrayal in his eyes ever since.

I want it all to be over so I can move on with my life and either stop trying to work things out with my brother or go ahead and get it resolved.

It's this feeling of living in between that's killing me.

I'm doing it for Nonna, but I wish I didn't have to decide my brother's fate.

I come into the main activity hub, passing nearer pastures, loafing barns, ranch hands working in our big arena, chicken barns, a row of bunkhouses, and a cluster of original homes built of low-slung adobe and Spanish tile roofing. The main house sits off one side, a sprawling building that Carter and I used to pretend was an old fort.

Crick is already out in front of the horse barn, standing near the hitching post, when I come to a stop.

"If you want to go, I'll put her up for you," he offers.

"Thanks," I say, taking him up on it. Considering Davis is coming up behind me, and Ellen's at home expecting me, it's an easy decision.

Turning away from the stiff wind, biting against my cheeks and making my eyes itch, I head for my pickup, settle inside, strip off my wet coat and chinks, then drag the driver's door closed.

This ranch. It's a heritage. It takes a crew. Cowboying is more than cows and riding. It's family, generations of family and tradition.

I'm suddenly in a shit mood and don't want to take that home with me.

The last thing Ellen needs is me worrying about Carter.

Instead of turning toward home to see her, I take a right off the main driveway, heading out to Echo Canyon, a place where time has traded elk trails for cattle trails for ATV trails. It's a bit of a drive, a few miles off the beaten track, but Nonna used to come here when she needed to think, and I came here with Ellen after Nonna died. It's always been spiritual and grounding.

I park the truck and take careful steps onto a slick outcrop, eroded stone blanketed with snow. A shelf overlooking a massive canyon, hundreds of feet deep, leading to an icy river.

As easy as it would be for me to head home and pretend nothing's bothering me, it's impossible to do that with Ellen. She knows me. If I'm worried, she's worried. Everything's spiraling out of control around us.

I take the ring I bought for her from my pocket and put it on my pinky finger. Not a million-dollar diamond, it's an engraved gold band—a baker's ring—she won't ever have to take off. I have found priceless acceptance and joy in building a life and bakery with her, but this land is in my blood, and blood runs as deep as love.

I try again to get my mood up before I go home.

It's a beautiful afternoon ahead of the coming storm. I'm lucky to have so much. Despite the frigid wind, the sun is out, warming my cheeks. I don't need the coat I left in the pickup. The cold makes me feel a little more alive.

I used to love coming here with Carter. We'd kick down the trails, eat massive cinnamon rolls for lunch, and barely make it into the house in time for chores and dinner. I used to think we'd live our lives running the ranch together. Operating things without him has felt entirely wrong, leaving me wishing I could go back 18 months and reclaim some parts of my old life.

Figuring out what special to offer at my steakhouse and how to fill in for staff who called off work used to seem stressful. The new owners have cheapened everything. Sometimes, I wish I hadn't sold it. Now that money's not an issue, I could offer to buy it back, but I no longer have time to run a restaurant, not if I expect to do a half-decent job as owner of a ranch the size of West Creek.

The sensation of being watched prickles my neck.

It's the eerie stillness. Winter in a place that's home to life you can't quite see but you know is there—sparrows fighting to survive bitter wind, prairie dogs and their shrinking habitat, and black-footed ferrets among America's most endangered species who hunt them for food.

But there's something else.

Behind me, in a vast basin of steppe grasslands, windswept ridges, and big sagebrush, a tall figure stands outlined against the horizon.

A sharp crack breaks the calm.

The shot echoes in the air as another one comes.

What the hell?

This guy is insane.

Thwack! A bullet whizzes past my ear an instant before the shot breaks the air with a *crack*.

This psycho is shooting *at me*.

My truck is too far—the open field in between is too wide.

Down the canyon's thousand-foot wall is a snaking river covered in ice and about a quarter mile west there's a small shelter hidden from above.

I slide into cascading rock, twisting my ankle under calf-high rubble. My fingers go raw against the snow before I catch a grip and perch on a ledge.

And at that moment, heavy snow really begins to fall.

CHAPTER 2

I PACE the creaky hardwood floor in my apartment over the bakery while staring at my phone's screen. I've sent Max a series of questions about dinner and where we're sleeping tonight. I've called and left two messages, cleaned up dinner, packed him a plate in the fridge, tried to read a crime thriller, and told myself not to worry. But, unlike me, Max is always early for everything. If he knew he was going to be late, he would have called. I walk to the kitchen, pour a cup of tea, and sip it while standing at the counter.

I love how he understands my personality, how patient and strong he is, and (bonus!) he's a fantastic cook who knows precisely the right flavor to balance out whatever I've imagined at my fabulous new bakery.

I need Max to come home so I can ask him what he thinks of

the latest cinnamon donuts I came up with. I double glazed them with toasted pecans. They might be perfect for our holiday crowd, but this is my first Christmas with the bakery, and he's lived here his whole life and has a better handle on the customers.

I need to show him everything is okay between us, because there's something else much more critical that I need to tell Max. A breath escapes my tight lips.

I need to tell him we're having a baby.

I should have mentioned it was a possibility before I took the test this morning. Still, we were so engrossed in the financial pundits' speculations about my father's collapse in a board meeting, and with Christa's trial it seemed like too much. The test complicated the knot in my stomach. Becoming a mother is . . . so momentous.

I need Max on my side and a mom to call for advice, except I'm unsure how Max will react to becoming a father while his life is so stressful, and my mom died nine years ago. His parents died when he was a teenager. We have no family to help us raise a child. We'll be first-time parents entirely on our own. I need Max to come home. We can make a plan, and maybe I'll stop shivering.

Warmth seeps into my hand from the mug. I've asked myself a million times if he said something about being late. Did he mention going to one of their remote ranges where only radios work?

He definitely didn't.

My phone chimes, and I nearly drop it in my fumble to see his reply.

It's a text from my father. Worry pinches deeper in my gut.

Ed Jasper: We need to talk.

Yes, I believe we do, but I can't handle him right now.

I sink to the window ledge and gaze out at the empty spot

where Max usually parks. My knee is shaking, and I press down on it to make it stop.

Did my father collapse in a board meeting? The financial experts are constantly getting things a little bit wrong.

My phone rings, and it's Father calling now because this is how he does things.

Ready to give him a blast to match the tension I've built within, I answer and press the phone to my ear. "What now?"

"I want you to come home." His voice is like a bullhorn.

I close my eyes and growl. "I don't care what you want."

"But you're in danger."

"I'm not."

"What's this about Carter Corbett?"

I lay my temple in my palm and pluck at my hair. I shouldn't have talked to Kent, the security guard Father assigned to watch me. Of course, Kent went straight to Father, sharing my request for help investigating the arsons.

"Why aren't you talking to me?" Father asks.

"I explained it to Kent."

He huffs into the speaker. "Explain it to me."

"I don't want to." I haven't even asked him if he actually collapsed at a board meeting.

He sighs. "I've tried to tell you these homestead idiots aren't trustworthy."

But I love Max. I trust him. *Where is he?*

My apartment window seat isn't warm, but the temperature isn't responsible for the wash of chills pricking my arms and thighs. I set the phone down and rub my hands over my legs.

Father's still on the line. I press it to my ear as he says, "A plane will be at the airport outside of town in the morning at seven."

"I won't be on it."

"I can't believe—"

"Believe it," I snap. "I'm not coming."

"Fine." Father hangs up, leaving me slightly sick, and it's

more than the strange, pregnant feeling in my abdomen. My phone chimes.

> Ed Jasper: Be on the plane if you want answers. I have information about the arsons.

No way I'm leaving without talking to Max about it.

But why did Father say I'm in danger?

He may be focused on his business and driven to get the gold out of Max's land, but he loves me in his domineering way. Like how he calls every few days, concedes to some of the conditions I put into his correspondence with Max, and insists on keeping his security team close even after he's said he disowned me. Maybe he has a reason to be worried about my safety.

Maybe I have a reason to be scared about Max not making it home.

Can a person be considered missing after only a few hours? I search the internet for an answer and find an article on steps to take.

A vacuum might as well be sucking at my insides. Max is always considerate. Not showing up for hours is so far out of the norm. When Mom died, she was on the side of the road. Her last breaths escaped before anyone found her. I grip my phone and consider calling the sheriff.

Last time I called local law enforcement for help, Carter was attempting to evict me. I got a voicemail asking me to leave a message. When I finally got a callback, it came with advice about learning to defend myself. I need more information before I start down that path again.

Max was headed to the ranch for a meeting with Davis. An arctic front is forecast to start tomorrow with wind chills predicted to put feels-like temperatures below zero. Frigid temperatures will be hard on their livestock, but drifting snow is the bigger concern. After big storms, they've found full-grown heifers forced into fence corners, where they suffocate in snow and die. Even their low-elevation pastures pose a risk, and they had cows to move. Maybe he's out with them?

Chilled all over, I call Kay the housekeeper and cook at the main ranch house.

When she answers, Christmas music is playing in the background, hopeful and loud.

I run my fingers over the ornament Max bought me last year. It's a picture of us playing in the snow. His smile has always been enough to make me romantic. A shadow of a beard on his cut jaw has me running a hand over my neck. I hold my voice calm. Instilled with Mom's southern grace, I explain that Max hasn't made it home and isn't answering calls. "Have you seen him?"

"He rode out to break ice off the springs in the low pastures, and at lunch he mentioned he might head over to see Carter at their place before he headed home." Her cheerful voice is melodic and soothing in my ear.

"Is everything alright?" Kay asks, lowering the music.

"How was his mood when he left?"

"I'd say he's worried about the trial and the cows."

I draw a calming breath. "So you haven't seen him since lunch?"

"You could call Carter."

"Okay, thanks." My voice sounds too high-pitched for the effortless grace I meant to project.

"I'll give you a call if I hear anything," she promises.

I get her to give me Carter's number before we hang up, then I collapse into the window seat and tuck my foot under my knee to keep it from shaking. Last time I saw Carter, he was at the courthouse telling Max to pull his head out of his ass.

I *need* to speak to him about Max. This is fine. I can handle a simple phone call.

I put myself in his position: already dissatisfied with their grandmother's decisions to split up their family's land and sell it to outsiders, he was understandably upset when she sold me their ancestors' original home, land that Max didn't want to be sold either. He loved it. His family used to picnic there and fish. It meant something to them. Their grandmother inadvertently put me in an awkward situation. I probably shouldn't have sprayed Carter in the face with bear spray while he was trying to evict me. Maybe he wouldn't have been so furious or determined to ensure there wasn't a house left for us to fight about.

My hand shakes. Rationalizing isn't quite working to make me feel better. I draw an enormous breath.

Carter's voice comes over the call. "You've got to be fucking kidding me. Max said if I even say 'hello' to you, he'll kill me."

"And now I'm calling you." Hoping it sounds sincere, I add, "Please tell me you've seen him recently."

"Princess, I haven't seen him since he was with you."

There's no missing the scorn in his choice to call me 'Princess,' a blandishment I've always hated because it implies I'm spoiled and fragile.

I force the annoyance out of my voice and say, "I'm worried that Max hasn't come home. He's always considerate, and it's been hours since he was supposed to be here. He's not responding to my texts or anything. He's been trying to figure out who started the fires. I don't know if he's in danger, but I thought of calling you for some reason."

"Okay," he says, and I can tell he's moving, a thump and harsh breathing, the jangle of keys.

"Do you know where Max is?" I wait for an answer but get only silence. "Where are you going?"

"You need to stay away from my brother."

"Why?"

The call goes silent. He hung up. Calling Carter was a mistake. Where is he going?

I grab the pocket-size .22 Beretta pistol from the top drawer of my dresser, the shotgun Max keeps by the bed, and my day bag. Standing on the landing of the second-story back door, I pause at the stairs. The alley is ice, and my car is snowed in. I have no clue where to go or what I'll find. The ranch roads aren't even plowed. Max will call. Or he'll show up in a few minutes. I back-step and lay all my stuff on the kitchen bar, expecting him to come in and razz me for gathering an arsenal I can barely use. I settle into the windowsill, phone in hand, watching for his headlights.

Moonlight outlines the sidewalk and shiny road. I will my phone to ring.

Wind whistles against the window, shaking it in the frame. I press my cheek against my knuckles, not wanting to sleep, knowing I will dream if I shut my eyes and let myself drift off.

I'd see Max fighting with Carter. They held each other at gunpoint after the attorney read their grandmother's will. Carter pressed his grandfather's shotgun to his brother's chest and pulled the trigger. Did he know it wasn't loaded for the same reasons Max knew the gun he'd selected had a shell in the chamber?

I ease away from the window and swipe a trembling hand across my forehead, trying to think. Instead, I bump into the coffee table and sink into the cushioned sofa.

When I finally get clear headed, my phone is in my hand. I'm calling Father.

When he answers, I say, "I need to ask you for a favor."

"About Carter?" Father sounds amused.

"It's about Max," I admit. "He hasn't come home."

He coughs, then says, "Good riddance."

"Father, that's unkind."

"What do you want me to do? Pray he comes home? You know I don't care whether he makes it in time for dinner."

"We're having an arctic front. The visibility is terrible, and I don't want to risk the roads in my car."

"And you're going to risk your life to find him?"

"Of course not. I thought you'd want to have someone from security come and drive me in a four-wheel drive."

"I've tried to tell you you're unsafe out there."

"I know."

"But you refuse to listen." His tone asks, *How are you even my daughter?*

I no longer know the answer, because if he thinks for one minute that I'm going to sit by and do nothing while Max is potentially in danger, he's out of his mind.

Outside the front windows, snow flurries have blanketed the road. The weatherman said this will be the first real snowstorm of the season.

"If you don't help me or have your team look for him, I'm going out to find him myself."

CHAPTER 3

MAX

I'll never make it down here for long, but above is someone planning to execute me. I should have risked it, headed for my truck.

I want to do that now, but to the right an outcropping tapers to nothing. To the left is a trail only a mountain goat could climb.

A diesel engine rumbles in the distance. A faint knock, two sounds—combustion and clatter, steel against cold fuel under high pressure. *Hum. Purr.* A droning *knock* coming closer then shutting off.

Ice crunching under my boots, I move up the snow-covered goat track. Shifting cobble cascades down the sheer face with each step.

Fifteen paces later, a trail heads up to another outcropping.

"Havin' fun yet?" a strange voice asks.

Cold enough to stumble, I suck myself up against the side of the wall, waiting for him to fire down. My fingers and face tingle with numbness as the freezing air begins to sink bone deep. I scan beyond the outcropping to the sky. If I could get above that angled rock and to my truck, I could get the handgun under the seat or the shovel behind the toolbox. Figure out who sent him.

"Like-ta never find your way out," he says.

I turn my face up. The outcropping dies against the sky's crystalline cloudbursts and vanishes into the sun.

Thwack. A bullet shatters the stone below me in a spray of grit and a fragrant earthy punch of rock dust. I step closer to the canyon wall. Shots rain down on the adjacent rock.

The shale below gives way to a shower of sedimentary shards.

Echoes break across the cliffs. Stone crashes, bounds, and glances off a trillion tons of canyon, frost heaving, rocks rolling, bullets shattering. The vibration alone is enough to move a mountain.

I skate a cobble field to a lower ledge, then beyond, tumbling down with a brutal blow to the thigh, a wrecked shoulder, and torn hands and arms. Every jolt is excruciating, but none of this will stop me. It's the fall that's coming that has me holding my breath.

I'm a somersault of limbs in motion.

Nothing's stopping me now.

I will not make it out of here alive.

But in a squirrelly, unfocused way, I stop.

Instead of falling, I float.

I close my eyes against a kaleidoscope of colors, trying to hear beyond the torrent of unleashed stone.

Vaguely, I consider Mother Nature could be in a good mood.

Carrying me on the wind.

Placing me in the hand of God.

With a thunderous crash, I thud onto a ledge large enough to stop my forward roll. My body explodes in pain. I cringe as my arm gives way in a sharp crack, my cheekbone and ribs scream. Breathing faster than normal. Sweating despite the snow, I try not to pass out and put weight on my good arm, testing my limbs. Weak and breathing hard, I cough blood, swipe a hand across my eyes, and then lie back, holding focus on the sky, trying to figure out how far I fell. My eyelids slide closed.

I wedge myself against the rock wall and stare at my phone's cracked screen; spots cloud my vision, tinged red, confirming what I already suspect. No service. Silence is broken only by howls, songs, hoots, and chirps of beasts stronger than me—wolf, mountain lion, coyote, badger, red fox, and raccoon.

Pressure builds in my chest. Dryness coats my throat. A low roar vibrates in my ears. I can't feel my hands and roll to one side, scooting toward the cliff. Beside me is another ledge, a small roofed shelter with no walls but hidden from the wind—something shiny on the carved underbelly of the outcropping. A long blade of some forgotten implement and a vintage Lucky Strike cigarette tin. I work it open with one hand, find a rolled note inside, and fight it flat.

> *Four days without food or water.*
> *Lost.*
> *Chaz Jacobs*
> *1938*

I shove the message in my pocket with thick, skinned, clumsy fingers and try to forget about the coming storm.

My breath quakes from between my lips. Figure I can make it back up after that bit of rest.

If I had half a chance, I'd take the blade from the ledge and gut the bastard like a deer, belly out, ass to heart.

Snow comes in big, fat flakes. As hideous as this odyssey has been, I tell myself I'm lucky. In agony but alive.

Sun brightens the sky white.

Down the canyon face is a racecourse of potential wreckage. Up is stone too steep to see beyond. I push to my feet, find the move biting back with dizziness, and resettle against the stone wall.

I groan against crushed ribs.

What did I do to deserve this?

I don't even know. Carter's furious. Maybe he paid someone at the sheriff's office to get Christa's case dismissed. Now that I've told him he still can't move back, he wants me out of the way?

Ellen's dad is at least that mad.

On top of that, I upset Sam Bowman at home as I reconsidered him as a suspect, basically accusing him of lighting his own house on fire while his family was inside.

The canyon face is a prison wall, the river below an icy hell. I tell myself to breathe. Blood on my knuckles, a throbbing face, the wind biting against my neck and ears, a reminder that a bitter arctic blizzard is still coming.

The stranger's shouted words echo in my mind as they did against the canyon walls.

"Like-ta never find your way out."

I will find him and make him pay.

I push my frozen fingers into my hot eyes.

Revenge is no reason to live. Not really. Fury isn't what drives me up the canyon. What propels me is Ellen's heart speaking to mine. "We could have all we want at another place, at a different time."

We should try that. Abandon everything and start over fresh. That's why I must live. To tell her. And to survive, I must claw my way out of here.

One good arm, a wrecked shoulder, bruised ribs, and two swollen ankles. With a grunt, I pull myself up the face, pushing hard, counting on millions of reps of push-ups, dips, and curls I've done for years in a struggle to control my temper. Now, I'm ordering myself to become furious and fight despite the pounding in my head and lack of energy. I have a sudden, maniacal urge to laugh at the irony, but even breathing hurts. I drag myself a short distance, switchbacking against impossible surfaces before resting on a pile of snow-covered stone. Minutes drag by in inches until the sun is down and it's almost dark. I have no heavy coat, food, water, or weapon.

CHAPTER 4

ELLEN

An hour after hanging up with Father, I've heard nothing more from him or Max. I pace the short distance across my apartment and stop at the tiny Christmas tree Max brought home a few weeks ago. It's one of those live ones, and we've been planning on planting it at the ranch, starting a tradition of putting lights on it every year.

I redial the main house. The phone rings through. I leave a message letting Kay know Max still hasn't come home and asking her to call me immediately.

I consider calling Father again. The last post I read about Father's health said he was already dead. The financial pundits are brutal all the time. They've reported he was dead twice before, but Father's never been sick.

As soon as he answers, I say, "If you don't send someone to help me, I'm going myself."

His amused huff comes from the speaker.

I lay my head forward on the cool kitchen counter. "This isn't funny at all."

"But it is." There's a chuckle in his voice.

"You're so evil."

"That's a hurtful thing for a daughter to say to her esteemed father." His voice is low and pained.

That's true . . . "But you're—"

"Kent has the whole team at the mine scouring the roadways."

"Oh." I deflate onto the barstool and prop my cheek on my hand. "You should have told me."

"It took time to arrange."

"Thank you. This means so much to me."

"You're welcome."

"I know some places they could check. Can you send someone—"

"*Ellen.*"

"You'll let me—"

"You stay where you are until Kent gets there. Then you get on that jet. I want to see you."

"But—"

"No buts." He hangs up.

I turn on the local news, check the weather, and see a slough of work and school delays. Closures run up and down the state. This storm has made a mess of things, and Max could be in it. A chill makes me head toward the floor vent, where the heater pumps out warm air. I stand there for a while, trying to tell myself that wherever he is, he's warm.

Then I sink to the floor and sit there, propped against the wall, watching the news and praying he's okay. I momentarily hug myself then let my arms fall away and stare at my phone. On any other average weekday, I'd be starting the bakery prep at

8:00 p.m. and finishing up by midnight or 1:00 a.m. It's a fairly typical routine now. I need to do something, but I rushed through all the bakery prep earlier this afternoon, planning to spend a relaxing night with Max so I could tell him.

The ache in my chest becomes so powerful, like someone is twisting the tubes in my heart.

I push to my feet and head for the kitchen, turn a burner on high, then stoop over to pull out my popcorn pot, loving the familiar creak of the oven door hinge and the weight of the Mom's four-quart dutch oven with thick sides and a heavy lid. I pour a few tablespoons of coconut oil into the bottom, add four popcorn kernels, and set the pot over the burner.

While waiting for the first promising pop, I melt butter in a small saucepan. Watching it liquefy and inhaling the savory creamy goodness make my mouth water. I've always been more into savory than sweet, reminding me of Mom's sourdough pancakes or her beautifully stenciled loaves of cheesy, crusty ploughman's dough, spread thickly with salted butter while still warm from the oven.

Getting four rapid pops, I add the remaining kernels, reset the lid, and give the pan a shake. Within about ten seconds the popping really starts.

For about a minute, I wait for the stragglers. I did this with Grandma and Mom all the time when I was little and now with Max, since it's a healthyish snack, and he's always thinking up creative ways to mix the flavors.

My comfort zone retreats as worry about Max makes my hands shake with the urge to grab my phone.

Instead, I pour the popped kernels into a bowl, drizzle them with butter, and dust them with turmeric, sea salt, black pepper, and nutritional yeast. Max made it this way the last time we had it together.

I set my snack on the coffee table, eat a few handfuls, and try to convince myself he'll drive up any minute.

Only he doesn't. I clean up the kitchen mess, then dial

Father's phone, getting no answer, I check the time and realize it's after midnight.

The news has changed to a late-night infomercial with some master hawker offering a way to make freeze-dried mini-hamburgers. I watch it until my eyes itch. I flop onto my side and bury my face against the couch, finally submitting to the need for sleep.

A diesel engine rumbles closer then cuts off with a final throat of bubbling exhaust, startling me awake and to the rear door.

Dawn lightens the sky.

A truck is newly parked in the alley, blue instead of white, and a Chevy, not a Ford. Not Max.

My eyes slide closed, puffy and sore from lack of sleep. I'm not sure what to do. Where is he?

Footsteps on the stairs have me gazing out again. Kent Goodwin, striding up.

Before he knocks, I'm poised. Do I open the door? He was there, protecting me after my first boyfriend stole my identity and drained my trust fund while he claimed to love me. Crazy that it was so long ago. Almost eight years.

Goodwin raps the old wood, his blows sending me four steps backward. Kent's presence was comforting, being near but not in sight. Despite his pathological shyness, he tried to kiss me once. I might convince him to help me look places they might not know to check. He seemed to care when I talked to him earlier. I draw the door in, stepping back to allow him inside. A frigid blast comes with him.

Gone is Goodwin's navy business suit, replaced with jeans, a gray t-shirt, a fluorescent outdoor jacket, and an ivory cowboy hat damp from snow. He's younger-looking when he's not so severely dressed, maybe a few years older than me.

His blue eyes rake over me—Max's t-shirt and Christmas-themed pajama shorts—making me feel naked before it lands on my head. I raise a hand to fluffy, unkempt hair mussed from sleep.

"Mornin.' Sorry to wake you, but a plane's waiting." He strings words like lyrics without a proper tune, then he smiles, bashful but not entirely sorry.

"I wasn't asleep." I clip my words and don't smile back.

"Let's get you to the airport to see your father." He mirrors my coolness.

I remember this about him now, the strange, awkward tension that wasn't entirely professional. At the time, when I was in such a tormented place after Peter's betrayal came to light publicly, Kent's attention had been flattering. I'd attributed my awkwardness to being extra sensitive about all men, looking for clues about where I'd gone wrong when I fell in love with Peter and clinging to hope that not all men were opportunists, seeking to know me because of Father's money.

Wishing for a bigger apartment where you can't see my bed from the kitchen, I head toward the bathroom and pull on a robe, hollering, "I'm not going."

"But the plane's waiting."

I dash a brush through my hair and catch my reflection in the mirror. My eyes look almost green. My lips could use a little color, but my expression is a yawning void.

My cell rings, and I nearly sprain my wrist to grab it from my pocket. The screen is lit with a photo of Father on his yacht. A chill washes over me. I drop the phone in my robe's pocket. He'll call again. Then he'll call Kent and order him to give me the phone. I can't avoid this for more than a few minutes.

I put the call on speaker.

"You need to get on that plane now." For once, Father's not a foghorn. Instead, his voice is low and quiet.

"But—"

"I'll explain everything when you get here."

For the first time in my life, I note something else in his tone. He's scared.

If Father is scared, I should be terrified. "What's going on?" I stare at the guns I amassed on the counter earlier. "What aren't you telling me?"

"Kent will escort you. Just do what he says. Please."

He never says please. Never. I swallow hard. The phone shakes in my hand.

"Tell me what's going on." My request is met with silence, and I ask, "You think Carter hurt Max?" When Father doesn't respond, I look to Kent.

He scrapes a hand over the counter near the guns. "It's hard to know what's going on with Max." I remember this side of Kent, self-righteous and a little chippy. Maybe I didn't like him.

Father starts to cough, a wet and rumbling roar that makes me cringe.

"Mr. Jasper," a woman says through the speaker, "let me adjust your pillow."

"Get on that plane," Father rasps, disconnecting the call.

I shove the phone in my robe pocket and turn to Kent. "What's my father going to explain when I get there?"

"Like-ta answer that, but it's not my story."

"What did you learn about Carter?"

"Nothing consequential."

"But you did learn something." I draw my shoulders back, unhunching.

"You're not going to come with me, are you?" he asks.

"Not unless you help me find Max." I've called everyone I can think of, and Kent's truck is ready to go, sitting right outside. "You wouldn't mind helping me?"

"Your father expects you on this flight."

"But I'm not leaving unless I know Max is okay, so maybe you should go ahead and go. I'll find someone else to help."

I move toward the door, draw it open, and motion for him to step out. It's stopped snowing completely. Only Kent's tracks show in the alley.

"Let's not disappoint your father. He's—"

"Well, then help me, Kent. Okay? I need you to do this, then I'll go. I'll do whatever you want once I talk to Max. My father won't even know."

"I don't have the authority to go against your father's—"

"Live on the wild side. It won't hurt anything for you to help me. Remember how you let me go to the beach that time? It was fun, and you never got in trouble. Please take me to the places he might be. We can check the private roads."

"Fine," he says. "We don't have much time."

A bit of tension eases from my neck and shoulders. I race to follow Kent's ushering hand. He reminds me to lock my door. His footsteps follow me down the stairs. He opens the door and waits with a tight smile as I climb into the passenger seat of his rented truck with the no-smoking sticker on the window. His fast driving speeds us toward the Corbetts' ranch, and I want to feel good about the decision I just made, but the icy roadway stretches ahead.

Snow is piled in drifts along the shoulders. The main roads have been plowed. I scan for Max's white truck and shiver despite my cashmere sweater and coat. Kent tailgates the car ahead of us, racing into the curve with enough momentum to squish me against the door.

I press a foot against the floorboard. "Slow down. You need to turn right here."

He stares straight ahead.

"Right there." I point at the road we just passed. "You're supposed to help me find Max."

He continues forward as I watch for a place wide enough to turn around, but it's two narrow lanes with a steep drop-off. He turns right toward the airport.

I put on my best power-broker voice. "I need to find Max, and you will help me because I'm not getting on that plane until I know he's safe."

Kent looks at me with professional blankness in his blue eyes.

I'm not above begging and start with, "Help me. Please, Kent. I can't leave until I know he's okay."

He parks then retrieves a tablet from the console between us and focuses on the screen for a long moment. Maybe he's considering my plea. He holds the tablet toward me, placing it in my hands, displaying someone's report about the arson investigation.

He says, "Based on what we found, Mr. Bowman's father was Archie Bowman. Archie died in jail on an arson conviction."

"So that article about Sam's dad is true?" Sam has seemed nice the few times he's come into the bakery for coffee. Could he have burned his house with his family inside? Max mentioned going to Sam's house the last time we talked.

I set the tablet on the console. A jet waits on the tiny airstrip. I try calling Max again but get his voicemail. I listen for a moment, wishing it was him, but I hang up rather than leave a message in front of Kent.

A young flight attendant, wearing a navy-blue suit and sunglasses, waits on the tarmac.

"I think you're worked up about nothin'." Kent's words are infuriating, suggesting my worry about Max is unfounded. He cracks the driver's door, approaches the truck's passenger side, and extends an impatient hand.

I head for the driver's seat and scramble over the console.

"Stop." Kent grabs my arm and leg and hauls me out of the truck.

"Let me go," I scream.

He pushes me against the freezing door by the upper arms. The door handle's hard edges cut into my back. "If you think I'll let you steal my truck, you're mistaken."

I stiffen against his touch and say, "Stop being a thug."

"You haven't even asked how sick your father is."

"Fine. How sick is my father?"

Kent steps back so we're once again at a professional

distance. "A nurse stays with him full-time. I can't say more than that. He wants to see you in person."

It makes sense Father would force me home if he's genuinely ill . . . He has a wet cough and a nurse with him full-time. It's just like how his father died. Sharp pain tightens my throat. But Father's forcing me into doing what he wants. Still, this domineering approach is nothing unusual for him.

Vulnerability can be kindness at times like this.

I could use all the strength and knowledge I've accumulated since coming here to confront him like I once planned. I might stop having nightmares about Father's mines. I'm haunted by the forged reports and what they mean to any families living nearby. If I hadn't done my part to subvert our reporting during the years I worked for him, I could forget about the damage Father's doing to mining towns worldwide and find satisfaction in running a charming bakery in a lovely mountain town. But won't this ugliness in my past impact my child? Won't it eventually ruin my relationship with Max?

A trip home could be a step toward fixing things between us and resetting the past. Max understands why I haven't completely cut ties with Father. Our baby could have one grandparent, even if Father has his shortcomings.

I draw a huge breath and attempt a compromise. "You promised to help me find Max."

Kent's brows lower. "I'd hate for you to miss seeing your father."

"You lied about taking me to find Max."

"Your mother passed away in less time than it's taken to have this conversation. I hate to make you go, but—"

"I'm truly sorry he's sick, but—"

Kent reaches past me into the passenger door then fumbles inside the console, retrieves his tablet, and works with it for a few seconds. Finally, he hands it to me. On the screen is a surveillance map of the area. Five dots move across the region. I touch the one closest to the ranch. The dot enlarges into a man's profile—a guard working for Father at his local mine.

"What are you trying to tell me?"

"I'm trying to get you to your father."

"I'm trying to find the man I love." I shiver and cross my arms, wrapping them tightly against my ribs.

"Fine," Kent drawls, dragging out his phone and scowling at it as he calls someone and engages the speaker. "Llorenç, tell Ms. Jasper what you're doing to locate Max Corbett."

"Sure, good morning, Ms. Jasper. We're checking the roadways and monitoring emergency channels for accident reports. And Adolfo's investigating the Vegas lead."

"What Vegas lead?"

"I told you that you're probably worked up and he's fine. Possibly in Vegas or—"

"You have no idea where he is." A frustrated breath escapes my nose. "I insist on checking the ranch roads."

"Llorenç will do it."

"But—"

"We both know that your father will call off the search if you don't get on this plane."

I draw an enormous breath. Of course he would. That's the game Father's playing.

The jet—Father's favored model—relatively small but with class-leading range, speed, and agility, can fly ten hours without stopping, easily reaching Father's investments in Africa, South America, Alaska, and Europe. I'd be in New York in a couple of hours.

The air crew is trying to keep it from freezing up despite the frigid weather.

At least I'd have phone service in the air. I'd be connected to better internet than the sketchy broadband at the bakery. I could keep trying to get Max on the phone while they look for him.

Kent's blue eyes are accusing. I don't want to get back in his truck either. I have no choice. This is my best chance at making sure Max is safe.

"You will leave your tablet with me so I can direct the search," I insist.

"Fine," Kent agrees.

Taking it, I walk from one undesirable situation toward another with Kent on my heels.

"Miss Jasper, welcome aboard." The attendant steps aside for me to pass.

"Thank you and good morning." I embody the gracious daughter my mother raised while I climb the stairs. With Kent settled in the captain's chair near the bar, I sequester in the private suite and collapse onto the bed, where I press the heels of my hands into my eyes. It's almost time for the bakery to open. I text Laura, my right hand at work, letting her know I got everything ready this morning before taking off for an impromptu trip to see my father. I thank her for stepping in and apologize for the short notice.

I dial Max again, and when he doesn't answer, I throw myself into orchestrating the search, sending Father's staff to the places I think he could be. Llorenç heads directly for Sam's house.

CHAPTER 5

MAX

I ᴛᴜᴄᴋ ɪɴᴛᴏ ᴀ ᴡᴇᴀᴛʜᴇʀᴇᴅ ᴄʟᴇꜰᴛ, but keeping still in fading sun and shade is almost more challenging than moving, so I mass a pile of not-quite-as-wet tinder. Shivering too hard to care about the stranger, I fish my cigar lighter out of my pocket and flick it alive, touching the flame to start a modest blaze—an inverted lookout, offering warmth but no salvation.

The stars above, which have guided me forever, seem distant in the half-light, the vast sky leaving me invisible against the bald and sloping stone. Every breath comes out shaky and raw.

I don't want to think about what's happening or even why.

It seems completely hopeless.

Fighting the pain, I settle two more sticks across the burgeoning flames then huddle against the stone shelter. A dead tree is about twenty feet away down the slope, beyond a snow-covered ledge I can't quite see well enough to trust.

It's white and brittle, like how my bones might look in a few years.

I grab the longer stick from the fire as a poker, rearranging the wood, then I force my hand steady, almost holding my breath with the effort as I sketch a hieroglyph in ash on the rock beside me. I imagine the crude sketches are hawks and ravens, destroying two-headed serpents with flared bodies and fisted talons—persistent effort beating superior obstacles.

Ellen looked so angelic when I last saw her, safe behind the counter in her bakery. I promised her everything would be okay.

The pain in my face, arm, and ribs is only slightly worse than the raw bite of the cold against my fingers, nose, and ears.

Working against the slippery brush and breathlessness, I drag a small branch back to my fire. Flames sizzle-lick the logs and twigs, creating damp heat and a humid amber luster of embers until the wind shifts direction and threatens to put it out.

Ellen's always talking about fire towers or going to the tree-house Pops built years ago. I imagine her watching for a distant beacon, but I am in a gorge. A fire would be invisible at the horizon.

Still, Carter will come here seeking me when he learns I'm missing, and he will find me if I'm marking the canyon.

Bold with hope, I gauntlet crawl off my ledge, clawing over sharp stones toward the tree. Minutes inch by with each impossible step as I drag it back and toss it onto the fire.

With torn jeans and smoke-filled lungs, I sit on the ledge as the fire takes on a life of its own, heating my skin until it's too hot. Perched there, breathless against the pain in my chest, with a charred throat, I imagine voices echoing above me, shouting, calling my name.

But it's not a fantasy.

Someone *is* here. Smelling smoke and looking for me—to save me or kill me.

I push, scramble toward the canyon face, then lose footing and fall, rolling toward the flames on a breath of exhaled, mother, fuck, fuck.

I am going down and down and down.

With a harrowing jolt and a crack of skull against stone, I land hard against a sharp rock. Engine noise is replaced by roaring in my ears and my own scream. My breaths come in jagged bursts. My eyes slide closed on a whispered groan.

I wake to Carter's voice, piercing the night. My stomach muscles, ribs, and neck strain with my breaths.

Cobbles roll down, followed by men with winches, torch lights, and rough hands. My brother's bearded face is shadowed by firelight. "You dumb fuck."

"Yeah." I grunt an exhale. "Thanks."

Somewhere along the way, I pass out again because I'm unaware of how I got here, sitting beside Carter in the truck. Breathing is impossible, but somehow I've gotten once-in-a-life-time lucky for at least the third time in my life.

When the shotgun my brother tried to kill me with wasn't loaded.

When Ellen decided to stick around and date me.

Right now, when my brother finds me almost dead and hauls me out of nowhere.

"You ought to go to the hospital," Carter says.

"Did you see who it was?"

He raises one eyebrow. How involved is he?

I barely manage to say, "Someone was shooting at me."

"Who?" Carter's tone is either incredulous or amused. "You're pretty banged up."

I'll tell you what I think, I say silently, laying my head on the seat. *I have no idea what I think.*

Pulling me from near sleep, Carter asks, "How'd you get out there?"

"I drove."

"Then where's your truck?"

I crack one eyelid open, finding shadows of light and a grid ceiling. Hospital machines beep around me, and it hurts to breathe. "Someone was shooting at me."

"Who was shooting at you?" Carter's tone is slow and concerned. Fingers squeeze my foot, then Carter adds, "He's been talking like this since we found him."

I lift my head, trying to see who else is in the room.

My seven-year-old nephew Logan is at the end of the bed, holding onto my toes.

"Hey, Moon." I lift a little farther.

"Hi." He gives me a timid wave.

"What've you been doing?"

"Dad got me a new trick saddle. I've been learning to upside down drag."

"I love that." I try to smile despite the pain in my face. Pride radiates off my nephew and makes me recall what it was like to be young and happy.

Pride also lights Carter's face. "I've been teaching him a bit of the whip stuff too. He's a natural like I was at that age."

While we were in high school, Carter snapped a lit cigarette out of my hand with his bullwhip, earning himself widespread notoriety and me a few sore fingers. Now, he's talking about himself again.

He's fantastic with his whip, and I'm glad to see him passing that on to his son, but I'm still furious at him. I fall back onto the pillow and tune him out.

"Where's Ellen?" I ask.

"Don't know," Carter says.

"Did you call her?"

"You said not to talk to her."

"You have my phone?" I ask, trying not to sound as angry at him as I feel.

"Battery's dead."

"Let me use yours."

When he doesn't move, I reach for the button on the bed, raise my head, and find the hospital phone on a cart a few feet out of reach. Stretching for it, I realize the full extent of fucked. Left arm is in a cast and sling. Right arm is hooked up to machines.

"Hand me the phone."

"Sure you want to do that?"

I glare at my brother. He lifts one shoulder, silently arguing because Logan is here.

I force myself higher against the mattress, twisting in the blankets, dragging the IV closer, clenching my jaw at the pain, and jerking the cart. I yank the phone and smash the buttons, dialing the bakery, since that's where I expect to find Ellen. She'd probably go to work to keep herself from going insane with worry.

The phone's trilling ring ends with Laura's cheerful answer. "The Old Press Room Bakery, how can I help you?"

"Is Ellen there?"

"Oh, hi, Max. She's not . . . She texted . . . She had to go to New York. Something about her dad being sick."

"Fuck." I close my eyes, realizing how wrong that sounded, and add, "Okay, thanks."

"Can I help?"

"No, it's fine. Everything's fine. I'll try her mobile."

"Okay, bye, Max."

I end the call, and Carter says, "You're going to let that girl tear us apart. You see that?" His tall posture, pressed shirt, and dark jeans combine with the "you're an idiot" look on his face, making my pulse pound.

"It's not her who's tearing us apart."

He turns to Logan and swipes a hand toward the door. "Come on, Moon."

"Thanks for hauling me out of there," I say to his retreat.

"Count on it." He throws up a bird.

"Always." I hate how badly that went. Our bond may be stronger than either of our wills. Still, who am I kidding? He's the one who started this. All Ellen did was accept Nonna's offer to homestead on land Carter didn't want her to sell. His dogs still scare Ellen. The first day they ever met, he let them scratch her car. He's never apologized.

"Prick," I mutter. But on the way to the hospital, he said something about my truck. "How'd you get out there?" I ask, "Where's my truck?"

"Don't care," he says from the hallway.

How big of a mistake am I making by letting him leave?

Unsure, I wait for him to go and then push the nurse call button.

When the R.N. comes into the room and asks how she can help, I straighten despite the pain. It's Jamie, a blonde girl I went to high school with. She still looks the same as she did back then, aside from her Christmas-themed scrubs and entirely professional expression. She used to be a real wiseacre, constantly mouthing off to other kids and sometimes even the teachers.

"How long will I be here?" I ask.

She focuses on the machine beside the bed.

"I'm ready to go."

Concern tipping toward annoyance, she sighs. "You're not. Your blood pressure is low. You've been coughing and have mental confusion . . ." She focuses on the computer near the bed then switches out a fluid bag hanging on the IV, pushes several buttons, then adds, "Someone with your injuries can get worse fast. If that someone was too far from the hospital or transported in a private vehicle, that person could die without making it to help."

"Sure, okay. I get it. Can you bring me a phone charger?"

Her frown softens. "Sure."

Once she's gone, I pick up the phone. Who to call? The sheriff? Detective Windt at the Wyoming Bureau Investigation? A private investigator? A security entourage?

I dial Ellen's mobile and get her voicemail. "Hey, Flynn, I . . . Call me when you get a chance. I heard from Laura that your dad's sick. Hope everything's okay. It's important. Call me. Love you." I fall asleep, thinking *Wish you were here.*

A sound wakes me. I crack an eyelid and squint at the overhead light. A youngish man wearing scrubs, earphones, and shoe covers runs a mop around the room, collecting discarded wrappers and dust in a final pass before he exits. I lean up to see, but pain clinches in my neck, fogging my mind. The sharp antiseptic smell turns my stomach. Groggy from pain medication and exhausted by the non-stop flow of people through the room, I sit up and groan.

The one person I wish was here hasn't called.

Ellen has no way to know where I am and no phone or room number at the hospital. I didn't even tell her I was in the hospital. I reach for my phone, find Jamie bought me a charger, power it on, and try Ellen. When she doesn't answer, I leave another message. Then, expecting her to call me back, I shift gears. Find my truck. I wait for the GPS vehicle tracking app to update while replaying the last hours of my life on a slow loop. Finally, getting the app running, I sign in, navigate to my truck, push the icon, and get this error message: *Ensure that your location services are set to On.*

To find my truck, I have to have my truck because I didn't bother to set it up correctly in the first place, but I'm pretty sure I did have it set up. Maybe someone switched that feature off? Is that possible? I have no idea.

My other option is to ask for help—contact someone at the ranch or report this whole fiasco to the authorities, but our local law enforcement doesn't have the best reputation. They're probably helping Carter. How else did they manage to lose crucial evidence and screw up a trial months in the making?

I push past gnawing uncertainty, pull up the security camera app on my phone, and scan the video for vehicles passing the main road after me. It's a chore made more difficult because of the tiny, cracked screen, blurry vision, ringing ears, and the number of questions barraging me to which I have no answer.

Christa's voice comes down the hall. "We can't just move into the ranch house without talking to him."

"I know, darlin'." Carter sounds as excited about talking to me as I feel about seeing him.

I could feign sleep, but I haven't spoken to Christa since before she was arraigned. I can't avoid this even if I want to.

My brother steps in, and she trails behind him. They stop at the end of the bed. Christa draws her braid over her shoulder. Her smile, though pained, softens her angular features.

Carter's stare says to watch my manners or watch out for his fist.

Hospital bed or not, he would make good on his threat, and I may love my brother a little more because of how much he loves his wife.

He pulls down the brim of his Stetson.

"Good to see you," I say to Christa.

"You too. How are you feeling?"

"The medication makes me feel strange, but hopefully I'll be off it soon."

"And get back home," she says.

"Can't wait," I reply.

"Speaking of home," Carter segues, "we want to talk to you about moving back to the ranch."

I knew he would do this. He can't wait until I leave the hospital to push his agenda. He wouldn't be here asking if Christa hadn't forced him. From the look on her face, a little annoyed and resigned, she wishes she hadn't insisted on getting involved.

Think like a shrink. Take time to breathe and collect your thoughts before conversing with your brother. Avoid escalating the situation with anger or hostility. It's possible they've both spent time behind bars for crimes they didn't commit. "Being in jail must have been hard," I say.

Carter draws in a breath and takes a step forward. Christa puts a hand on his arm, holding him back.

"I'm sorry to upset you. I meant what I said about it being difficult. If you are innocent, that would make it so much worse, and with no trial, how can we ever move forward?" When no one moves, it turns into a ramble. "I'm unsure how to fix this. I have no idea how to make it right, but I want to try. Ellen suggested we investigate on our own."

Christa scoots into Carter's side. Her voice is tight enough to crack. "That's fine."

"Okay."

"It's really fine. Ask me whatever you want to know."

"So you're going to interrogate my wife?" Carter asks.

"I'm trying to get facts. We've hardly talked since this started. You want me to trust you but refuse to give me any reason to do it."

"How about you trust me because we're family?"

I may regret this. "That's the only reason I'm talking to you now."

"So if we do everything you say and answer all your questions, you'll let us move back to the ranch?"

"If Ellen says it's okay and we all work it out, then maybe."

Carter tilts his head, his lip curling. "And what tricks do we have to do now to earn our 'maybe?'"

"How about you tell me where my truck is?" I suggest, attempting to be lighthearted, but I'm only half in jest. He either saved my life or tried to kill me—or both. I'm not sure I know my brother anymore.

One corner of his mouth ticks up. "You genuinely don't know?"

"No clue."

"I figured you walked out there like Nonna did that time."

"So, you're saying my truck wasn't at the turnaround?"

"That's what I said."

"He must have taken it."

"Or maybe the medication is making you a little paranoid."

"You think I went down in Echo Canyon for the hell of it?"

His forehead wrinkles. He glances at Christa. "You were yelling at me in the driveway at the courthouse. We can't move back. The case was dismissed erroneously. The sheriff's incompetence doesn't change anything. It was all my fault. I figured it was one more day when you were upset enough that you weren't making sense."

"I spent the entire morning trying to figure out who started the fires and why they did it. I went to the Bowmans' house. I talked to Sam and Detective Windt. I've been trying to prove Christa didn't do it and stirring up a whole mess of history."

Christa brings one hand to her temple and whispers, "Thank you."

"They're still talking about refiling the charges," Carter says.

"What happened to her diary?" I ask.

"It was all circumstantial evidence," Christa says. "There was nothing in there—"

"Then why does it need to disappear to make the case disappear?"

Carter leers forward, barely restraining his rage. "Why did they ever file the charges in the first place?"

Christa pulls him back and holds onto his hand. "It's okay. I want to prove I'm innocent too. So we must answer questions even if people don't believe us."

Maybe I *am* a bigger asshole than I realize, because it genuinely sounds like she's telling the truth.

CHAPTER 6

ELLEN

THE TURBULENCE WAS SO bad during take off that it was impossible to do anything other than remain strapped in my seat. But now that we've reached elevation, I scroll through Kent's tablet, seeking answers. I land on an investigation into Max, detailing his days and logging his internet search history.

What the heck is this about?

Father has been scrutinizing the personal details of my life and spying on Max. We already sort of knew this since he's had Kent at the bakery for the past few days, but this level of invasion is toxic. If it's not illegal, it should be. It can't be allowed to go on.

I'm considering dialing Father when Llorenç calls to say he's at Sam's house. There's no sign of Max's truck, and from the driveway no one's driven near the house since the snow started falling hard. He waits for me to tell him what I want him to do next.

"Try to find out if Max was there and what they talked about," I reply, pulling Kent's tablet closer as the dots move across the screen, members of Father's security staff from the mine scouring roadways.

Llorenç tells me he's put the call on speaker inside his pocket, confirms I can hear, then plods through the snow with grunting breaths.

"It's cold out here," he says, heading up to the porch. Boots heavy against the steps, he stops and knocks on the door.

When Sam answers, Llorenç introduces himself and asks, "Have you seen Max Corbett?"

"What's this about?"

"We're looking for Mr. Corbett, checking the places he's been."

"Is Max okay?" Sam sounds genuinely worried.

"Probably so, have you seen him?"

"He was here yesterday morning."

"And how was he during that visit?"

"Who did you say you are?"

"Llorenç Marín. I work in security at the South Gulch Mine. We're looking for Max Corbett."

"You think something happened to him?"

"What did you talk about while he was here?"

"Why is that your business?" Sam asks.

"We're just worried about Mr. Corbett."

"And you decided to come here? Are we being targeted, investigated?"

Llorenç says nothing.

Sam says, "Until you can explain why you're here in a way that makes sense, I'm through answering your questions."

"Is that all you wanted to know?" Llorenç asks me. I can imagine him leaning down to speak into his pocket.

What a mess. I feel bad for sending people out there based on nothing more than gossip.

"Sam, this is Ellen Jasper from the bakery. Max didn't come home last night, and with the storm, we're checking all the places he's been. I'm sorry for how it's coming across, but we'd be grateful if you know anything to help us find him."

"Oh, well, in that case, we can round up all the homesteaders and put out a search party. Someone should have said something."

He's right; I might have called them for help instead of Father. Max has mentioned my independent streak. He says I need to try to trust people a little more. Not everyone wants to get close to me because of Father's money, especially not around Higgins, but I still have a hard time with it.

"Would you do that now?" I ask Sam.

"Of course."

I fill him in on how long Max has been gone.

"We'll put it on our social media pages and ask anyone who may have seen him to contact you," Sam says.

I hang up with Llorenç and stare at Kent's tablet.

By the time we're over Lake Michigan, I'm digging into Kent's search history. His investigative efforts lead me to the secretary of state's office and a rabbit trail of permit applications, connecting Carter to a limited liability company with land adjacent to Echo Canyon.

While it's not evidence of a connection to Sam or the fires, it seems like it could be significant. It's not something Max has mentioned.

Max says his brother is just as set against mining as he is, but Carter's been dead broke since their grandmother cut him out of her will.

It's funny, in a sad way, what money does to people. Or, in Carter's case, what a lack of money may have done.

Two messages arrive from Max, and then the phone rings. I scramble to answer.

"Flynn." His voice is so comforting.

I close my eyes, know he's safe, and hear him like he's beside me. "I've been trying to get a hold of you. You're okay?"

"I'm in the hospital, but I'm fine."

"You're in the hospital?" I bolt off the bed and pace across the tiny room.

"Well . . . Some guy was shooting at me, and I ended up in Echo Canyon all banged up."

I draw in a shuddered gasp. "Oh my God! What? What happened?"

"I'll be out of here today or pretty soon, I'm sure. Laura told me you're headed to New York. How are you?"

"Who would shoot at you?" I stare out the window at the ground 40,000 feet below.

"I'm not sure yet."

A bottomless pit opens in my stomach. I whirl toward the bed and scroll through the development permit. "Have you called the sheriff?"

"Not yet. I'm trying to figure it out."

"Do you think it was Carter?"

"I don't know. He found me."

My breath hitches slightly. "Carter found you?"

"I'd still be down there if he hadn't shown up with a bunch of ranch hands."

"Wow. I'm so glad they did. You're sure you're okay?"

"Yeah. Fine. Really." He's definitely lying.

My nostrils flare. I take a couple of deep breaths and smell the conditioned air, something savory they must have cooked in the main cabin, and my own unshowered skin. "I'm coming home."

"How's your dad?" Max asks.

I groan. "I'm not sure yet. I can turn around as long as Father's staff doesn't stop me."

"Would they really stop you?" Concern mars his voice.

"I doubt it," I say, despite my worries. "It's just that it sounds like he's not doing very well. He's being really pushy."

"When isn't he?" Max half-laughs, but it's a pained noise.

"But this is different. He sounded scared on the phone, and his staff was adamant that I needed to see him today. I think he's very sick."

"I hope he's not."

"You're okay?" I ask.

"Yeah." He sighs.

I want to be there with him. "I left you about a hundred messages. You probably got flooded by them."

"My phone is messed up. The screen is cracked in the middle."

"Did they not show up?"

"Not yet."

"But they would have come through by now. Wouldn't they? Are you getting other messages?" Unless Father's had people tampering with Max's phone the same way they found the internet search history. Could they do that? "You need to change all your passcodes."

"Why?" He uses his mom's birthday, and her memory is crucial to him.

"I'm sorry. My father's been tracking your internet search history."

"Huh. Okay. He told you this recently?"

"I saw something on Kent's tablet since I got on the jet. I was using it to direct the search so they could help me look for you."

"I wish you hadn't gotten them involved." I can imagine the look on his face, pained and slightly annoyed.

"It was a last resort. I even called Carter."

"You talked to Carter?"

"I didn't know what else to do. Kay gave me his phone number."

"So you talked to Carter?"

"You're repeating what I'm saying. Yes. I talked to him."

"Sorry. It's . . . My brother came in a minute ago."

"Oh. I'll let you go."

"Let me talk to him for a few minutes. I'll call you."

"Okay, but I found something about Carter." I hurry to explain the permit application adjacent to Echo Canyon.

"What kind of development?" Max asks.

"I don't know yet. Maybe mining. It's scheduled for a hearing in August."

"I'll come back right now."

"You should see your dad. I know that's been weighing on you."

"You're sure?"

"I'm sure."

"I love you." I need to tell him I'm pregnant. My tongue sticks to the roof of my mouth. I force it free and blurt, "I need to tell you something important as soon as you have a minute to talk privately."

"Okay. I love you, Flynn. I'll call you soon."

"Talk soon." The words hurt. I text Sam and thank him for offering to help, letting him know that Max is okay.

I continue researching using Kent's tablet until the jet touches down at Teterboro and begins taxiing.

A knock sounds on the door. The jet has stopped.

The knock grows more insistent. "Miss Jasper, are you ready to deplane?"

"I'll be right out." Taking my feet, I check my appearance in the mirror. This is a different life than the one I left behind, and I'm not the same woman I was when I left. I don't miss the cocktail parties dragging toward dawn, being fawned over by men I never planned to marry, brunches with political players, or afternoons in the Hamptons, Westchester, Father's country house, or yacht. Hours I wasn't schmoozing someone were spent at his office forging mining records as part of Father's elaborate charade. It's not as if by just being here my past life could infect me once again.

I can manage myself long enough to see Father and go home. A low buzz of anxiety starts in my ear, sending a shiver of fear through me.

Opening the door, Kent's smiling face confronts me.

He extends one hand and says, "I need my tablet."

I return it then walk past him.

His footsteps follow me off the jet, his breath warming my neck.

I stop at the bottom of the airstair and turn.

He pulls me into him and moves forward. His hands are cupping my neck and cheek. I shove him as he moves forward. Our lips collide. He opens his mouth, giving me a taste of whiskey he must have had in flight.

I push him hard enough that my hands slip off his arms. I flail against the air as my shoe slips on the bottom step. "What the fuck was that?"

He's looking past me at the camera, with a smile.

I slap him so hard that my hand stings.

CHAPTER 7

MAX

Ellen disconnects our call, leaving me glaring at Carter as he glares back. He deleted her messages off my phone. She's accusing her dad, but I'm sure it was him.

Knowing what the guilty look on his face means, I ask, "What were you thinking?"

"That you're not thinking. Look at you, lovey-dovey—let's buy a box of candy over this girl whose father is wrecking our family. It's sickening. Somebody has to look out for you."

I grip the bedrail hard, shoving it with one arm until it's out of the way, then kick my legs out of bed and drag the IV stand forward with my free arm. My feet hit the floor, and I cringe.

He laughs, not a full roar but a chuckle.

I step forward, lumbering across the shiny floor, regretting it immediately because pain shoots up my injured right leg. "Why do you insist on fucking with me?"

He steps forward. "I'm looking out for you."

"You're an idiot if you think tampering with my relationships is looking out for me."

"Did you just call me an idiot?" He's right in my face.

Christa grips his arm, pulling him back. "You both need to stop."

Carter looks down at her then back at me. He lets her move him into the visitor's chair, but he's still half-smiling.

What the hell am I thinking even talking to Carter? He may have dragged me out of a canyon, but letting them return to the ranch would be a huge mistake. Nothing is settled between us.

"You want what you can't have," he says, his tone plain as Pops's used to be while ranting. "Since you were four, you've been like this, dreaming of getting out of here, too moody to see happiness is in front of you."

Christa chimes in with, "I was the same way when I left, then I came home and things got better."

He draws her onto the chair beside him. "You have it all right here but can't see it because you're wrapped up with Ellen. Stop trying to get what you can't have. Just stop, and you'll be happy."

"Stop telling me who to love. It won't go well."

"But you're not seeing her for what she is."

"Don't judge her because of her dad."

"I'm not. Have you considered how things would be between us if she'd left Maker's when I asked her to?"

"You had no right to bully her into leaving. Blame Nonna if you want to blame someone." Bitterness makes my voice low.

He helps Christa onto the chair arm and then comes at me. "Would you have bought land when you knew it was sacred to a family fighting over whether it was sold?"

"She didn't know."

He smirks.

"Honest to God, she didn't. Stop acting like she has ulterior motives. Just leave us alone and stop trying to wreck things."

"I will once you face the facts."

Anger makes me want to fight with him, but the weakness in my limbs, pounding in my head, and racing of my heart combine to make me step back until I'm resting against the footboard.

He puts a hand on my shoulder.

I look him in the eye. My older brother. "You turned off the GPS in my truck too?"

His head jerks back. "No."

"And you expect me to believe that?"

"I expect you to believe that." He's back in my face. "Did you just accuse me of trying to kill you?"

"No."

"Well, then, it must be me. I'm having difficulty understanding why you'd accuse me of fucking with your truck."

Dr. Campela walks in and takes us in with an unamused frown. She turns to Carter. "The hospital has a visitor management policy, and the yelling carried down the hall. I'll have to document this as a level-one incident, bringing it to the attention of the other staff. In the meantime, I'm going to ask you to leave."

"We were just headed home." He starts for the door.

"Do not go to the ranch. Do you hear me? Not until we sort out why you're deleting messages off my phone."

Christa walks out with her hand on his arm, talking in his ear, likely trying to calm him down, and I'm sorry for how this impacts her and Logan. Our family is a mess, and I'm not improving it.

Once they're out of sight, I parrot my eighty-year-old grandmother's pleas after she had a stroke and attempt to convince Dr. Campela I'm fit to go home. "How soon can you make that happen?"

She pushes her glasses up and pinches the bridge of her nose.

"You lost blood and are dehydrated. You probably feel okay now because of the IV fluids and medications, but you'll remain weak for a few days."

"I can be weak at home."

"If you want to go home, then you go home." Her words are what I want to hear, but her tone says I'd be a moron to do it.

"So that's it?"

"You'd be discharged against medical advice. Your blood pressure is low. I'd prefer to keep you admitted until we're sure we've stopped any internal bleeding. You would need to limit your activities, stay in bed, and have someone close by to keep an eye on you and bring you back to the hospital if you get short of breath, dizzy, rapid heart rate, have any complications. Even then, it's marginally unsafe and not recommended."

"Okay." I'm dizzy with shortness of breath and a rapid heart rate, but how can I stay here when I should be doing something to figure out who tried to kill me?

As she leaves the room, I sink into the well-worn visitor's chair. The TV, silently showing the Cheyenne news, has nothing to compare with the drama in my hometown.

I call Kay, the ranch cook responsible for keeping my manners tuned after Mom died and teaching me to dance. She's nearly seventy, the same woman Nonna called for help in difficult circumstances, such as being confined to a hospital bed when she didn't want to be there.

After I tell Kay I'm recruiting a hospital getaway driver, she snickers then promises to bring me clothes, which will probably make me feel like I'm being dressed for elementary school all over again—having me looking like a John Wayne impersonator.

Before we disconnect, I ask, "Have you seen Carter?"

"He's been here with Logan and Christa most of the day. I cooked their supper."

"Okay."

"He said you told them it would be alright."

Not wanting to draw her into the argument, I ask, "Any idea where my truck is?"

"Over by the horse barn."

Over by the horse barn? "Don't touch it, okay?"

"Okay. I'll be there to get you soon."

I settle back in the vinyl chair, amend my request to include loose clothes, then end the call and dial Detective Windt to fill him in on someone's efforts to kill me. Explaining the last few days will require me to admit I was investigating Christa's case, implying I'm not sure they got it right. Maybe they didn't.

I end the call before he answers and search the internet for private detectives instead, finding a guy from Jackson who agrees to meet me at the ranch later in the afternoon.

Kay walks in as we finalize the details and pinches her mouth into a firm line as we end the call.

"You're banged up." She runs a finger around the hair at my ear.

"Give me a few days. I'll be good as new." I'm trying not to think about it.

"That cut on your cheek will scar."

"Makes me look rugged." I give her my best smile, probably making me look deranged.

A hospital administrator comes in with paperwork. A tech removes my IV, and I change into too-large sweats behind the curtain. Bruising covers my torso and legs, but I'm in decent shape besides that and my arm and cheek. And my headache. My entire body hurts. Leaving one arm under since my left arm is in a sling, I walk—more like hobble—out of the hospital and into the passenger seat of Kay's crossover.

She turns on the radio—a local news blowtorch informs us of the latest in human trafficking. Snowy prairie slides by outside the window.

I pull out my phone to text Ellen, "Carter's the one who deleted the messages off my phone." Then I send her a gif of the dog we've been talking about getting, a golden retriever like the one she had when she was little. Only this dog burrows into the bed, practically kicking the guy off the edge of the mattress to nuzzle beside his girl.

She replies with a laughing face emoji, and then a few seconds later she sends a snapshot of another article about her dad. This one has comments below from pundits speculating that he's already dead. They're ruthless.

I text back, "You'll get to see him soon," and she replies, "I'd rather be with you. How are you?" I reply, "Just got out of the hospital, headed to the ranch."

She calls, and when I answer, she asks, "They discharged you?"

"Yeah." A white lie I shouldn't have told. Still, I need to figure out who tried to kill me. "I'm feeling pretty good."

This earns me a cartoon eyebrow from Kay, which I shrug off with a "what did you expect" smirk.

"I'm so glad. I need to talk to you about something, but I'm on a helicopter. We're about to take off."

"Kay's driving me home. We'll talk tonight after you see your dad?"

"I'll call you."

At the main house, Kay helps me inside and then stays in the kitchen while I limp toward the library. Christa is talking on the phone while propped against the massive stone fireplace in the great room.

"Even Logan thinks maybe his mom lit the Bowmans' home on fire." She looks up as I walk in, offers a tight smile, then says, "Okay, Dad, I'd better go. I'll call you later." Then she tucks the phone in her pocket with embarrassment etched on her face. Even Logan isn't sure if she started the fires, and the entire situation seems wrong. I will do everything I can to figure this out. And if it turns out they're not responsible for the other four fires, I'll write a check to repay whatever all this has cost money-wise.

But until then they need to leave.

"Carter's here too?" I ask.

"Yeah, sorry." She gives me a tight smile. "I know you said not to come."

I lean against the chimney, scoot onto the hearth, and say, "Carter can't keep doing the stuff he's doing. Can you talk to him, save us a fight? Get him to move back to your place at Benson's Pond. Until we figure this out, it's the only choice."

She draws in a big breath. "I don't want to be the intermediary."

"But he'll listen to you."

"At this rate, you two will be shooting at each other again."

"Give us a few hours." I attempt a smirk. That whole memory of us pawing through Pops's gun collection like maniacs makes me cringe.

"You're going to have to figure out how to get along."

"I know." It's either that or cut ties altogether.

"I'll talk to him, buy you both a few days to cool off, and let you heal up."

"Thanks," I say, but I'm thinking she may be the only one who can get him to be reasonable.

She starts to speak then stops.

I ask, "What do you know about a development deal near Echo Canyon?"

She fusses with the end of her braid. "Nothing. What is it?"

"I'm not sure. Just something I heard."

"Heard about what?" Carter asks from down the hall, just beyond view.

"Do you know about a development near Echo Canyon?" Christa asks him.

He scrapes a hand down his beard and then looks at me hard. "What are you doing out of the hospital?"

"Came to make sure you're not going to try and move in just because I'm not here to stop you."

He steps up to where I'm sitting, glowering at me. "I spent hours looking for you. Pulled you out of—"

"I know, but that doesn't give you license to invade my privacy or orchestrate my love life."

"It's all about this girl."

"It's all about you thinking you're in charge."

Carter's shoulders bunch.

Christa stands and touches his elbow. "We need to give Max a few days. Then we can come back and talk."

"Okay, darlin'," he says, but he's looking at me over her head as she shoves him out of the room with a silent reprimand that I take to mean, "You want to dictate policy and act like the badass in charge? You better be ready to back it up."

CHAPTER 8

KENT FOLLOWS after me with boots that clap against the concrete apron. Half of me wants to sprint toward the photographer and give them something really stunning to put on their news feed, but a more seasoned part of me knows it would only make things worse.

Still, it's very unpleasant and made worrisome by a nagging sense that Father has put Kent up to this. He's trying to undermine my relationship with Max, and he's using Kent as a pawn because we have a tiny bit of history from a part of my past I'd love to forget.

I should never have trusted Father to help me find Max.

I definitely can't believe a word Kent says about anything.

The exclusive private jet terminal is tiny in size and a huge perk, limiting visitors to the extremely wealthy clientèle. A waiting helicopter is emblazoned with Father's logo on the door.

"You're not welcome inside," I say to Kent before meeting the pilot.

Of course, Kent follows me, regardless.

The sleek interior with posh cream-colored seats and a bar built into the console is large enough to carry me and a small cheerleading squad.

I stop and face Kent. Saying his name, I wait for him to meet my gaze before adding, "I don't know what my father has told you or what game he has you playing, but if you try to get on this helicopter with me, I will file a police report."

"Noted," he says, rubbing his square jaw like he's just taken a punch.

I meet the pilot, climb aboard, and sit rigidly against the cold leather upholstery, waiting.

Kent remains outside, happily speaking with the pilot, telling a long story about how he can't wait to get down to Florida to see his mother. How they're planning to share a chartered fishing boat with another one of Father's employees and wouldn't the pilot like to join them in the sunshine. It's an innocent chat that sets my teeth on edge and makes the hair on my neck prickle. Father is behind this.

There's no other explanation. I've never experienced such unprofessional behavior from anyone under Father's employment. It's absurd and infuriating.

Being photographed, being violated, and even being photographed while being violated aren't new experiences after everything that happened with Peter selling photos of us together to finance his defense attorney. I'd hoped that part of my life was over, and I hate that it's not.

I'm waiting for Kent to press the pilot to let him aboard and press me into filing charges against him. With every passing moment, my breathing becomes faster. The crushing anxiety I've almost gotten over since leaving this life comes roaring back. I grip the armrests until my fingers bite into the hard plastic under the cushion. I imagine the half moons they make in the leather and concentrate on my breathing until I can almost forget that Kent's outside, waiting to push me toward a confrontation.

I miss my happy life. I miss Max and the way having him beside me makes me feel safer and happier. I need to go back home and make sure he's okay. I need to find out why someone was trying to kill him. I place one hand on my stomach and draw a calming breath, then another, and more, imagining that I can hear Max's steady heartbeat instead of the annoying voices and whipping rotors of the chopper landing beside us.

Max texts me a silly photo of a golden retriever that I've been saying we should get. Only, with everything going on in both of our lives, now probably isn't the time.

I need to tell him about Kent, but he's in the hospital. If I tell Max another man kissed me, he'll want to come here. He would confront Kent, but he doesn't need to be stressing over this. I'm ashamed of letting it happen, of trusting Father when I should know better.

I send him a laughing face emoji and a photo of the latest report about Father then ask how he's doing. He replies that he just got out of the hospital and is headed to the ranch.

I call and when he answers, I ask, "They discharged you?"

"Yeah. I'm feeling pretty good."

"Thank God, sweetheart. I'm so glad to hear that you're out. I've been really worried about you. I need to tell you a few things, but I'm on a helicopter. We're about to go to my father's building."

The pilot yells at Kent, breaking away with a shouted apology as he excuses himself and shuts me inside with another bashful apology about the delay.

Max says, "Kay's driving me home. We'll talk tonight after you see your dad?"

I agree to call him and we hang up.

As the helicopter takes off for the short flight between Teterboro and Manhattan, I stare out the window at Kent. His form shrinks on the tarmac below. I can still feel him looking at me despite the tinted window. The tension in my body reawakens, a buzzing warning, like a rattlesnake you can't see.

My phone rings, and it's a Wyoming caller. Not Max's number but someone calling from the ranch. I'd give out my favorite muffin recipe to have Max's voice in my ear again. Maybe he's calling from the house phone.

Even though it's loud and not strictly proper to talk on the phone in the air, I pull off my noise-canceling headset and answer.

"This is Davis, the West Creek farm foreman," a man's voice says.

I turn my head into the seat to hear. "Oh, yes, of course, Davis. I know who you are. We've met but not spoken, right?"

"That's right. Laura's my niece. She thinks you're great, and I know this is a strange phone call, but I wanted to say Max was near death when we pulled him out of Echo Canyon. Kay and I have been thinking and talking ever since. This is similar to when Janet died, with nobody around, Carter being the one to come upon her injured."

"I remember." Max was immediately worried after his grandmother fell at night while working in her garden.

"And she died," Davis says.

"Yes, I know." Cold fear washes my arms and hands. I strain harder to hear.

"Well . . . I'm not saying . . . I don't know what I'm saying. I'm just thinking, and Max is still in the hospital. Carter's always around since we found Max, so I can't talk to him, but Carter's also started moving into the main house here at the ranch. I just thought you should know things are haywire."

"Yeah . . . We . . . Thank you for the call. I'll talk to Max."

"Maybe it would be best if you don't mention I called when you talk to Max."

"Um. . . Why not?"

"I'm unsure what good it would do. Maybe I shouldn't have said anything."

"No, I'm glad you called, and I'll try not to mention your name. Okay?"

"I hope it turns out I'm wrong. This family has been through so much already."

"I know. Thanks again. I better go."

I disconnect the call and sit, bouncing my knee, suddenly wanting to go home more than anything. Why doesn't he just text Max if he wants to reach him? Max says he's fine and out of the hospital. Davis says it's much worse—*near death.*

I turn toward the window, grip the door handle, and will the helicopter to touch the East River heliport as it bumps the landing. As soon as the rotors quiet, I resist the urge to throw the door open so I can see Father and get back home.

Still, once the crew opens the door, I sprint the pier toward Father's towering black glass building. I'm winded when I approach the doorman.

Plastering on my most professional face, I ask him to help me get up to Father's floor.

He ushers me toward the security guard behind a sleek desk in the chrome and black lobby. The guard presses buttons and hands me a keycard, giving me access to restricted parts of the building. I continue past, present my card at the elevator, and almost lose the food I didn't eat during the lightning ride to the top floor, home to Father's executive suite.

I'm queasy with nerves and morning sickness. I haven't eaten in hours. I enter the foyer and want to turn back without facing Father. I shouldn't be here without Max, but here I am.

And Father can't get away with what he's doing. It's time for me to tell him.

A deep atrium of polished, etched glass and chrome is directly in front. On three sides are doors. A clear one leads into Father's executive suite, a heavy mahogany one to his residence, and the last to a set of stairs leading down sixty floors.

I head toward the business end of the space and greet his longtime secretary, Adelle Castro.

She stands behind her desk and gives me a judgmental once over. "He's expecting you."

She's put up with Father for so long—a trooper, efficient as high-octane fuel. The sort of woman a man like Father can depend on to keep his schedule ticking along on time. Her short hair is dyed jet black and coiffed in the style of my deceased grandmother. Her white silk shirt has tiny beige spots, coordinating with the timeless Jackie O-style scarf tied around her neck. I hope he pays her exceptionally well. It looks like she hasn't smiled since before I was born.

With a characteristically grim look, she ushers me into his office. Then she scurries out, closing the heavy glass door behind her with a soul-sucking vacuum sound, like I've entered another atmosphere. It's caused by Father's special filters in the space to purify the air, since he sometimes smokes cigars up here while entertaining.

He's settled on his semi-circular sofa with one ankle crossed over his knee. His signature navy-blue suit still shouts authority, but he's so thin that it could be dressing a scarecrow. Still, there's no nurse here. I'm hit with warring sentiments, shifting between resentment, sadness, and love. And maybe now I understand what Adelle's judgmental look meant.

His skin is so white that his graying eyebrows stand out, and his beard stubble contrasts his chin.

The financial pundits are right. He's dying.

He stands and wraps me in a bear hug as if nothing has been strained between us. He still smells like peppermint gum and holds me like he's in control, but coming here brings home how much of my life is different from when I left. I feel different. Stronger and sure of what I want.

Once he releases me, I sit straight-backed against a chair across from him and try to look as put together as I did in our last corporate headshots. His stoic expression is unreadable.

"How are you?" I ask.

"Fine."

"You didn't sound fine during our last phone call," I say.

Father leans over his knees, posture slumped.

I stare out the big windows and then down at the million-dollar rug covering a marble floor.

Things between us weren't always so bad. Before Mom died, he was domineering, sometimes manipulative, but loving. When she died, he was a wreck, just like I was. I might sometimes hate my father, but he held me when I hurt. He defended me publicly after Peter's betrayal came to light. Still, Father's the reason I went to Wyoming in the first place. He's trying to ruin my relationship with Max. He disowned me but continues to keep me from living as I'd like.

I meet his weary blue eyes.

Father says, "I'm sorry. I've never said I'm sorry, but I've been thinking since you left, and I am sorry."

"For?" I clench my jaw, thinking through the last few hours— Kent's behavior in Wyoming then kissing me as we exited the plane and what he said about Max. I use everything Father taught me during the six years I worked for him to analyze him.

He's unblinking and tight-knuckled. He says, "It's stomach cancer that has spread into my lungs."

"What do the doctors say?"

"Pff." He lets out a discordant breath.

"I'm sorry to hear you're so sick."

He rests against the leather chair. "I mishandled things with the farm."

Mishandled! He demolished Mom's family home and left it in heaps of rubble. That's not mishandling. It's destructive! If he hadn't been so set on keeping me from spending time there, our relationship wouldn't have imploded.

"I regret it," he says.

A time existed when Father's admission would have meant everything to me, but now I say, "It's in the past."

"It's affecting us now."

"Because you're still doing the same things."

"And you're not?" He steeples his fingers.

"I haven't done anything that compares." Still, I turned in the undoctored monitoring report on the Zelda Mine and started a massive investigation into his business dealings that he conveniently lied his way out of. He cut off all my access to money. Our relationship has been on a downhill slide ever since.

He clears his throat. "Let's say you finance a charity leading the way in mineral processing innovations, and instead, the charity becomes a conservation center focused on stopping mining," he posits. "And you are left considering, 'Stopping mining is exactly the opposite of what I supported.' Can they do that? How can they go and do that?"

He frequently talks in circles when trying to avoid the facts. It's always annoyed me. I wouldn't have turned in the Zelda report like that, but he destroyed her old home and sent me on a quest for independence via a Wyoming homestead.

He would upend the earth to make money, and Max would rather forget there's gold than risk the land. Everything about my life here contradicts what I left behind.

I notch my folded hands between my knees and lean forward, holding my tone firm but gentle. "I have too many things on my mind to take a meandering approach. If you want to talk with me, you must speak plainly."

"If you listened, you'd hear something important."

"Is this what we're doing today? You sounded afraid on the phone." I wait for one full breath before taking my feet and moving toward the door. "I don't need to be here for this. I flew across the country, knowing Max was at risk and with Kent making travel uncomfortable. I can't believe I fell for your bullshit all over again."

"You can fire Kent." Father gazes at me, unblinking. "You can fire anyone at the company you want to fire."

"Oh, yeah, I'm sure." What game is he playing now?

"It's about to be your company," Father says.

"But—"

"All you have to do is return to work at Cross Mountain."

"What do you mean, 'it's about to be my company?'" I ask.

"Just what I said."

"Why would you give me your business if you know I'll reverse your decisions?"

"Because you're my daughter." His voice is bitter. "Even if you're befriending my enemies, I love you."

I take a deep breath.

He's selling me the way he sells investors on the nonsense deals he's hoping to get off his books. He's had Kent spying on my life, extensively researching me as a target, he's prepared responses to my objections, he automatically dominates every conversation, and now he's letting me sit in silence, stewing over an offer that is exactly the thing it would take—the only possible enticement—to get me to walk away from my happy life.

"This is bait, right?" I ask.

Amusement causes his lips to pull up on one side. "It's not bait."

"Then what is it?"

"This is your father." He lifts his hand then draws it down in front of himself as if displaying a product. Except, he's so frail and clearly sick.

"And why did you have Kent kiss me at the airport?"

Father's bushy gray brows draw low over his eyes, causing them the hollow even more.

"You want to drive a wedge in my relationship with Max."

"I just want you to consider the proposal in front of you."

"So you're unaware of Kent's behavior?" I ask.

"Kent sometimes uses unorthodox tactics."

"And you approve."

"It gets results."

"And you don't care about the costs?"

"Pff."

My phone chimes with a message from Gena, my former assistant.

Gena Wellins: *Looks like you're making a splash with your home-coming. Glad to have you back.*

She's sent a photo spread of Kent kissing me. If Max sees this, he'll be furious at Kent mostly but also maybe at me.

I tell myself to breathe and summon a solution from my professional brain, but worse, what about when I tell Max about Father's offer to bequeath me his company?

An icy panic creeps up from my feet and hands toward my chest.

Max won't be thrilled, but he'll understand why I'm even considering the idea. He'll help me figure out if anything Father's saying makes sense.

Because if there's a chance I can fix the mines, I'm not sure I can ignore it.

CHAPTER 9

MAX

"YOU NEED to go back to the hospital," Kay says from her perch near my childhood bed. It's light outside. I can't recall how long I've been lying here.

I turn toward her. "What time is it?"

"If you need us to keep Carter out while you're in the hospital, Davis will help me do it."

"I know." They shouldn't have to fight my battles.

"Then let's load you in the back seat."

"No."

"Then I'm calling in a home nurse."

I kick my feet over the side of the bed.

She springs out of her chair. "Oh no, you don't. Stubborn or stupid, either way, you stay in bed."

"Fine, hire a nurse. Call Dr. Campela and ask her to recommend somebody." Too exhausted to move, I keep moving, forcing myself forward despite the pain and dizziness.

"You're going to end up back at the hospital."

My phone alerts me with a new message.

"My investigator's here." I move past Kay and out the veranda door. It's maybe four o'clock based on the sun, plenty of daylight left to get some answers, though a frigid wind is coming from the west. I turn back to get a coat, find Kay holding it out, and pause while she tosses it over my shoulders.

One arm still in a sling, I don't mess with the zipper before limping out to meet the investigator. Dressed in jeans, a collared shirt, and a heavy jacket, he has short-cut hair and an exercise fanatic's build.

"Wow," he says before we exchange hellos. "You're in bad bad shape."

"A walking corpse, from how people keep lookin' at me and saying stuff like that."

"Well . . ." He lets the words trail off, introduces himself as Dick Kalpakoff, then asks what he can do.

"Tell me who last drove this pickup." I walk toward my truck, expecting him to follow, which he does, matching my turtle pace.

He fingerprints me and then starts on the truck. While he's inside dusting for more prints, Carter walks up and holds out his flask. "You need whiskey?"

I should ask him what he's still doing here, but a drink might chase away this shiver. I take Carter's flask and swallow a burning draw. More alive and stupid, I struggle to recap the lid. Not liking how dizzy I am, I stare at the horizon. It shimmers then spins. I put one hand on the truck, reset the lid, and hand Carter's flask back to him.

He tucks it in his jacket pocket. "I've been thinking. What if the shooter was someone from the South Gulch Mine? Not an employee, necessarily, but someone with access to that property. One of Ed Jasper's people?"

"This meddling again?"

He crosses his arms and says, "They've got access coming in the back way to the turnaround. It could have been someone from over there. They wouldn't have had to come through one of our normal gates. Could have stayed off the cameras."

I blink against my spotting vision. Carter seems to sway. How badly did I mess up leaving the hospital? Or was it something in his flask? Still, I say, "I keep meaning to look at the cameras."

"I've spent the last four hours reviewing the footage with Christa. There's nothing out of the ordinary, and whoever parked your truck picked a place between cameras and left by staying between the house and the treehouse."

"Maybe they walked out." He could have done it as easily as anyone.

"Maybe."

"It makes sense you're saying this."

"Because you think I have an agenda."

"Because I *know* you have an agenda."

"Alright, fine. I have an agenda: looking out for my numb-skulled, half-dead brother."

"Looking out for me. That's what I'd call it."

He shakes his head, takes a step back, and then holds his hands palms out. "This is the same thing that happened with the fires. Because I care and get upset, everybody thinks I'm doing things I shouldn't do. Well, you know what? You were all wrong before, and you're wrong now."

He stomps off, skirting the iciest patches of road.

Someone could come from the South Gulch Mine into the backside of our property without raising anyone's notice, but so could whoever's involved in the development project Ellen mentioned. Owning a ranch as big as a national park makes me vulnerable to countless issues.

Dick says, "I've got all the prints, and the mess is pretty cleaned up." He lets me know it's okay to drive it or have it detailed or whatever I want to do next and that he'll have more information once he gets back to his office.

"Is that it?" he asks.

"I also want to talk to you about an old investigation into four arsons and a development permit on the other side of our property." More sore and winded with each step, I hobble over the terracotta tile toward Nonna's office with Dick beside me.

Once there, Dick settles on Nonna's stiff-backed antique couch while I lean on a tall wooden file cabinet and thumb through old records in the middle drawer. I need any information Nonna had about the fires. Carter had hired an investigator back then. Preoccupied with running my restaurant and refusing to get really involved, I never read the report, but I find a copy tucked into a manila file folder and pull it out.

I consider handing it over to Dick, letting him tell me what he thinks. Instead, I settle across from him in Nonna's old leather chair and start to read it aloud, which goes well until he holds up one hand.

"I can't understand you."

"Huh, okay." I start again, but each breath hurts. I focus and enunciate like I'm giving a speech.

He lifts the other hand. "You're turning red and skipping words. Maybe you should consider getting medical attention."

"Probably." I hold out the report. "How about you read it, tell me what you think, and let me know how the truck fingerprints turn out."

"Sure." His eyebrows draw together. "Want me to drive you or call someone or . . ."

"It's fine, there's someone here to look in on me."

We're caught in a loop of reassurances until I call Kay on the intercom and make her tell him I'm okay—which she reluctantly does, promising there's a nurse on the way.

Once he's gone, I lie back against Nonna's chair, close my

eyes, and try to control the pain and slow my breathing by daydreaming about nothing and everything.

I take the ring I bought for Ellen from my pocket and put it on my pinky finger.

With my cheek against the chair, I feel time slip.

I see myself as a boy afraid of storms, crying the house was coming down then arguing with Carter when he called me a liar. Memories skip forward to Carter at Nonna's funeral, surrounded by a group of ranchers, but among the men is Ellen's father with his stiff shoulders and pious expression, saying he's there in Nonna's remembrance. He hates us because of his lawsuit with Pops all those years ago, but if West Creek falls, it won't be his doing. It will be from the rotten chasm that's hollowed out our center. Corbetts fighting ourselves. It would take little more than a spark to ignite an apocalypse of kith and kin.

In the distance, my phone's ringing. I dig it out of my pocket. Ellen's photo fills the screen, showing her smiling at me during a monumental flour fight at her bakery.

I answer. "Hey, Flynn."

"Max, sweetheart. How are you?"

"Good." I lie because she doesn't need to worry.

"You sound a little tired."

"Exhausted."

"Wish I was there."

"Wish you were here."

She laughs, then, "You sound a little drunk."

"Just sleepy." I close my eyes. Sleep sounds great. Really awesome.

"Max." Her voice is so sweet and soft that I can almost picture her saying my name. "Sweetheart. Max."

"Yeah."

"You're okay?"

"I miss you . . . It's not a stretch to say I need you. Love, please . . ."

I ache for Ellen. Her lips, her heart, her physical comfort. Her understanding and the softness of her voice. A warmth grows in my stomach and radiates outward, making me reach for her, not finding her in bed beside me. I squint at the overhead light, trying to see what time it is without fully waking up.

My throat is as sore as it's ever been in my life. I stretch for the glass of water Kay left on the side table and keep reaching. I lean up, realizing the sterile walls, stiff sheets, and antiseptic smell. With a grunt, I try to sit all the way up, meeting the limit of a small tube coming out of my armpit on my right side, where it pinches against a bandage. My left arm is still in a cast and sling. There's pink fluid coming out of the tube. I free it from the sheets then locate the up button on the guardrail. Even holding it down hurts because my fingers are still sore. The extent of my injuries would draw a laugh if they weren't so bona fide and painful.

"You okay?" It's Nurse Jamie coming in. She messes with something on the counter across from me.

"Yeah." It's light outside, probably morning. I lie back on the pillow. The grid ceiling is way too white. "What am I doing back here?"

"You had hemothorax."

"Huh."

"Blood collected in the pleural cavity, between your chest wall and your lungs. They fixed it with exploratory laparoscopic surgery and have been giving you more blood."

"So what now?"

"You stay here until Dr. Campela orders a discharge."

"Huh."

"You're gonna 'huh' over and over?"

"What do you want me to say?"

"Gee, I don't know." She puts her hands on her hips. "How about 'I shouldn't have insisted on going home against doctor's orders? I won't go home until after the chest tube is out?'"

"Yeah, that."

She focuses on the computer near the bed, typing sharply for a few seconds then refocusing on me. "Seriously, you were in shock. You're a complete idiot."

"I know."

"Okay." She heads toward the door.

"Thanks for keeping me alive." I can't even manage a grin.

"It was a small bleed. They didn't see it on the imaging at first, but there might be more issues. Injuries like this usually happen in car accidents. Blood vessels are ruptured by a fall or high-speed collision."

"Like tumbling down a cliff," I ask.

"Exactly, so you're going to have to take it easy. Stay put for a while."

"I'll be on my best behavior." I mean it, though it's almost unbearable to imagine staying in a hospital bed while my life disintegrates. Still, the pain is a lot better than it was. It's easier to breathe.

Once she's gone, I retrieve my phone and call Ellen.

She answers, "Max, sweetheart. I'm so worried about you."

"I'm worried about you too."

"I'm . . . I almost said I'm fine, but I'm not even close to fine. Are you well enough to talk to me? A lot is going on, and I have a ton I need to explain. When we talked last night, you sounded bad. Kay said you've been in surgery."

"I'm out now. I'm fine."

"Oh, good. I really need to tell you some things."

"Okay."

"Well, I . . . This is going to surprise you and not in a good way. I was walking off the jet right after I got off the phone with you yesterday, and Kent was trying to . . . Well, he shocked me. He kissed me. I've never had any member of our staff do anything like that. I think my father's trying to make it seem like

I'm cheating on you. I will fire Kent if—but I need to talk to you about that."

I summon a reaction that doesn't include letting my temper flare or hurting her feelings. She didn't want to be kissed. She's trying to deal with something unwelcome and outside of her control.

"How can you fire him if you no longer work there?" I ask, despite the growing glow of fury in my stomach.

"My father wants me to stay here and take over his company. He's very sick and said I can fire Kent if I accept the role. Of course, I would rather be there, but this is a chance to fix the past, and . . ."

"And that's important to you," I reply, pushing past the knot in my throat.

"It is."

"What are you going to do?"

"What do you want me to do?"

I tell myself this isn't Ellen saying we've talked about how to make it work a hundred times and never found a way. This isn't her asking me to be that man who lets her walk away: "no hard feelings darlin', no tears." I'm not sure I could be that man. Carter's words, "You want what you can't have," seem truer now than ever.

Still, what do I say?

I'm trying to figure out how to do anything about a guy grabbing her and kissing her against her will while I'm hooked up to tubes and barely able to hobble around without people acting like I'm taking my life in my hands.

"Davis said you were near death when they pulled you out of Echo Canyon." Her quick subject change sends me into a spiral. That guy.

"Davis said that?" My voice is sharper than I meant it to be.

"He called to say he hoped everything was okay with my father."

"You know Davis?" I nudge my toe against the footboard.

"He's Laura's uncle."

"Huh. But why did he call you?"

"He's worried Carter might have had something to do with your nonna's fall and hinted that Carter finding you was too convenient."

"But Carter saved my life."

"Maybe he was having regrets?"

"Or maybe it was somebody else."

"Sure, it could have been."'

"Did you call Windt?"

"I started to, but if they got it wrong with the arsons before, they might keep looking at Carter and Christa when it could be someone else. I hired an investigator."

"Oh. That makes sense."

"If this guy doesn't find anything useful from the prints he took today, I'll call Windt and fill him in."

"What did the shooter look like?"

"He was tall and about a football field away. I never got a good look at him."

"You'd have recognized him if it was Carter?"

"Yeah. It wasn't anyone I know. His voice was different, slow, and strange."

Christa comes into the room with her cousin, Skyler—one of my long-term annoyances from childhood and someone Christa has repeatedly tried to fix me up with over the years. I like Christa, but I can't handle her cousin.

"I've got company," I tell Ellen. "I love you, but I'd better go. I'll call you back when we can talk some more."

Ellen says she loves me too, in her sweet way.

Skyler squeezes Christa's arm. "They're so cute. Aren't they cute how they talk to each other?"

Barely managing to avoid asking them to leave, I grit out, "Give me a break, and don't talk about Ellen."

"I like her," Skyler says.

I have zero energy for this. "Why are you here?"

"We wanted to show you something." Christa motions to Skyler, nudging her close to the bed.

Skyler holds her phone toward me. "I'm not trying to gossip, but I thought you should see this, if you haven't already."

On the screen is a photo of Ellen kissing Kent. He's wearing a straw Stetson as they exit a jet. Somewhere deep inside I'm getting angry, really hot and ready to erupt, and these two are in front of me looking like targets.

I try to stop the surge of fury by asking myself these three questions: *Will getting angry help? Is getting angry now useful? Can I keep myself from getting angry?*

Part of me wants to roar out of bed, order them out of the room, combat them by trying to defend Ellen's character, or get frustrated about being presented with a situation I know very little about. Instead, I hold my voice steady and take the quickest route toward getting them to leave. "I have no opinion about it at all."

Skyler gazes from my face to her phone. She puts it back in her purse.

A little smug, I ask, "Is that all?"

She looks at Christa, who lifts one shoulder.

Skyler twists her hands together. "It's just that people talk around here. I've been hurt so many times by gossip. Christa has too. I deal with it at the salon, and people have been talking about Ellen, reading the news about her, since her dad's so famous, you know?"

I hadn't considered this angle on their visit. It's such a small town. Even before Ellen moved here and we started dating, people always talked about our family.

Skyler paces to the visitor's chair and back. "I can tell she didn't want to kiss that guy. He was on top of her, and she was pushing him away. Her body language was wrong. What should I tell people about you and her? I mean, do you want me to say anything? Maybe I can stop them from gossiping or making things worse when she comes home."

Christa says, "We want to hold them accountable for what they're saying and help if we can."

"Thank you," is what I say, but I mean more. I thought they were here to ruin things, and now I'm just trying to think of what to say, but it's like finding out I have family when I thought they were all gone.

CHAPTER 10

ELLEN

PERCHED on the lowest step in the fire exit, I chew on a tasteless vegan granola bar, stare at the door leading me out of Father's building, and clutch my phone. I've been sitting in this position since I ran downstairs after leaving Father's office.

I didn't really say what I needed to say to Max about the incident with Kent. I'm not really sure what to think about Kent. Was he following orders? Acting on his own? A combination of both?

The only thing I do know is that I don't want to think about Kent.

Max said he missed me. He wanted me to come home.

Surrounded by cold concrete walls and steel stairs, buzzing starts deep in my eardrums. A low vibration. It's like a bee growing closer—maybe it's panic. I can't draw a full breath. Someone tried to kill Max, and it's barely sinking in. This is a real threat, more legitimate than their half-baked brotherly antagonism.

My phone rings, and I answer. Laura's cheerful voice over-powers the vibration. She says one of our deliveries is late, but she's talked to the supplier and has changed the planned special to use things we have on hand. I thank her for holding things together.

Tension ebbs from my neck and shoulders. I miss the simplicity of that life and how it connected me to Mom. But the buzzing is still there, a hive inside my skull. How could I have been solely focused on things I can trust Laura to handle? I thank her profusely, plan on giving her a big raise, and end the call.

I need to focus and rely on years of producing results under stress while working for Father. Keep it basic. Consider my fears and attack each one until they're all manageable. I take the stairs two at a time toward his suite.

I'm still unsure what the next steps are when I reach the glass wall of his office. He's alone at his desk. Snippets of conversation carry through the partially closed door. Before he disowned me, I would have been welcome no matter what conversation Father was having. He was schooling me to one day assume his role. I catch a phrase. ". . . threaten my family . . . Ever."

I'm the only person Father would call family. I walk closer, spine-tingling, straining my hearing.

"You hurt my family. I will hurt yours." The voice coming over the speaker sounds just like Max. I grip a hand around my throat against a painful stab. And yet. No. Max would never hurt me. That's insane. It's this buzzing in my head. The voices are distorted through the glass. I step to the door and crack it farther open.

Father says, "You started this."

Fear roots me to the floor, making everything seem slower.

My heartbeat and breathing seem to pause. I push every faculty, wait for Father to respond, for his caller to issue a retort.

"I'll end it," the voice says, and something about his tone is so familiar but definitely not Max. It's Carter on the phone with Father.

"I've already ended it." Father's tone is a finality.

Carter snorts. "Can't you see I don't want to hurt your daughter?"

Father hangs up the phone, wordlessly staring at me. He's so pale it's as if he's already seeing himself in a grave. I hate him for interfering with my life. I never should have come back here. But what if Carter was trying to hurt me? He's definitely capable. The buzzing grows so loud I tug my earlobe. Swallowing the knotting sensation in my throat, I force my voice to come out strong.

"You will tell me what's going on, or you're dead to me already."

He stands and comes around the desk, holding his hands out, moving forward, sending me skittering back. "Calm down."

"Stay away from me."

"God damn it, Ellen." Father sits against the top of his desk, gripping the edge with either hand. "You asked me to help you. I called Carter and tried to negotiate a deal with him. He accused me of trying to kill his brother. I laughed because it's ludicrous that he would accuse me of such a thing, then I mentioned he assaulted my daughter. He became more upset and repeated his accusation, then . . . You heard the rest."

He is good at this, spinning stories and selling the narrative. I move to the window, staring out at the city, trying to think, seeking answers without hitting pay dirt. Did Father try to kill Max? He's not a murderer. However, he is devious and manipulative. Maybe it's a coincidence or circumstantial evidence that's led Father and Carter to accuse each other.

Father would never knowingly hurt me. He wouldn't harm someone I love, but would he hurt someone he thought might harm me to protect me? I think maybe, yes. And he's been hurting Max for a while in other ways. A strange sense of loss settles over me.

All I know is that I know only what Father wants me to know.

I take the stairs to the basement home of Father's security staff, present my keycard at a blank door, and enter the dispatch room. With environmentalists protesting in front of the building occasionally, he prioritizes personal protection. After the phone call I just heard, I should too.

A youngish Black man in a blue suit and starched white shirt sits staring at computer monitors.

He looks up and lifts his chin. "Evening, Ms. Jasper."

"Good evening." I wish I'd brought him something with caffeine. While he's entirely professional, I imagine how tedious the job would be. "Is your whole shift spent sitting down here?"

"Yeah." He smiles. "I like seeing the world from a bird's eye view."

"That's a different perspective than I imagined." The room is smaller than the closet in my apartment, with stark walls, commercial carpet, only Father's picture, the company logo, and a flag as decoration.

"It's better than being up there." He points at the monitor. Kent interacts with another guard. I jolt like he can see me then relax and study him. The other guy ignores him as Kent continues talking. Maybe Kent has boundary issues, and I'm not the only one he's making uncomfortable.

"Does he annoy everyone?" I ask.

The guard stifles a laugh then shifts in his chair, refocusing on the monitor.

"You don't have to answer. Let me say he annoys me and leave it at that."

He tilts his head and leans back in his rolling chair, focused on me. "He's been gloating to everyone about you coming back and kissing him at the airport."

If that doesn't ice the cake, nothing will. I can't believe I used to find him attractive. I cringe at the memories I've been trying to ignore. I touched his hand once, and that day on the beach, I let him walk with me, right beside me like a boyfriend. Maybe years ago, I led him on. It was a mistake.

I move toward the door, then past it into the depth of the space, down the hall, past a break room, offices, a recording room, a conference room, and into the armory.

Father denies organizing the attack on Max, but Kent was in town. He came to get me. Maybe the timing doesn't line up for Kent to have taken a shot at Max himself. Still, he showed me all the staff he had in the area. A tingle runs down my throat and unsettles my already tender stomach.

Still, a few hours ago, I was considering it could have been Sam. It may have been Carter. I need to be careful about who I accuse.

From a rack of handguns, I select a .22 pistol bigger than the one at home and stand holding the grip, fingering the trigger. Suddenly, I'm freezing despite the heat coming into the space from shiny overhead ducts. Get this done, prove I can protect myself, and go home.

Max explained that knowing the range of my weapon and being comfortable with how it's used is my best bet at protecting myself by shooting safely and accurately. He spent hours patiently letting me pick out the gun I wanted from a catalog and went with me when it came in on order at R&S Ammo. Even though he almost laughed at the tiny size of it, he agreed it made sense after I explained I could carry it in my purse without ruining my posture. He'd said it was good I knew my priorities, and he loved that about me.

Swallowing the tingle in my throat, I move into the range and stand in the first lane. Foam lines the walls, and the back is shielded with rubber to stop the projectiles. I move the paper target backward, eyeing the digital readout to reach my maximum practice distance of 50 yards. Positioning my grip and focusing, I shoot and replace targets until I can consistently create two-inch groups without the red dot sight I have on my gun at home.

I move the target in and go again, firing faster, imagining someone shooting at me and forcing myself to hit it. I repeat this until I am sure I could shoot someone coming after me if I had to quickly pull the pistol out of my purse. Then I move the target to six feet. I imagine the pressure and focus it would take to get the gun up before an attacker could take it from me.

Shell casings cover the floor around me. I'm warm and angry but not powerful or confident. If I had to shoot someone, I'd probably hit them in the knee.

I reset the gun and ammo where I found them and walk dazed out of the range.

Kent stands on the other side of the door.

I pull up short, barely managing to avoid a collision.

He smiles. "Like-ta wore a hole in that rubber."

I move to pass him.

He steps into me, blocking my path.

I'd like to punch him in the nose. I glare at him. His after-shave is sweet and way too strong. I swallow down the sickness rising up from my stomach and groan. Holding out my hands as a barrier between us, I squeeze past.

Easy breezy, I walk ahead of Kent with my power-broker face in place. The security guard I met earlier sits behind his moni-tors, watching the screens. He gazes up at me with a conflicted expression. Confusion. Concern. I'm not quite sure.

My phone chimes.

Ed Jasper: Board meeting at nine o'clock.

He includes a link to a press release appointing me to take his place as Chairman and CEO of Cross Mountain Capital.

I haven't even said yes! This isn't fair. It's obnoxious.

Hating how the elevator makes my stomach roil, I launch up the stairs toward his office. Kent's footfalls no longer echo behind me.

Exertion from climbing combines with anger to make my breath hot—my pulse hammers. I'm breathless, sweating, and outraged.

As the majority shareholder with voting rights, Father has the legal authority to make the change even if his board rejects the decision. He would replace them if they objected, which they will. It will be incredibly unpopular for Father to tap me as his successor, especially given my recent experience is running a small bakery, not a massive New York mining conglomerate.

How is he positioning this? Does he expect me to follow his agenda?

Three floors to go. My dressy shoes pound the stairs, echoing in the long, narrow well.

The only way I'd consider taking over is if he gives me irrevocable authority to fix all the out-of-compliance reporting and remediate the mines.

Two floors to go.

Maybe I will finally stop having nightmares. Suppose I go home now, miss the press conference, and the chance to make things right. I'll regret it forever.

I come into the atrium and head into Father's office. Adelle isn't at her desk. I continue past, seeking Father in his office without finding him and then heading out the way I came and entering his residence. The heavy mahogany door of his suite snicks closed, leaving me feeling isolated in his silent home, with massive rooms stuffed with expensive artifacts, like trophies won and put on display to record his life and accomplishments.

Every choice that takes me toward Father's agenda will lead me farther from Max. I need to talk to him before I do anything.

Swiveling slowly, I present my keycard at the door and wait for the light to turn green.

I present my card again and again. Nothing.

And it hits me. Exit doors are not supposed to have keycards. This is a significant code violation, but more than that I'm trapped in Father's residence.

CHAPTER 11

MAX

I FLIP through Dick's report. Various fingerprints were on my truck's door handles, console, and passenger side. Dick says my fingerprints on the wheel and shifter imply that I'm the last one who drove it. Even if someone else had gripped the wheel while wearing gloves, he thinks my fingerprints would have been more smudged, and there weren't any other good prints on the wheel or shifter.

Summarizing the investigation into Sam Bowman, he concludes Sam could have started the fire at his home but not the other fires. There were four fires all at the same time, and Sam was trapped inside a burning house. It had to be someone else, or he had help. Dick wrote, "Why do you think the authorities got it wrong?" Okay. Avoid that thought spiral. I scroll to the next page.

Developers adjacent to Echo Canyon have applied for permits to strip-mine for gold. But Dick makes no connection to Carter. How does Ellen know he's involved? Is she involved? Is her dad involved? Maybe I should ask Jamie if the medications cause paranoia.

I dial Dick and start in. "Any connection between the strip-mining permit and my brother, Carter Corbett?"

"Not that I found. I can dig if you want."

"I think, yeah. Dig into that and . . . Ah . . . Take another look at my truck. See if there's any way someone could have moved it without driving it, like maybe they towed it."

"They'd have had to put it in gear."

"True, but, Dick, someone moved it miles from where I left it."

"They're doing a pretty good job covering." There's a question in his tone: "You're sure you didn't forget where you left it?"

"I hit my head pretty hard, but I'm not losing my mind."

"I'll take another look."

"Thanks, and do it today, okay?"

"Investigations take time," Dick says, droning on, saying nothing. It comes across like a lot of assurances without much meaning. God's truthing and fact of the mattering until I'm forced to concede that my expectations are unreasonable.

We hang up. My eyes glaze making the grid ceiling blur.

Carter's voice comes down the hall, talking to Jamie.

"Stop harassing my patients," she says, passing in the hall as he walks in the door.

"How are you?" Carter asks, tugging off his hat.

"Frustrated with a lot of stuff."

"Like what?" He props his Stetson on the windowsill behind him, sloughs his coat, and sits in the visitor's chair with his legs stretched like a lion relaxing.

"Long day?" I ask, deflecting. How can I bring up the things frustrating me without having it turn out badly? It may be impossible.

"Been working with Logan and Jake. They're learning a bunch of tricks. We've been talking. Maybe we could all ride this year. With you too."

It would be awesome to ride with my nephew and his friend, but I mumble a non-committal "Maybe" nonetheless.

He sits up a little straighter. His eyes and expressions match mine. "Let's cut the bullshit." He's in a blunt mood, and maybe that's a good thing.

"Alright."

"You first."

"No, you first."

"A typical little brother move." He gives me a wry grin. "But okay. I'm cross with you about many things but also worried about you."

I heave a sigh. "Tell me what you're worried about first then what annoys you."

"This relationship you're in." He pauses. "I see you getting tense, but I'm not trying to make you upset. I'm not saying Ellen is the problem. Not her as a person."

I unclench my hand from the bedrail. "Just say what you want to say so we don't have to discuss it anymore."

Carter's eyes widen and then settle to something like amusement. "Her dad called me, telling me to stay away from her. I told him to stay away from you. He said he didn't want Ellen around you, that you being near her put you in danger."

"That doesn't prove he did this." I want him to have not done this.

"How do you know he didn't do it?" Carter asks dryly. "He's threatening you with the mines. He's hated our family for decades because of whatever Pops got mixed up with. He harassed Nonna, trying to drive her into her grave with his attempts to bankrupt us. Here you come and shack up with his daughter. You think he's pleased with you?"

I think he despises me, but I don't want to admit that to my brother. Maybe it's pride or hope that one day I'll be welcomed by the father of the woman I love. Carter's waiting for me to answer. I say, "Let's discuss the development permit near Echo Canyon."

"That's how you're going to play this?" He looks at me hard for a long time until I look away.

I grit out. "You make sense, and you're right. You're saying things I don't want to hear, but I hear you. Okay?"

He nods then leans forward, riveting his attention on the floor between his boots.

I poke his bearlike form with a question. "You going to tell me about this deal at Echo Canyon, or are you planning to wait for me to figure it out?"

Without sitting up, he lifts his head, eyes shining. "I fucked up."

In times like this, Dad always let silence carry the moment, lingering in the bottom notes of sound. The critical care floor is quiet but alive with machines beeping and low murmurs of speech. It's a place intended for healing and here I am with my brother, hopefully headed toward some sort of diplomatic conversation. Whatever he's done, he regrets it.

"Let me help you," I offer.

"I'm not sure you can."

"Try me. At least tell me what's going on."

I watch him, hoping for a blink or a sigh, some sign that he's going to let me in. He stands and puts on his hat.

"So you're not going to tell me."

He drops into the chair with his elbows on his knees, leaning forward as he talks. "Years ago, before I went to Laramie, I signed a deal with Abner."

"He called me the other day," I reply, filling the silence. I don't add that he asked me to go hunting or that I've refused to go. Carter already knows I've cut ties with Abner. He's just too strange for me, and that was before Carter used Abner as an alibi after he hurt Ellen, saying they'd gone up to Alaska for a hunting trip while Carter was lighting Ellen's house on fire.

"You go out to his place in Ballford?" he asks.

I give him a look. *Don't even get me started on why I wouldn't have gone.* He's an idiot to have gotten mixed up with Abner.

Carter scuffs his boot across the polished floor. "In exchange for him buying the tannery to help Christa, I helped Abner buy some land. At the time, I wasn't sure what it was. Just a limited liability company he didn't want his name on. I knew the parcel was near the ranch but didn't know what it was about until later."

"Okay," I prod.

"It turned out Ed was behind the deal, just using Abner. Pops and Nonna wouldn't let the land go through the lease expansion clause, and Ed's lawsuit had been in court for years. They would have fought it longer, not wanting him to win, and then they had a chance to sell to Abner and me. They let it happen, but even though I have legal responsibility for the company, I have no ownership or control."

"So, actually the land is Ed's?"

"Yeah. Exactly."

"But why are you still involved?"

"I don't fully understand it. I've tried to get out of it, but they keep sending me stuff with my name on it. Christa says it's messed up legally. People a lot more educated than we are wrote the contracts, and I have no resources to figure it out, so I'm along for the ride, trying not to fuck up any more than I already have."

"You've been talking to Ed for how long?"

"Since Nonna's funeral."

"And what's going on now—with the strip-mining permit?"

"I refused to sign off on it. His attorneys keep sending me letters, trying to serve me with paperwork." He looks up again and grins. "But good luck to them trying to find me."

I choke out a laugh because I can see him leading process

servers on a chase, but it's a pained sound. We should have talked a lot more before now.

"You could have told me."

"You can't do anything about it either."

"Maybe not, but you should have told me."

"Would you have wanted to hear?" His tone says what he doesn't, that I'm sleeping with Ed's daughter.

His assumption pisses me off enough that my voice is gravel. "I would have listened. Ellen would have helped you."

"Like she's helping you now?"

Annoyance pounds at my temples, spreading behind my eyes. We're headed toward a fight, and I'm powerless to stop it from coming, like watching clouds build on the horizon. I ask, "Do you have any concept of how much she knows about mining permits?"

"And you think that means I should trust her?"

I despise these arguments with Carter. He won't listen when I tell him Ellen's not like her dad. He's stuck on repeat and keeping me away from her. I don't even want to be here talking to him, but he's still talking, droning on about how everything between us would be better if I let him take over Dad's quarter horse program at the ranch. He wants to go to the equine heritage auction in Amarillo. I lean into the pillow.

Nothing will change unless I change.

I reconsider the clause from Nonna's will, she'd planned that if something happened to me, the ranch would be divided up and sold with the proceeds going to charity.

A sinking feeling settles in my gut.

If I expect to have the life I want with Ellen, I have to fight for it, even if it means I'll be the one who sells my family's legacy. I will miss Logan if I can't get square with Carter.

He stops talking and looks at me for a response.

I have no idea what he just said.

If I tell Carter what I'm thinking, I will see the ugly person he can be.

"You gonna talk to me?" he asks.

"If I tell you what I'm thinking, you'll be pissed, and I don't want that."

I struggle out of bed and into the visitor's chair. The shiny floor reflects the overhead lights. Reconciliation is implausible when every conversation I have with Carter goes in circles.

I've had things my way, attempting to satisfy everyone and satisfying no one. I locate a national realty brokerage in Jackson focused on selling large rural estates. They connect me with an agent who explains they'll present photos of the property on their website and in magazines. They discuss showcasing it on their television show, the land, house, and substantial price in the listing.

Within minutes of hanging up, I'm staring at an agreement on my phone. My entire body revolts at the idea, making me jumpy as a silverfish. This is not the right thing to do. And it's not that Carter will be furious or that I haven't talked to him beforehand. It sits wrong in my heart and my gut, like I've eaten something sour that will make me pay a heavy price at some point in the future. I scroll through the email. They've got some lingering questions to finish the disclosures.

I should talk to Ellen about this before making a decision. But what if she says we should sell?

It's wrong for Logan, for whatever kids Carter may have in the future, and for whatever kids I may one day have.

My phone rings. Davis calling me back from yesterday. Maybe I'll learn why he called her.

He answers, speaking about the issues he's been having with a neighboring property over a fence alignment, projected water allocations, and crop rotations for next spring. When he's done, I ask him questions about the disclosures, when a few buildings were built, and how many acres we had in hay last season.

When he runs out of things to say, I ask, "Did you call my girlfriend, Ellen Jasper?"

Silence makes the line sound empty, like when my radio loses signal as I pass between mountains. I add, "She said you called her."

I pull the phone back to see if the call has dropped.

He exhales loudly. "Kay and I have been thinking and talking. This is similar to when your grandmother died, with nobody around. Carter is the one who found her. I'm not saying . . . I don't know what I'm saying. I'm just thinking . . ."

"And instead of talking to me, you decided to scare my girlfriend into believing my brother's trying to kill me."

He doesn't say anything.

I'm trying to imagine a scenario where Davis tried to come by the hospital to see me, found Carter here, and instead called Ellen out of the goodness of his heart.

I'm coming up blank, but Davis's voice is all wrong for the shooter, and he's a better shot than most. Probably wouldn't have missed if he'd been meaning to kill me.

"You could have texted me or called."

"It's a hypothetical worry, a thought gone to the extreme," says Davis.

"Of course," I reply, but I'm thinking as we hang up, *This isn't over yet.*

I text Ellen three photos of us together during trips we've taken away from here and a message. "Wish I was with you."

I'm completing the remaining disclosures and considering how our conversation about selling might go when my phone alerts me with a new text, and I'm so grateful for the distraction that tension ebbs from my ribs and torso.

But the text from Ellen says, *Help. Kent.*

CHAPTER 12

ELLEN

THE HEAVY MAHOGANY door of Father's suite cracks open, and the metallic click of the latch vibrates in my bones. Kent stands ready to enter.

My breathing quickens. He never used to be so forward or frightening.

He closes the door behind him and stands in the entry. "When you told me about Carter, I knew you needed me to keep you safe."

"I don't need you to do that."

His cobalt eyes are accusing.

I step back. My heel meets a table leg. I skitter past it and edge behind Father's favorite leather chair.

Kent stalks toward me, faintly amused. He enjoys seeing me afraid.

I glare at him, standing my ground. "What are you saying about Carter?"

Father taught me that half the battle is about fooling people into thinking you still have the reins. Kent can't know he's scaring me, that the calm I plaster on my face is an attempt to control the conversation.

"When's the last time you smiled?" His grave voice makes my skin itch.

I lean against the chair's back. "I smile all the time."

"I don't like it when you lie." He takes a step closer. "You were almost mine."

I clench my hands into the cool leather. The buzzing restarts in my ears. It's hard to even look at Kent, but I will meet his eyes and force my words to come out steady. "What made you think I was yours?"

"You liked me."

"I did like you." My belly fizzes. I take two steps backward toward the hallway. "But that was so long ago. Sorry if I sent you the wrong messages, but I'm in a relationship."

"I've watched you be so hungry for love and attention, for someone to care for you."

"Lots of people care for me."

"Not the right way."

A slither of fear snakes down my spine.

For an instant, something about his eyes makes me think he's imagining that day we spent together on the beach.

"Peter took advantage of you," he says.

"That's true." The humming in my ears makes it hard to concentrate.

"You were so afraid of everything."

"He robbed me."

"You loved him."

My stomach flops. "It was a mistake."

"You were just a girl who didn't know any better."

"Maybe, but I have Max now." I press my hand against my stomach, trying to steady the subconscious spinning.

Kent closes the distance between us and stands sickeningly close with his protruding Adam's apple and stiff white shirt. "Your father says he's a hack."

"Don't talk about Max."

"I don't want to talk about him either."

I clamp my jaw hard enough that my muscles twinge. I could excuse myself, but that would require going farther into Father's residence. I could shout for Father to see if he's in his room. I could ask Kent if he knows why my keycard won't work.

I slip my hand into my back pocket. Without looking, I start what I hope is the emergency SOS sequence, pressing the buttons on either side of my phone. Father will be angry at me for making a spectacle. An alarm will sound before it dials for help.

Kent puts his hand on my forearm near the elbow.

I step all the way to the glass and cross my arms over my chest.

He holds his hands up. "Don't be scared. I've talked to your father about you so many times. Did you know he sees all your photos when I show them to him on your Instagram?" He extends his hand toward my cheek.

"Please don't touch me."

His jaw tightens, making the muscles flex like a fist. Heat builds in my chest like a chemical reaction, an expansion of sadness and fear combining under pressure. It has to be released. I want to threaten Kent and say *the police are on the way*, but this tactic failed when Carter tried to evict me. Would it provoke Kent?

I edge toward Father's room, unsure if he's home. "I need to check on my father."

Kent reaches for my wrist, and I sprint down the hallway, past the lounge where Father taught me how to entertain men, fixing drinks and flirting while he sold them on deals.

He grabs my elbow hard, dragging me into the room and wedging me against a long leather sofa, circling me with one arm, drawing me into his chest.

I turn my cheek from his square jaw and whisper, "You're making a bad impression."

He breathes softly near my mouth. Even the smell of him is making bile rise in my throat—a sickly sweet aftershave.

"Have you considered how I might feel about having you touch me when I don't want you to?"

He eases his grip, not pinning me but still gripping my arm.

I want to twist away from him and run. Instead, I slowly shift, trying not to provoke him.

His lips turn up. "Your father said a man like me could teach you things about business."

My pulse flares, sending a wave of fierce heat over me. I can't handle much more before I crack. My defenses are all over the place. Fight. Scream. Run. It's a chant in my head, pounding with my pulse. But I remain perfectly still. Breathe. Think. Act.

I put another inch between us, sliding along the sofa edge, and plaster on my most appropriate face—a genuine curiosity about this man making me uncomfortable—while I try to shove down a heavy side of *I want to escape.*

In my most cheerful voice, I ask, "Your mother lives in Florida, right?"

"She's been staying at your father's house in St. Augustine."

"It's a lovely house." My voice is high and tight.

"It's right on the coastal highway," Kent says.

I finally break away from his hand. He reaches for my hair, letting a few strands slide between his fingers.

Warnings blare through me. Father sometimes does generous things for his staff. He's the first to say he wouldn't be where he is without the people he trusts. Still, it's surprising that Kent is that close to Father.

My choices in dealing with Kent so far have not been right.

Very wrong.

Very exceedingly wrong.

The best thing you can do when someone makes you uncomfortable, I learned while waltzing with men whose hands roamed as they fed on fat contracts offered by Father: Be true to yourself.

I scrunch my nose. "I'm surprised he's not letting her stay at his harbor house. It's much nicer."

Kent frowns and steps away, tilting his head and looking toward Father's room.

Maybe Father *is* there. "That's where he would stay if he wanted to day cruise," I add, scooting along the couch until we're over a foot apart.

"You'll never believe it, but he's got a rhinoceros head in his study. It's huge, like a throne room, full of the beasts he shot while on safari. It used to terrify me when I was a girl." I take another step back. "We should ask Father to tell you about it. Maybe he'll let you see it sometime."

Kent grabs for my wrist.

I lurch away. "I'm going to check on him, right now."

My phone chirps.

I slip it from my pocket and read the message while hurrying into Father's room.

Max Corbett: Wish I was with you

My fingers shake as I try to text. Kent loops his arm around me.

I want to say, *Me too. You have no idea.* I start to respond.

Kent reaches for my phone.

I hit send just as Kent takes it. It's ringing as he walks beside me, gripping me above my elbow.

I glare at him.

He puts my phone in his pocket, and it stops ringing. Max must be confused and worried.

"Want to let go of me?" I twist against his hand.

He squeezes tighter then releases his grasp. We're almost to Father's bedroom. Will Father be there?

I steady myself and ask, "I guess you're pretty close to my father?"

"Like-ta think so. He's been lonely since you left. I got you home without a fight, just like I promised him."

I release a discordant scoff at his gloating and my stupidity. I never should have gotten on the jet. But oddly, now, I think of Max calling me, of Kent shoving the phone in his pocket and how the phone stopped ringing. It's unlikely, but hope makes me think Max is on the line. Maybe he can hear us talking.

We're finally in the sitting room outside Father's bedroom, a small space cluttered with a lifetime of junk, some of it Father's, some collected by Mom before she died. If I hadn't gotten on the jet, I wouldn't know how sick Father is.

"Like your father's style," Kent says. "Tell me more about his harbor house."

I talk for Max now, in case he is listening. He understands me better than most people. I start making things up that Max will understand. "Father has a security guard living there named Kent too, like you, but his last name isn't Goodwin like yours."

Kent tilts his head, scrutinizing me.

"He mounted antlers around the exterior walls. It's all stone, and there's a courtyard in the middle, like a fortress. You can't get out even when you want to."

"Where is it?"

When I don't answer, Kent crosses his arms. It's oddly satisfying to frustrate him. I can't say it's in New York, even though that's where I am.

"Right on the water," I finally say.

"What city?"

"Off the coast."

"So—the Bahamas."

"Sort of."

Father's nurse speaks from just beyond the doorway. "Mr. Jasper went to sleep right after he ate, and now he won't wake up."

CHAPTER 13

MAX

I'M EAVESDROPPING on the strangest conversation of my life and trying to understand what I'm hearing while staring at Ellen's text. *Help. Kent*

"Like-ta think so," a man says, prickling the hair on my neck. Kent is *Like-ta*. The soreness in my throat transforms into fluttering like I've swallowed a beetle and its wings are tickling my windpipe.

I jab my finger into the nurse call button and lurch out of bed.

Without thinking it through, I'm pulling on sweatpants, jerking off my hospital gown.

Ellen is with the guy who tried to kill me, and she's asked me for help. But how can I get to her when she's 2000 miles away? I grab the hospital phone and dial 911.

"What's your emergency?" the operator asks. On the other line, Ellen's voice shakes.

"This is Max Corbett. My girlfriend is in New York, and she's being harassed by a man named Kent Goodwin. He tried to kill me—"

"And you're calling from the hospital in Wesley?" she sounds incredulous.

"This isn't a hoax. I'm in the hospital because he tried to kill me here in Pultney County. My girlfriend is in Manhattan, and she's being harassed."

"Please hold."

I pace, awkward lurching steps from the bed as far as the tube in my ribs will allow me to go and then back. I sink into the visitor's chair. Ellen's voice emerges from the speaker, fake and clipped. She's afraid.

I stand and push the nurse call button.

The 911 operator comes back on the line. "Can you please tell me the address where your girlfriend is located?"

"Uh. Sure. It's um . . ." I open the finder app on my phone. She installed it last fall when she ran the marathon in Jackson so I could locate her on the course. A map appears on the screen, showing she's in her dad's building. I give the operator the address, and she puts me back on hold.

Ellen's voice isn't coming through anymore. Will they even believe me? It's a little hard to explain. I probably should have reported everything that happened before now.

I untape the IV, slide the needle out then focus on the chest tube. It's going to hurt. Removing it myself could go very wrong.

"What are you doing?" Jamie rushes through the doorway.

"I need to go," I tell her as I text Kay, asking her to have someone help her bring me my truck immediately.

Jamie glances at my phone, reads my message, and tilts her head. "You're serious."

I start working at the tape around the tube, running into a somewhat swollen area under my arm. The bruising around my tattoo is a grotesque version of the artist's intent. "Either you're taking this out, or I will."

Her face crinkles in sympathetic pain. "I can't. I mean . . . I'd get fired."

"Tell me how to do it."

"You're serious?"

"Help me."

"Air could leak back into the pleural space and collapse your lung, or you could get sepsis. Either could kill you."

I work at the soft padding around the tube.

"Get back in bed." She holds her hands as if to push me but doesn't. I peel the stuck-on tape, cringing at the sensation like it will rip my skin. "I have zero time."

Jaime starts toward the door. "Get back in bed, or I'm calling someone to help."

I yank the bandage off then lean down to look in my armpit. A stitch holds the tube in place. I need scissors.

She hurries back. "You have to lie down. There's a procedure to do the removal safely."

My phone connection with Ellen has dropped.

I start dialing her back and follow Jamie's instructions. I return to the bed and lie down as she outlines several steps, including bending my knees and getting the bed to a specific position. It takes about a minute. I'm listening to the 911 static and getting closer to taking the tube out myself.

Before I'm entirely situated, four more nurses are in the room, asking, "What's happening?" Hospitals must have protocols for guys like me. Like a silent alarm at the bank. Either that or Jamie called someone while she was near the door.

Dr. Campela comes in next. I'm half-focused on her and half-focused on the operator, who hasn't returned to the call, as the doctor spells out the next steps if I want to be discharged, something about an x-ray and oxygen monitoring, but I can't let anything happen to Ellen.

"So I've got someone for you," the operator says then

connects me to another dispatch center. I start over, explaining while the nurses trail toward the door.

"Don't go." I start on the tube again. Everything the operator says comes across as a lot of, "Sure, we understand." "We're listening." Only, from the pitch of her voice, it sounds like she's watching cat videos. I'm sure she's not, but I've been in our local dispatch office, and it's a little like that.

Ellen asked me for help, and I'm ready to do something more for her.

They've just finished removing the chest tube, closing the sutures, and applying new bandages at the site and where my IV used to be. Four hospital staff members are gazing at me like I'm the stupidest asshole they've ever seen. I convinced them to let me finish the call with 911 and remove the tube.

Maybe I am out of my mind because they're doing their best to help me, but Ellen is at risk. I should have told her to come home. It's just like the day she texted me that Carter was there to evict her. I should have been there then.

Dr. Campela moves to the foot of the bed. She's holding a file, studying something. Finally, she looks up. "I would have discharged you already if I thought you would follow the home care instructions."

I sit straight against the stiff sheets and attempt to appear cooperative. "I will follow most of your instructions."

She continues, slow and droning, about how I'll need to recuperate, take the medications they've prescribed, and have people around to watch me as I could still pass out unexpectedly.

I'm out of bed as soon as Kay's in the room. I grit my teeth against the pain. I can feel Ellen's fear in the way my heart races.

I scribble a signature on a form then hobble out of the hospital beside Kay.

"There are some real estate agents at the ranch." Her voice is inquisitive, but her brows are arched.

"Some outfit from Jackson?" How are they already poking around without my permission? It's insane. I'll call them as soon as I don't have so much on my mind.

"Carter's talking to them with Davis."

I can't deal with everything at once, and I notch this worry somewhere near the bottom of my brain. As soon as we're out the doors, a blast of icy wind hits me. I tuck into my shoulder and stalk toward my truck.

Kay's car is right beside mine. I wait for her to get in.

"Are you headed to the ranch?" she asks.

"Not right away, but you should go ahead."

"I'll follow you." Worry mars the ensuing silence.

I stare at my phone.

"Is everything alright?" Kay asks.

Maybe I should tell her what's going on, but no. She's not going to be able to help. I let her know I'll see her at the main house at some point then wait for her to drive away. Sitting behind the wheel of my truck, I'm somewhat more in control. I maintain a safe speed out of the hospital. By the time I'm headed down a windy two-lane road toward the highway, I'm going 90.

Right about now, I realize maybe I should fly.

Driving to New York will take too long, even going way too fast. Commercial flights won't get me there until tomorrow.

I try her dad's building and get a receptionist who refuses to put me through to security. It seems they've had a fair number of pranksters. So I call Ellen's friend Babs and explain what's happening.

"I'll let you know how it goes. Or I'll go over there."

I thank her. She promises to update me, and we hang up.

I'm a few miles outside of Higgins when Carter calls.

He'll start in about the real estate guys poking around. I speak before he can. "Don't. I'm not talking about it now."

The line goes eerily quiet. He must either be able to tell I mean it, or he's worried I'm actually selling. Or perhaps he's just too stunned to say what he'd planned on saying.

He finally asks, "What's wrong?"

I grunt. Should I tell him? He's the one I would typically call in a situation like this. He's the one I called when I almost killed the drunk driver who killed our parents. Carter would get it.

Filling the silence, he exhales, low and slow. "Kay peeled out of here a little while ago, leaving tracks like the devil was chasing her. I can tell from the noise that you're driving, which means you're out of the hospital again. I haven't done anything to get you rattled. Who's jerked your chain this time?"

I focus on the double yellow line stretching toward infinity.

"Where are you headed?" he asks. "I'll meet you there."

I lay it all out for him: what I heard, what I worry about, what I'm thinking about doing.

"I get it." His voice is earnest, and I believe he does. It's like he's the older brother he used to be, and he listens as I talk. That's why I decide to take his advice, despite all the reasons I probably shouldn't.

———

I'm sitting on Abner's jet, heading out of Ballford, Wyoming, population one, for Teterboro airport, population big city.

The jet is almost entirely beige inside except for the carpet, probably made of real gold.

Abner would commission a jet too expensive to own, with carpet that weighs as much as a car.

Since grade school, he's been an odd one. Now, he's rich, invested well in something about global warming, and playing pilot wearing a golf shirt, slacks, and shiny shoes. A guy who shaves his head to a military cut even though he's not enlisted or balding. Finicky. Eccentric. Emotional. I'd half-expect him to have a flight attendant with sleek blond hair and cherry red lipstick wearing a tailored desert-camo uniform, like this is all part of a music video he's conjured to wow people, but it's just him and me on the jet.

He eyeballs me. I won't apologize for my sweats, and there's not much I can do about the messed-up state of my face. What's going on in my head and heart is even worse. He offers me a drink. I thank him but refuse.

A bitter taste coats my tongue. Probably because the hospital food was terrible, not because I have zero control over how this unfolds, or because Abner knows I need him now more than he needs me. I'm lying to myself, and I wouldn't say I like that, but Ellen is in danger.

I'd *like to* be there already.

Am I an idiot to get mixed up with Abner? Absolutely. Do I have a choice? I couldn't think of one that seemed better.

Sitting on Abner's private runway, a broad strip of concrete, you almost wouldn't know anything was out here if you managed to miss his tower house—a house stacked on top of a house, with another smaller house on top and so on, all the way up to a tiny house on top like a cuckoo clock. He built a pagoda-like structure that most men would be afraid to enter—where a kid could wreak havoc, dropping things from above.

If Abner could convince a woman to have a kid with him, his house would be on the news with a story about some moment that went wrong.

Hope this doesn't end up in the news.

I haven't heard a word from Babs. Even though I've texted her a few times for an update, I have no idea if Ellen is okay. Maybe asking Babs to get involved was a mistake. I may have put her in danger too.

I'm trying not to bounce my knee. I could call Carter to see if he's had any luck contacting Ellen's dad. He's done me a kind-ness by being willing to talk about my relationship with Ellen without lecturing because this has always been us.

When the shit gets thick, we're still brothers. He even offered to come with me. Of course, I told him no.

I'm ready to forget how wrong this could go. Hopefully, I don't end up right back where I was when I met Ellen, having almost killed a man, allowing my brother to go to jail for my crime, then living with the weight of what I'd done.

Abner asks, "You ready?"

He's looking at me expectantly. I can only guess he's hoping to build suspense.

I shrug.

He manipulates controls, propelling the jet forward and pressing me back in the seat until the accelerating tension tugs on my face. Carter had mentioned Abner's affinity for jets with short runway and high-altitude performance. *He's your best bet of getting there before nightfall*, my brother had said.

I glance over at Abner. He's got a wicked grin.

"Have you got our landing figured out?" I ask, messing with him since he's inclined to screw with me. "Seems like you're just learning to fly this thing."

He runs a hand over his buzzed head. "You're still a daredevil, aren't you? You were when we were kids."

"I guess."

"It's not a big deal." He flips several switches on the console. Next, he grabs a pillow beside him and props his head against it, turning his cheek like he plans to nap.

"You woke me when you called," he says.

We're careening through the sky. He closes his eyes. I scan the open snow-covered prairie and craggy peaks and think of Carter making a deal with Abner, the strip mining he's mixed up with, and Ellen's dad.

"How do you know Ed Jasper?" I ask.

He tucks into his pillow. An alarm blares from the console. The digital readouts are all foreign—no clue what they mean. I'm a little ill at the idea of crashing, having no way to stop the situation from unfolding, mainly because of what it means if I don't get to New York.

Abner's pretending to be asleep.

I grab him by the ear and pull him up. He's still that kid from class who never knew when things he did weren't funny. He grins at me, toothy and amused. "Me sleeping with you staring out was too creepy for you?"

"I wouldn't say I liked it."

He tucks the pillow back where he got it, letting the alarm buzz its grating warning. "How often do you think commercial pilots fall asleep in the air?"

"Can't say I gave it much thought. How about you answer my question?"

"Fine." He resettles his hands on the controls and gazes straight ahead at the horizon. As he lifts the nose, the alarm finally turns off. "The guy's a weirdo."

"And that's it?"

He shrugs. What a weasel.

"Abner, what'd you get Carter mixed up with?" I'm not too fond of it when Abner doesn't respond. I'm thinking, *Don't make me remind you what an asshole I can be.* He's just the kind of guy to mess with a person who threatens him without realizing the full implications of his choices, so I say, "I can tell Ed's got something over you, so why not tell me what it is, and we can get it straightened out?"

CHAPTER 14

ELLEN

THE NURSE PRESSES the phone to her ear, like she's listening closely for instructions.

Kent is at my side, but not touching me anymore. He's probably waiting to see if Father's awake.

I hurry toward the bed and grip Father's hand, giving it a tug. It's the first time in forever that we've held hands, maybe two decades. His fingers are warm, curled around mine, and his fatherly grip is comforting like he's still here and will wake up any moment.

Only he doesn't move—droplets of sweat bead on his upper lip and forehead.

The nurse speaks into the phone, "Let me know when they get to the elevators. Everything's ready. Just get here."

"What's going on?" My voice holds a tremor.

"We're requesting emergency transport."

"I heard you say he ate."

"He ate fine then said he was full and tired."

"Has this happened before?"

Kent steps closer and leans over the bed.

I wedge myself into a rolling cart to keep my distance.

Behind me, on the side table, is Father's mobile. Kent stares at my phone like he's trying to unlock it. I could ask for it back, but I don't want to talk to him or even be near him. I don't want him to ask about the text I sent to Max. I edge over and slide Father's mobile into my waistband.

Kent looks up.

I squeeze Father's hand. "Can you hear me?"

His eyes flutter but don't open. *Wake up! Please don't die. We haven't even talked.*

"The emergency response is downstairs," the nurse says.

I turn to Kent. "Would you go out and show them the way inside?"

He looks at me with impassive slate-blue eyes.

The computerized voice of Father's electronic smart assistant comes over the intercom in his bedroom. "Board meeting in twenty minutes."

"I better go." I hold my hands, trying to get past him without touching him.

The corner of his mouth lifts. I give him a scorching look. He smiles. I scowl, holding my breath as I pass. He's present behind me. His footsteps are close as I hurry toward Father's front door, but I refuse to look back.

Crap! My key card doesn't work. I race around the corner, past Father's leather chair and toward the exit. If I can't get it open, I may have to beg Kent to let me out.

I glance backward.

He's slowed but is still coming. I stumble over the edge of the rug. My knees crack against the stone floor. My palms sting. I push to my feet and run to the door then try my card as I yank on the handle.

Voices echo from beyond the door of Father's residence. Someone is working at the latch from the outside.

CHAPTER 15

MAX

ABNER LEANS OVER and gazes out the window at the ground below for so long that I look too. The plane is screaming along at a nice clip, the jet stream pushing us east. We might land in an hour or so. The apricot seed of tension stuck in my throat eases. We've been talking. So far, I've learned a few things about Abner. This is his second-fastest jet, and he really hated it when I sold my restaurant.

"I want you to cook for me," he says.

That's not likely to happen. Still, he dropped everything to fly me across the country. "What do you want me to cook?" I ask.

"How about that Greek salad you made for my wedding."

"That was like, what five years ago, and it was *your wedding.*

You remember the salad?" I'm not even sure I remember the salad.

"I'm vegan," he says.

"Since when?" I ask.

"About two weeks. I decided to switch after I went to a summit about how adopting a vegan diet is the biggest single way to reduce planetary impact."

"Good luck with that," I say, neglecting to point out that his love of flying is probably an issue as well. To each their own.

"How'd you meet Ed?" I ask instead.

"You're going to make me that salad?" His eyes bore into mine.

"I'll send you the recipe."

"Do it right now."

"Okay." As he flies, I type something slightly made up into a message, a quick and simple salad, tomatoes, cucumbers, red onion, dill, parsley, and dressing. It's my basic go-to catering salad minus the feta cheese, and send it to him. Once it's sent I say, "You'll need to find tomatoes at their peak for it to be really good."

"I put in a heat sink at the house and have about a million tomatoes right now."

"I'm impressed." Not wanting to dive deeper into his odd house, I ask, "What about Ed? Where'd you meet him?"

"At a climate fundraiser."

"Why was he there?"

"I don't know. He literally bummed cigars off everyone all night. He ended up smoking cheap Maduros because it became a running joke."

"You just talked and smoked $8 cigars?"

"He was funny about it. We eventually ended up playing bridge until he lost. We still play over the internet every once in a while, but he gets shitty when he loses, so we haven't played in a few weeks."

"What about this development permit that Carter's gotten himself mixed up with?"

Gazing out, he says, "Ed offered me a deal, and I took it."

I stare at Abner's thin face and pasty white skin. Seriously, what tricks does Ed know? Abner's a pretty wily character.

"Why did you take it?" I ask.

"It got uncomfortable."

Who knows what Abner got himself mixed up with? Instead of pushing him to tell me something he's unlikely to share, I ask, "So you called Carter and convinced him to get involved?"

Abner doesn't look at me, but he starts to talk. "I'd been waiting for the right moment and never figured out how to convince him to do it, but Ed kept calling and talking, and then Carter called me for help, and the pieces fell into place. Sort of like you called me today. I've been asking you to hunt with me, golf, or whatever." He grins, making my skin crawl like I'm leaning out over the sky, gazing down, making me want to go back in time and not call him for help.

My phone rings. It's Carter. I answer and shuffle into the back of the jet. Maybe it annoys Abner, but I'm tired of his half-assed manipulation. I want to get there and see Ellen, wrap her in my arms, and never let go. Carter starts talking about his efforts to contact Ed. He's left messages with Ed's secretary but gotten nowhere.

Then Carter starts in about other stuff. He's slightly sympathetic about my feelings for Ellen. Christa's been talking to him, but he's still pissed about the real estate agents.

"What the hell are you thinking?" he asks.

"There's too much on my mind to fight with you too."

"You want my advice?"

No. "Sure." I add, "Yes." Having help right now would be great.

"You're the luckiest one."

I snort a pained laugh. "You're insane. Have you seen me lately?"

"You're luckier than Christa, who's spent months accused of crimes she didn't commit. You're luckier than Skyler, who's been waitressing in Jackson to help pay Christa's legal bills, and you're luckier than me, who's constantly kissing somebody's ass to get half a chance at what you have."

He's right, of course. Silence lingers between us—my neck prickles. Abner's standing in the cockpit doorway, watching, listening, and pissing me off. I need to say something to my brother. I'm unsure what, but I'm building toward an apology. As much as I've believed he owes me one, I expect mine is just as overdue. I start forming the words.

"I gotta go." His voice is tense.

Gotta go set somebody else straight on how lucky they are.

"Kay's screaming about the horse barn being on fire," he says, fraught.

My gut hollows. Panic swells inside me. The horses in danger will put Carter in danger. He's not only a volunteer firefighter, but he's also the kind of person who values horses and dogs with more esteem than most people. "Let me know."

And he hung up. I draw a frustrated breath and slip the phone into my baggy pocket with a shaky hand.

We don't need anything else to go wrong right now. How much of this is Ed's fault? As much as it pains me to think it, much of it is somehow my fault. I'm trying to find answers to the questions rolling around in my head while texting Babs. How many things can go wrong before we all end up part of something tragic?

We retake our seats, and I ask Abner, "What's going on with the land you and Carter are mixed up with?"

"Nothing really."

"There's an active permit application for strip mining," I counter. It's an intense and invasive method, creating runoff water that has to be stored in massive tailings dams used to capture the by-products, which are often acidic, toxic, or radioactive.

"Why don't you tell me what's going on before you start to really piss me off?" I ask.

He tugs at his shirt collar. Then picks a piece of lint off his sleeve.

"Abner."

His eyes pop a little wide then he stares at me while he bites the inside of his cheek. "Ed's just tormenting him by making him stay on the board."

"Just for fun?"

"I think it has more to do with you dating Ed's daughter."

As Abner continues talking, I focus hard despite the pounding worry and zero in on the final thing he says, "Ed's been asking questions about you too. Like where you like to go and what kind of things you like to do. He's been trying to get me to take you out hunting with this guy named Kent. He even said his daughter . . . Ellen, right?"

He looks at me and then says, "Yeah, Ellen, Ed says she's got you right where he wants you. This whole deal will work out how he's been planning since she first moved to the area for her 'high profile' assignment."

"Abner . . ." I control my voice. Anger builds until I can't hold it inside. ". . . you think this is a game, don't you, and now you're making shit up to get me mad?"

"I'd say Ed's after getting his hands on all West Creek," Abner says then begins talking to air traffic control and flying the jet, orchestrating our approach, so I let him focus. He pulls out his phone and scrolls through it while fine-tuning the landing. Finally, he hands the phone over to me.

Older pictures of Ellen with Kent. They're smiling. Her hand is on his arm. Her face is raised to his.

Abner laughs a devilish little chuckle.

My phone rings—Ed Jasper's name scrolls across the caller ID.

The air that should be coming in and out of my lungs has gotten caught somewhere in between. While I struggle to breathe, Abner brings the jet down smoothly and taxis toward a boutique-style terminal for private planes.

I want to choke somebody, but I'm choking instead. Pressure builds in my chest, and dryness coats my throat. My situation draws an ironic, maniacal urge to laugh, but instead I answer the phone and hear Ellen's voice. "Max, sweetheart."

"Yeah."

"The police are here with Babs. She told me you're on your way. Are you really out of the hospital?" Ellen asks, and I think: *This is good.*

She's no longer in danger.

A weight falls from my shoulders. "What was happening when you texted me?" I ask.

"It's a bit of a long story. I want to tell you, but everything's okay now, and I can tell you about it when you get here?"

"Yeah," I reply. "We're landing at Teterboro."

"What? You're in Teterboro already?"

"I got your text."

"And you understood me. Gah, I'm amazed. Speechless. Sweetheart, I have so much I need to tell you. It will be fantastic to see you. I'm so glad you're well enough to come. I can't believe you're in Teterboro. You're crazy, you know that?"

"Crazy about you," I say, cheesy as ever. A smile grows inside me. "It will be great to see you."

She lets out a sigh, and I can imagine her tugging her ear the way she does when she's really stressed.

I want to ease whatever's bothering her, but I'm unsure where to start. "What's worrying you most right now?" I ask.

"I'm considering taking the position my father offered, but I'm not sure if I should," she says.

It's hard to consider what this might mean for us. I'm barely coming to terms with an attempt on my life, Carter's call, and learning the horse barn is on fire. Add in Abner's ambitious attempts at manipulation, and I'm a ball of raw nerves like those thin, rusty-red worms that mass together. You drop them in an aquarium, and fish pick them apart in a mad rush.

I'm unsure where all the threats are coming from, but it's the uncertainty in Ellen's voice, the questioning tone of her words, that slices deep and leaves me wide open. She's asking me what she should do.

Before I say anything, she asks, "Max, are you still there?"

"Sorry, yeah. I'm just a little surprised and glad you're safe. Tell me about the job."

"I'd be assuming control of the operations. He's given me complete control of everything while he's medically unable to manage things himself."

"Is he . . ." Once again, I'm out of my element. I want to ask, if he's dying like the pundits say, but that's harsh.

"My father's headed to the hospital, and if I'm going to do this, I need to go into a board meeting. I need to ask HR to start the process of firing Kent, and I'd need to get one of Father's attorneys to start the filings for a restraining order, but I'm not sure if I should."

"But this is the chance you've been talking about for months, right?"

"Yeah, it's everything I've wanted. If he is dying and is going to hand me unrestricted control, then I can fix the mines."

"Then get out there and do it."

"You think I should?" she asks.

"For sure, Flynn. I think you were made to do this."

"I guess so. Okay, then I better go," she says. "I love you."

"I love you too," I reply. She's energized with a purpose she's talked about but never had a chance to explore, and she's grabbing onto it and moving away from the life we've built.

I could ask her about the photos on Abner's phone. He's watching me with one eyebrow arched. I could be jealous of Kent because of how she used to look at him, angry she's suddenly talking about upending our life, or self-pitying that I love a woman who's moving on from what I thought she wanted.

But I know better. Ellen's not trying to hurt me. She trusts me enough to ask me about things that matter to us, like what's going on with Kent. I'm about to ask her to explain it to me now.

"I need to go the board meeting. I'll call again in a few minutes," she says.

I stare at the phone after she disconnects, then I thank Abner for the spur-of-the-minute ride and hobble across the airfield toward the concierge desk.

New York is where her heart is.

This hotshot is who she is. She loves me. She loves her dad and has regrets about the past. And her dad sent someone to kill me, and who knows where that guy is now? It's pretty screwed up if I say so myself. What do I do?

I enter the terminal's automatic parting doors and ask a stranger for advice about transportation to her dad's building then grab a waiting commuter helicopter. Sitting alone in the passenger cab seating six, I use my phone to find her location and then navigate toward her from the heliport where we will land.

Despite the aviation headset and cabin soundproofing, the chopper is louder than our biggest harvester under a heavy load hauling ass through a field. As the aircraft lifts off, I start to see the silver lining.

If Ellen can love a man like her dad, no wonder she can love a man like me—with a past and a complicated family. It would take Sherlock Holmes's genius to figure us out, but she understands.

Carter calls likely with an update on the fire. I pull off my noise-canceling headset and answer.

He clears his throat and says, "The fire's just about extinguished. We got all the horses out. They're scared but safe. It was . . . I can't believe someone lit it while I was right here, on the property."

I don't say anything. I can imagine the look on Carter's face —a mixture of shock, confusion, and defeat—the silence carries immense sorrow, like his life has been reduced to a series of catastrophes counted by the number of times he hasn't lived up to his own expectations.

A fever creeps up my throat and into my nose. All of these things have done things to him, and I sniff back the burning threat of having him hear my pain.

He clears his throat and moves on, saying Dick is also there now. His voice is thick with his own unstated emotions. "I authorized him to call in an arson expert from Cheyenne. You'll get the bill."

This is almost the same action he took last time there were fires. Back then, I thought he was prime suspect number one. And now I'm not sure who could have lit the fires I once suspected he'd set. I'm thankful for my brother. He's taking charge and doing the right thing. Maybe that's all he was doing back then, but all I could see was what he'd done to Ellen and *how* he was going about getting his points across to our grandparents' other homesteaders.

I raise my voice over the chopper's rotor noise. "I'm sorry. I should have said this long ago, but you deserve better than you've gotten from me. Even if we frequently disagree, when it matters, I trust you. I want to figure out how to make things between us right again."

"I can barely hear you, but I think I get it," he says.

"Good. I better go." I end the call, gaze at the map showing Ellen's location. The dot has moved. She's possibly not in her dad's building any longer.

My phone rings again.

When I answer, Davis says, "We've had a fire at the horse barn . . ."

The helicopter settles on a waterfront pad adjacent to a crowded cityscape. The location dot moves as I wait for someone to open the door.

Davis is still talking about the extent of the damage, the rescue efforts, mainly things Carter has already said. When he runs out of things to say, I ask, "Did you talk to Carter? I've put him in charge of the investigation."

He sighs. "What if Carter and Christa are back at it again? I'm not saying they did anything. I don't know anything for sure. I'm just wondering . . ."

"Of course," I reply, but I'm thinking as we hang up. *Davis's offhand accusations answer some questions about why Nonna accused Carter.*

He's always hated my brother. With how he's always treated me like I've been given something I don't really respect or deserve, I don't believe he cares for me much either. After the call's over, I text Carter. *Have Dick investigate Davis.*

The pilot opens the door as my phone rings again. It's Dick, maybe with an update on the investigation.

I send him to voicemail and call Ellen. When she doesn't answer, I call the number she called me from earlier.

"Kent has my phone," she says when I ask if she switched numbers. She promises to fill me in on everything that's gone on with Kent and her dad as soon as she gets a break and adds, "I'm headed to the hospital in Father's car. They're admitting him. I'll add you to the visitor list and send you my location too."

With a sweet "I love you," she hangs up. She's going to be occupied with her dad for a while. Still, I'm too edgy to slow my heart's racing, much less the forward momentum of this day.

I thank the pilot then hurry down the wharf toward the city. An icy December wind makes me wish I'd brought my coat. I tuck the pistol into my waistband and hobble forward.

My boot heels scuff against the wide sidewalk while pedestrians hurry past—the crowd parts. People stare, and it's likely more than the boots and sweats fashion statement. Maybe it's the bulging gun, the crazed look on my face, or my half-dead appearance. I could call someone for help, the law, or a security entourage. A woman pulls out a phone to take a photo of me. It's probably illegal for me to carry a gun here. I tuck it into my boot despite my swollen ankle and turn between two buildings, heading toward a busier street.

Part of me is still worried about having Ellen see me like this, but a more significant part isn't willing to wait to hold her again. I'll feel better as soon as I have her close.

Reaching a crowded curb, the two location dots remain on my phone. One will lead me toward Ellen and the other toward the guy who tried to kill me.

I'm still deciding which direction to go as I hail a cab.

Kent's a trained security expert. My arm's still in a cast and sling. When a car stops, I crack the passenger door, settle onto the worn seat, and tug the door shut. The driver smiles at me in the mirror.

I extend my phone and point with swollen fingers.

CHAPTER 16

ELLEN

Father has been awake since he arrived in the ambulance. Softness relaxes the lines around his blue eyes since they started the morphine drip. They've explained it may help with his shortness of breath, pain, and anxiety. It dilates the blood vessels in his lungs and allows him to breathe more deeply, but they've also warned him the morphine could impact him in unforeseen ways, overloading his organs and quickening his death. He's decided this is as far as he wants to take the treatments and plans to die the way he's lived.

I already know some of Father's story, shared when I was eleven, to help me understand that Father knows the culture of poverty and has made incredible gains—stealing clients and lying and kissing every ass he had to kiss to claw his way out from Appalachian culture, which he hates for its fatalistic outlook and encouragement of dullness, languor, and sloth. It's a sadly optimistic story of American success, but it doesn't answer the puzzle inside me.

For much of my life, I felt Father resented me for taking Mom away from him. Since she's been gone, it's been a reversal, where he's realized we have certain similarities—being business-minded and driven toward set goals—and he's tried to remake me into his protégé—despite my reluctance to assume the role.

This is my chance to say whatever needs to be said, yet I can't find words to start a conversation.

Father seems just as happy to let the silence linger.

Even the TV is on mute.

Voices travel into the room from the hallway, but none belong to Max.

My hands tremor. I wedge them under my thighs before catching Father's stare and straightening my gray pencil skirt. On the outside, I appear somewhat okay. But I can't help glancing at the door for Kent.

HR went to deliver the paperwork, but no one could find him. If he comes in, I'll head for the hallway, then the nurses' station, and keep going until I find a security guard. He has my phone with every personal detail of my life locked inside. Maybe he's figured out how to unlock it. He seemed technically knowl-edgeable. I draw a breath and remind myself that they're working on a restraining order, even if the attorney helping me says the process takes time. The police know Kent has my phone. They'll locate him.

Father shifts against his pillow. Instead of speaking to him about what's weighing on me and risking starting a fight, I say, "Will you tell me about your life?"

"Oh, bullshit," he says, "what is this about? My obituary?"

Hurt, I shake my head. "I just want to glimpse how you became the businessman you are and understand the things that matter to you."

"So what? You want me to . . ."

"Tell me about being young and in love with Mom."

He smiles. Even in his diminished health, his blue eyes light up, making his face seem younger. "Your mother was the best thing that ever happened to me. She had organized an exhibit at the museum in Richmond, and I was there to meet someone else, but within a few minutes, I knew I would marry her."

"That's what she always said too."

"Really?" He sounds amused at the idea.

"Did she not tell you that?"

He tugs up the sheet. "I always wondered if she would have married me if it hadn't been for you being on the way, but she swore she loved me."

"She did. That's what she always said." But Mom wasn't happy with their arrangement. "She got this look in her eye whenever you were around, but then you left."

"I left, and your mother stayed."

"You wanted her to come with you to New York?"

"In the worst way, but she hated the city."

"I know." Mom adored Appalachia—a lush land of voluptuous summers, woodsmoke winters, and breathtaking autumns and springs. She loved its people, its myths, and the mountain culture that raised her. She wanted to raise me there, and she did it until Father insisted on sending me to Connecticut for boarding school. If I decide to stay here, I'm asking Max to sacrifice what he loves.

I lean forward, resting my elbows on my knees, and say, "You're asking me to come back and take things over, and I'd like to understand why."

He lets his head fall on the pillow.

I begin to speak, and he closes his eyes, but I don't let it stop me. "I'd prefer to be back in Wyoming at my bakery, but if you're offering me a chance to clean up the mines and be the kind of owner I wish you'd been then I'll do this."

The contentment passes from Father's face as his lips tighten into a scowl.

He stares at me. "You're like your mother. She disapproved of how I made the money I earned, but she enjoyed spending what I put into her bank account on frivolous artwork made by the very Appalachian trash I spent my youth trying to escape."

"You think that's what I'm doing?"

"That is what you're doing."

"I don't ask you for money."

"But you're undermining my business, befriending my enemies, standing in the way of my project."

"You've been harassing Max, and you don't even know him," I say, voicing a longtime issue I've had with my father.

"I know his type." Father bites off the last syllable with venom.

"What type is that?"

"A podunk hack who inherited some land. He has no idea what it takes to make a dollar, much less a million."

Kent said Father called Max a hack. I don't try to stop the fury from building into pressure, forcing words from my throat. "Well, I'm pregnant with Max's baby. You're going to have a grandchild."

"Pff." Father turns his face toward the windows.

"I love him." Tears well in my eyes, heating my nose. I grip the chair and fight the urge to leave the room.

"He's no better than Peter was," Father says.

"Is that right? Max is no better than a con artist jailed for stealing my identity."

"We had this same conversation about Peter."

"We did not."

"What else do you want me to say? Congratulations?"

I storm out of Father's hospital room and into the adjoining family room.

Father's voice follows. "I want to say some things."

I chew on my thumbnail and feel nothing. No answers, no solutions. He may be angry and resentful, but he's dying. My thumb feels detached, and so does my body as I slowly walk back into Father's room and retake the chair.

He offers me a small smile, his power play complete.

"I told you that it was important to me that I leave you with some wisdom." His voice is low and raspy, tired. His body is aware of the choice he's made and is losing its strength along with his will to live.

I lean closer.

He starts to speak. "You don't have to shout to get your point across. You stay relaxed and handle all conflict professionally and decisively. You start something, you need to be prepared to finish it. Every time you find yourself in a situation starting to get out of hand, that's your chance to take charge."

He really does want to share some last vestiges of wisdom, and it makes me sad that this is the advice he thinks I need. Still, I say, "I've seen you do what you're telling me to do."

His eyes light up. "Some people describe me as manipulative because I listen and act in my best interests, while they pay lobbyists to buy politicians who make Byzantine rules favoring their businesses."

"You are a bit scheming," I reply, unwilling to let him white-wash all he's done wrong.

He's as calculating as ever. "They don't like it, but it's the number one way to get rich."

"And you are quite rich," I reply.

"I am quite rich."

"A picture of American success."

"Some people say it didn't happen that way."

"But it did. That's the way it happened." I squeeze his hand, and I'm only half-lying when I reassure him. He worked amaz-ingly hard, and although he hurt a lot of people along the way, he helped a lot of people too, donating to worthwhile causes and allowing Mom and me to do that on his behalf. Now, he's asking me to continue his legacy. I've allowed him to get away with doing things he never should have done. He won't tell me what he expects me to do once he's gone.

He closes his eyes and says, "You've been a good daughter to me."

I sit beside him as he drifts into a fitful sleep.

I'm not sure how long passes, but the TV has moved on from one business show to another.

I stand and check my phone. Still nothing from Max.

CHAPTER 17

MAX

When the taxi stops under a shiny curved canopy, I pay the driver, tip him for getting me here in one piece, and readjust the pistol in my boot. I crack the door open and gaze at the location dot on my phone.

Now's the time when I want to feel better than I do about the decision I just made.

I leave the busy sidewalk and pass through automatic doors. Trading a cold December day for the polished hospital lobby, I'm dialing Ellen's new number when she calls.

I answer, letting her know I'm downstairs. She says her dad's sleeping and she'll come out and meet me.

Following Kent would have been a mistake. Tugging off my baseball cap, I wait at the bank of elevators.

A few people come in and out. The car behind me dings. I turn, hoping to see Ellen.

When she emerges, one side of my mouth starts raising. It's so good to see her. She's stoic, giving me an intense perusal.

I stand before her.

She's dressed in a sleek gray suit with a skirt ending above her knees. Pearls grace her neck, and high-heeled black shoes draw my eye to her legs. Amazingly put together and elegant. Just the sight of her makes me momentarily stop breathing. Entirely different from the woman I'm used to seeing every morning but also entirely the woman I love.

She shakes her head.

I stand a little straighter.

"You've been lying to me about how badly you're hurt." Her breath hitches.

"It's really fine."

"And you're here."

I look like roadkill. "I am."

"You've been lying to me." She breaks eye contact.

"It's all superficial. Not as bad as it looks. I'm pretty wrecked from belly-flopping a canyon, but they discharged me properly this time."

"You're still lying." I love her voice and let her soft syllables calm my frayed nerves.

"I don't want you to worry." I reach for her as she comes forward, settling into my embrace with her arms around my waist, making me feel like I'm finally home. I relax against her as she squeezes. It hurts a little. My body tenses involuntarily.

"Should we get a doctor?"

"Dr. Campela said I'm fine. I just need the pharmacy to fill a few prescriptions, and I'll be on track with following her discharge orders. We can do that here."

She tugs me down the hall to the outpatient pharmacy, and I force myself to go a little faster than my limp would prefer, but I don't want her to stress. If I was truly worried about having left the hospital the way I did, I'd stop in at the ER, but I'm fine. Much better. Maybe it's because she's here with me. We drop off paperwork and plan to pick up the meds in under an hour. Holding hands, we enter the first elevator that opens. She pushes the floor number and rests against the railing. Finally, her lips turn up into a beautiful smile.

"I'm so glad you're here."

I shift until we're touching hips, our fingers intertwined. A relaxed, contented sort of sound comes with her exhale. I send her a genuine smile. She lays her hand on my cheek then kisses me slowly and softly.

I nuzzle into her neck and whisper, "What do you say we escape for about an hour? We could get some lunch and just catch up with each other?"

Her eyes light up. "I know a place we can go, and it's close. You'll love it."

She waits for doors to open then, like a little kid, pushes the button to send us back down to the lobby where she drags me out onto the main street, wide traffic lanes, packed sidewalks, panhandlers, and shoppers, along with guys in suits and a woman walking her dog.

It's nothing like our usual routine, but it's also a lot like it because she's always excited about new restaurants, the menus, and little details at places showing potential.

Except nothing about this looks all that great. Folding security bars over dirty storefronts and car exhaust combined with the smell of millions of people crammed together in a small space.

She stops in front of a shop with black tinted windows.

"Why are you taking me into a grungy bar?" I ask.

"You're going to laugh when you figure it out."

I open the door for her, glimpsing inside before she walks in, and it's still a little dim and overcrowded. We're forced to cram against the front glass because it's so jammed, and on the back wall is a gratified pig that instantly makes sense. It's the place her friend Babs saved from going under. The things she did here brought her enough credibility that she eventually started a consulting firm, specializing in helping restaurants.

"You brought me to the pigs in a blanket place," I say.

"They're hot dog rolls," she says, accusingly.

"They're pigs in a blanket." I grin.

She spins to face me, smiling so wide. "And you're going to love them."

"I probably will, but they're usually hard and dry. A little gross." We've had this conversation many times and talked about making the trip but hadn't gotten around to it.

"These are soft and fluffy." Her expression goes a little lusty, the way she looks when she thinks about sex or really good bread.

"They taste like breadsticks with hot dogs inside," she says.

"Okay, that's gross."

She grabs my hand and tugs me out of the way as a group walks past us out the door. "It's *not* gross. You have to try it first."

"This is a New York hotspot?" I ask, amused. I'm unsure people in Wyoming would go for it.

"This is one of like 40 locations."

"That's awesome."

"I know, right? And the owners are super sweet. Not that we're likely to see them, but still it's fun, don't you think?"

"Seeing you happy is fun."

"I need you like this," she says.

I raise a hand to her cheek and press a soft kiss to her forehead.

She tugs me toward an open table she spots near the bathroom, and while I save the table she strolls up to the bar.

I spin the cardboard coaster on the scratched wooden tabletop and let my attention linger on her, watching the little things, taking glimpses anytime someone moves out of the way. How she stands with her right hip swayed to one side, the way she leans against the bar, tipping forward in her high heels. The shape of her ass under her skirt and the modest length, ending above her knees, make her even sexier.

She's talking, motioning with her hands, causing the entire staff to swivel toward her, and it's not just how pretty she is or that soft lilt of her voice that makes everyone want to do whatever she asks.

She faces me, smiling wide. She's done something.

"What happened up there?" I ask when she returns.

She sinks into the chair across from me, props her elbows on the table, and steeples her hands in front of her lips.

"What'd you do?"

"I ordered one of everything." She giggles.

It's hilarious how excited she is about this. I like it. I was satisfied with being single for a long time because I didn't want to be around people who made me feel more lonely. Love is about finding someone who makes you better than you are alone. That's what Ellen does to me with these silly, crazy things that make her personality shine. I think she feels the same way but needs different things from me.

We catch up while they make all the food she's ordered, both of us refusing to speak of the heavy topics that would drag us back down.

Two servers show up with trays of everything from pigs in a blanket to seasonal salads someone must have carefully sourced. It's a mixture that actually works in a strange way.

But across the table, Ellen looks a little green. She puts her hand over her nose then closes her eyes for a few breaths.

She loads up her plate but picks at her food, not actually eating anything.

"You okay?" I ask.

"I'm fine. I'm good."

I've never seen her quite like this. She's lying, and that makes me not want to eat either, even though she insists I should, and I'm pretty hungry. The hot dog rolls are actually tolerable.

"I told you so," she says as she shoves her plate away.

"It's good," I reply, wanting to take some of the strain from her. I'm just unsure how I can.

On the way back, we slip into all the shit that's been going on, things we really can't avoid forever no matter how much we want to. Kent and the restraining order she's working on getting, Carter and the horse barn fire, the worry she has about what her dad might be asking her to do, a lot of things that are critical for us, life-threatening, and yet almost completely outside of our control.

When we reach our floor, we exit the elevator, and she takes us toward a private room adjacent to her dad's room. A nurse meets us in the hall, letting Ellen know her dad's asked for her. She says she'll be right there but lingers beside me as the nurse heads back.

She puts her hands on my shoulders and tilts her face up, her eyes a little wet. "Thank you so much for coming here and for wanting to feed me and catch up and have fun."

"You're welcome," I reply, even though it feels like she's the one who fed me, took me someplace fun, and then didn't eat.

I'm trying to figure out how to take some of the strain from her shoulders when she says, I want to talk to you more about things with Kent, what we should do about whatever my father wants, and what it might mean if you can work things out with Carter." She pauses and blinks. "I mean, if you can, will you stay with me, whatever comes next?"

"Of course." Even if I'm a little concerned that she felt the need to ask. "Don't you know I'd do anything for you?"

She wraps her arms around my waist in a loose embrace, like we're strangers slow dancing. Only there's nothing strange about it. She's everything I ever wanted, and I hope she knows it. She says, "I know you will stay with me, but maybe I needed to ask you to be here with me, and I needed to tell you I need you. I was hoping you could stay with me and help me survive this. Okay? I can't do it right without you."

Her words are a puzzle piece locking into place. I should ask her to marry me. I should get everything figured out with Carter and make that happen now, even before I go back home.

She tugs on the collar of my shirt, still waiting for me to reply. I lift one eyebrow and half-smile at this woman who has everything and yet wants me. "You're sure you want me here with you?"

Playfully tilting head, she sizes me up. Even as the crease returns between her brows, she tries to play the worry off with a grin. "I mean—your ass is still pretty perfect."

I grin back then draw her hand up and kiss it. "At least that's cleared up."

My phone rings with a call from Dick. Ellen takes the interruption as her cue to see her dad while I answer.

Dick starts with a report about the fires. He's learned Sam Bowman left his old hometown on poor terms, but it's also circumstantial evidence. With the help of the expert he hired, he's figured out the fire in the horse barn was started by a match in a trail of diesel fuel poured down the center of the aisles. Whoever set the fire knew where the cameras were located and how to shut them off. He mentions Carter's request that he consider Davis a suspect and says, "I'm still looking into it, but I can say, based on what I've heard so far, Davis has a flimsy alibi for this latest fire. He said he was at his dead brother's grave over in the cemetery, all alone."

"He said his dead brother's grave is in our cemetery?"

"That's what he said." Dick concludes, "That's all I've got, but I'll look into him some more and call you."

An hour later, a driver in a town car picks us up at the hospital and drops us at her dad's building.

For the first time, I see what Ellen's life was like before I knew her.

I always thought my family was pretty well off, with a house that made people gawk and land spread across miles. Traditions that make us miserable but also privileged. But her dad's building is all black and chrome and glass. Everything is grandiose and shiny. There must be hundreds of people working out of this location alone.

Ellen's apartment is near the top floor, stunning and modern, located among arguably the highest-priced real estate in the world. She unlocks the heavy paneled door with a keycard and waits for me to walk in—an open space with tall ceilings and oversized windows. I heard somewhere one of these apartments sold for over two hundred million dollars. I think of the ring I bought for her, still in my pocket.

An article I read right after we met weighs on my mind. A picture of Ellen wearing a white bikini, backdropped by an endless ocean, and a caption about some guy who'd proposed to her with a million-dollar ring.

I sink onto her couch in one corner of a large living room and scan her bookcase, seeking familiarity in her selection of novels and cookbooks, knowing her because of this small detail.

"Anything you want to do tonight?" She settles beside me and stares out the window into the cityscape. It's so casual and domestic it hits me hard. She's one in a billion—a girl who has everything and asks me what I'd like.

"This." I pull her toward me, fitting her back into my uninjured shoulder. It's so good to have her against me. Still, she's worried and readjusts not to bear weight against my side. I trace the soft skin on her upper arm.

"What do you want to do for dinner?" she asks.

"I want you to wear the skirt you're wearing right now." I run my pinky up her thigh, past the hem. At least I have one finger that isn't sore.

She twists so she can grin at me. "That's not even an answer."

I hold a lock of her hair and hope she doesn't cut it because she's trying to fit someone's mold of her professional appearance. Maybe she misses living here.

She's waiting for me to say something about dinner. I know what she's thinking. She wants me to be at ease in this place that reminds me of how miserable I was attending college in San Diego. That was the last time I tried to leave Wyoming for more than a few days.

She twines her small fingers with mine, and I draw her hand up and place a kiss on the back.

Maybe I'll need to find her a fancy ring after all. Or maybe she won't want something as simple as I can offer.

I can't even look her in the face for fear her eyes will tell me a truth I'm not ready to learn.

CHAPTER 18

ELLEN

MAX HAS BEEN ALTERNATING between trying to be strong for me, acting like he's got this all under control, and being willing to do whatever it takes to make me happy. He's got to be hurting and exhausted and probably not really in the mood to be here.

He's frowning, a slight downturn at the corners of his mouth as he gazes out the window at the cityscape of blocky buildings gray and layered against the night sky. The sun is past the horizon, but an afterglow lingers. Maybe it's too early for dinner since he's still adjusting to the time zones.

"What are you thinking right now?" I ask.

He gives me an unreadable look then solemnly says, "I like your place. It's nice—like *really* nice. I might get used to it, lounge around all day, and let people bring me stuff while living off my girlfriend."

I snort a laugh because he would never do that, but still his words have an edge.

He's hurting and trying not to show it.

I lean into him and whisper. "I'm sorry, sweetheart. Living here would put me into a position I've never really wanted, and it would hurt you too."

"Would it?" One side of his lips has this mischievous little lift.

"You're sexy when you do that," I admit.

He smiles wider and says, "When you were on the side of the road, fixing your tire, I kept thinking, one of these days, I'm going to figure out how to get that woman to take me home with her."

I half-laugh then grimace. I want to say that he doesn't have to pretend for me, but I understand what he's trying to do.

He wants to allow me to decide what I want without feeling pressured. He needs me to prove I want him as much as I believe he wants me.

Careful of his hurt arm, I push up to my knees.

His good arm loops around my waist, pulling me forward as I lean into him.

He gives me a gentle kiss then breaks away and says my name, his expression tender.

"What?" I ask.

"Are you feeling okay?"

"Yeah."

"But you hardly ate anything at that pig in a blanket place."

"They're hot dog rolls." I smile tightly to stifle a groan. I couldn't tell him at the hot dog restaurant. It would have been ridiculous. Pulling him up so we're standing, I lift my chin and make him look at me.

His slate-gray eyes and chiseled jaw have always made me swoon. The kind of gorgeous that made my breath catch the first time I ever saw him.

I inhale deeply, shoulders drawing up with the breath, then exhale, saying, "I'm pregnant."

His forehead is drawn, creating a slight crease between his eyebrows. "You're pregnant?"

"I should have already told you. There have been a couple of times I almost did . . . I hope you won't . . ." I let the words trail off, but my mind finishes the thought. *Please don't be upset.* We've talked about what it would be like to have kids. We both want that, but the conversations always ended with a mutual understanding that we would get married and start a family once things were settled.

He pulls me toward him, wrapping my waist in his good arm and whispering into my hair. "Do you want this?"

"Yes. Of course I do. I'm just worried and—"

He stops me with a kiss. Well, not actually stopping me since I become absorbed and appreciative.

Max knows how to kiss. He knows how to make me whimper and how to make me moan. How to make me melt and drive me so wild I forget my surroundings and everything but the taste of his mouth and the tender weight of his hands on my skin, twined in my hair.

He pulls back slowly, working his fingers into his pocket. He drops to one knee, and the sweetness of his soft eyes. The depth of his voice as he says, "I know you're worried, Flynn, and I don't want to scare you or make any of this harder for you, but I want to ask if you'll do me the honor of becoming my wife."

The sudden joy inside me comes out as a vigorous nod.

His hand shakes as he holds out a thin gold band.

I finally manage to say, "Yeah."

"Yeah?" He tilts his head to look up at me.

"Yes! Of course, yes."

A genuine smile breaks over his handsome face.

I lift one shoulder. "Did you think I might say no?"

He stands facing me. "I wanted it to be . . . I wanted to do it once everything was settled and I could promise you I wouldn't be trying to forgive my brother. He's been such a prick to you. I wanted to take you somewhere, romance you, and make it a surprise and special."

"This is perfectly us—it's exactly how people like us would get engaged. Isn't it?"

"It's how we got engaged," he says with a small crease between his eyebrows.

"I love you for trying to fix things with your brother, and things might always be a little complicated where you're involved. Everything doesn't have to be settled for us, does it?"

"I guess not." One corner of his lips raises. He reaches for my palm, turns it up, drops an engraved gold band into my hand, and asks, "What do you think of the ring? I could get a different one."

"I love it because you picked it out and had it in your pocket and because I can bake without taking it off."

He smiles on a sighing exhale and then takes the ring from my hand.

I meet his smoky gray eyes.

With a lingering touch, he runs a finger down my wrist to the curve of my thumb, teasing me with soft strokes, sending a current of longing through my limbs.

"I can guess when it happened," he says with awareness in his eyes.

Of course he can. A blush rises into my cheeks. I've never been on the pill because of a genetic predisposition for blood clots, and it seems we're both recalling the same wild night. We were at his old house, by the lake. We hadn't been there in a few months and had just gone over to make sure nothing would freeze with winter really coming on strong. But once we got there, we didn't want to leave. It was where we really got close as we began dating, and I started talking to him about how much I'd wanted to be with him back then. Things evolved, we didn't have any condoms, and I said it didn't matter. The idea of being together completely bare was a forbidden fantasy that we took as far as it would go, deciding since we'd done it once that we should do it a few more times in front of his fireplace, and in his bed with the star map on the ceiling, and on the kitchen counter.

He places my palm over his heart and says, "Thank you."

And those two words say so much more. He sees this baby as a gift.

I crush him into me. He lets out a small groan. I'm squeezing him too tight.

I take a few steps back. "You've been through hell and still came to find me."

"Seems to be a habit of mine."

I smack him because he ran into my old house, thinking I might have been inside after his brother set it on fire. This is the second time Max has put himself through the worst for me. Still, I'm so glad he's here. I wouldn't change a thing except to make sure no one ever tries to hurt him again.

The doorbell rings. I stare at it unmoving. I haven't lived here in a long time, but I can't recall hearing anyone ever ring the doorbell. My house phone rings next, trilling an eerie omen from every room. It might be someone with news about Father. I move toward it then stop.

"You want me to get it?" he asks.

"It could be Kent." I sound more afraid than I mean to.

He steps around me. "I'll get it."

"Or it could be someone with the restraining order paperwork." I pull his arm and stand in front of him, unwilling to let him put himself in danger for me, even as I'm also incredibly grateful he's willing.

He shakes his head. "I know you're brave, but will you let me? It'd make me feel a whole lot better."

"I love you, but let me look through the peephole first. Okay?"

I step to the door. The visitor is dressed formally in dark

slacks and a stiff white shirt. His hair is the gray of a man in his late fifties. I don't recognize him. The phone stops ringing.

"It's an older man in a suit," I tell Max as I open the door.

"Ms. Jasper," the man says. "I'm William Butler of McCarthy, Butler, and Kline. I'm the attorney handling your father's estate."

"Oh."

He hands me a yellow envelope with my name typewritten on a white label. I nod and grip the door edge.

Mr. Butler is silent momentarily, then he goes on, "Your father was a great man. I respected him. I'm so sorry this is how it is, but . . . I'm afraid he's gone. You don't have to worry about the details. We'll handle funeral arrangements and press releases based on your father's instructions."

As hard as I try, I can no longer remember the attorney's name. He said it when he introduced himself to Max and me. He's still talking, but I have difficulty following him. Father's truly gone. I choke on a breath. The attorney asks if I want him to stay and help explain what the will means, but I shake my head and blink.

Max gets his card and tells him we'll call him if there are any questions. When the door is closed, I set the envelope on the small table near the door where the maid usually leaves mail or notes. Max reaches out, gripping me around the waist a moment before I realize my knees are weak.

We stand there in the foyer for a while. I'm not sure how long. I try to count the time by how his heart thumps against my ear.

Steady and solid. I'm safer and more at ease than I would be without his support. Apparently, sometimes, when a relative dies, an attorney delivers their final wishes, or at least that's what's happened to me. It's still sinking in.

This is how Father would die, the same way Mom died. I never got to say the last things I would have said. I thought I had more time or that they would have called me.

"Why did they not call me?" I ask Max.

"I don't know, Flynn."

He holds me up and guides me to the sofa, where I wedge myself against his side. He sits beside me, slowly unwinding my tension until my back is against the cushion and my feet are in his lap.

My nautical chart depicts the harbor's channels and coves on the TV. True North is there—and Max is here.

He says he will stay if I'm going to, but if we stay here, we will miss what we've left at home. I have a whole life there, and he has the ranch. Our baby could grow up there. As the sun lowers against the horizon, I grab the will off the table near the door and slide the pages out on my way back toward the sofa.

Max sits beside me, saying nothing.

I read until my eyes glaze.

Of course, Father included stipulations, attempts to control his legacy from the grave, a meticulous list of tasks he'd like to see me focus on. However, reading the power of attorney, there's no legal constraint. I don't have to do as he's asked.

Regardless, most of what he's requested aligns with what I would do. However, I would do a few things that would drive him crazy, like hiring a third party to go through our compliance and give me an objective opinion about how we can fix the mess.

Some of the energy leaks out of me as I flip the pages of legalese. Simple words conveying a mountain of responsibility. I wordlessly pass the packet to Max, who sits against the cushions and reads in his characteristic way—his brows slightly knitted as he leans against the sofa cushions.

"It looks like a chance to do what you've wanted," Max says.

"Yeah, it is. I could make a real difference." Still, if I decide to stay here, I'm asking Max to sacrifice a lot. "Is staying here worth it to you? I know it's not ideal."

"Let me make sure I'm clear on what you're asking."

"Okay."

He frowns and sets the papers aside before asking, "This is where you'll be?"

"If I decide to stay."

"Then of course being here is worth it to me. I love you. I don't want to live away from you, and if that wasn't enough, we're about to have a baby."

I stare at him across the short distance between us. His arm in a cast and sling, the cut and bruising on his cheek. I've been so preoccupied with my pain that I haven't even asked him what he went through, and from his looks, Davis was right that Max might have died.

I could have lost him.

God, I love him so much. The thought forms, and then I'm reaching for him, forcing him to set the papers aside. I cling to him and cry.

CHAPTER 19

ELLEN

I BLINK against the light outside. Max is still in bed with me. His bare chest is tanned and strong—a work of masculine art smattered with bluish-purple bruises and the small bandage on his right side where the chest tube used to be. Combined, he's even more irresistibly rugged. I intertwine my hands over my belly to quell the temptation. I'd love to nuzzle beside him, but he's been restless.

He's finally sleeping soundly.

I slide out of bed, shower quickly, and towel off. Closing the door to muffle the sound, I blow out my wet hair then finish my makeup. I like the curve of my mouth when I think about Max being here with me.

His tousled brown hair, sleepy face, and the slope of his hips under the sheet have me longing to head back to bed, but I slip past him to the closet.

It's Tuesday, so I dress in work-casual attire—a knee-length gray skirt, a white blouse, and a jacket in case I leave the building. Heading toward the kitchen, I consider what it will be like to raise children with Max. A smile grows inside me. He'll be dedicated. It will be entirely different from my childhood. We'll be in the kitchen a lot. But maybe that won't work either; not if I'm taking on Father's company, trying to run a bakery, and being a mother. Nothing about this is fair, but what am I supposed to do?

I take the elevator up, bypassing my office for Father's suite. Last time I was on Father's floor, Kent was harassing me. I haven't heard from him. Maybe I never will. With a restraining order, a doorman, and security guards watching for him, it's unlikely he'll be back.

Still, I'm a little nervous when I enter the foyer. I head toward the glass door and greet Adelle.

Behind her desk are countless arrangements and plants sent in condolence.

She stands and gives me a once-over.

I hadn't seen Father in so long that even though I miss him I expect the loss hits her even harder in some ways. They were in constant contact. Wishing I had something to say but unwilling to share my thoughts, I come up with a void. Father's dead, and it feels like a dreadful dream. He was a hard man in many ways, but he was lovable too. He and Adelle worked together for years. Maybe she knew him better than anyone. He wrote her into his will as an alternate—as the person to step in and manage things on behalf of a charitable foundation in his name—if I refused to accept his bequeath.

"I'm sorry for your loss," she says, handing me a red-manila file organizer. Not a hint of sorrow peeks through her iron-clad demeanor. Her face doesn't even wrinkle. But her words and fortitude combine to hollow the area between my heart and stomach, making me wilt.

I square my shoulders and meet her dark eyes. "I'm sorry for your loss as well. It must be incredibly difficult to see me here instead of him."

Our connection holds for a long moment then falters. She plants one hand on her desk, leans forward, and bows her head. Her breathing is steady and controlled but audible over the heater.

When she gazes up at me again, pain is etched into the creases around her mouth and the wet shine of her eyes.

I set the folder on the corner of her desk and move toward her, pulling her into an embrace. We hold each other tightly enough to speak without words.

She breaks free of me and smooths her blouse.

Then, with a characteristically grim look, she dismisses me and resumes her role, sitting proudly behind her desk and tapping her keyboard.

I pick up the folder and take measured steps toward Father's office. The heavy glass door seems to bear the weight of his life, and the soul-sucking vacuum makes me feel hollow. Inside, it still smells like he was just here, the familiar peppermint scent combining with the lingering sweetness of a cigar. A scrap of white paper is balled on the floor just inside, like a discarded receipt. I scoop it up and then flatten it, but the paper is larger and thicker than a receipt. Big blocky letters show inside.

YOU'VE CAUSED THIS.

What the . . . how? Caused what? I go entirely still and scan the space for Kent. I swear the air moves around me, but it's me moving. I'm trembling from the inside. Father's office is the same—the semi-circular sofa, the straight-backed chair where I always sat, his massive desk, papers still strewn over the surface. The cigar smell really isn't that strong.

With a distressing tension in my body, I scrutinize Father's office as he might have—the big windows, the million-dollar rug covering a marble floor. The space is a statement of power and wealth, representing the man himself. However, many people had reasons to dislike him, and Father was never quite as put together as he liked to appear. He didn't have cameras in his executive suite for exactly that reason.

It's reasonable to think he might have caused many things that made people displeased with him, and the note was in his office. Papers cover the keyboard, and I scan message slips from Adelle about upcoming meetings and missed calls. Some are well wishes from friends and colleagues she must have placed there in the last hours before he passed.

Shaken, I return to Adelle's desk. "Has anyone been in my father's office?"

She glances up from her typing. "Not that I know of. Is something out of place?"

I extend the note and say, "Just this. Any idea what it is?"

"Hmm." She tilts her head and reads it aloud. "You've caused this."

"It was on the floor inside."

"I don't know. It's a little odd. It may be left over from the cleaning crew, or that air conditioner of his is so powerful. It tends to blow things around. He was always up to something, planning ways to plant seeds for his projects. Maybe he wrote it."

I wrap it in my palm and say, "You're probably right."

She offers me a knowing smile. "Can you still smell his cigars in there?"

"Mmhmm," I admit, although I'd thought maybe it was my heightened senses that had made the room seem like he'd just been in there smoking.

I return to Father's office, take his chair, and stare at the note with my folded hands notched between my knees.

It wasn't brilliant to imagine Kent would simply disappear or that I could fire him without some retaliation, but when you're a billionaire living at the top of your building, you expect a certain amount of security.

The air conditioner kicks on with a whoosh, and I startle in my chair. I will stay here and spend the time necessary to convince myself the note is meaningless. It's hard to believe Kent would risk breaking into Father's office to deliver a note.

Maybe it's nothing, like Adelle said.

I read and sort, robotically making my way through the stack. I'm unwilling to part with anything and set papers aside in a pile, one by one, until I reach a torn-off envelope and stop to read.

Ellen
  Send Kent

I set the scrap beside the crumpled note. The writing doesn't match. My hand trembles as I sort the remaining items, but nothing else out of the ordinary rests in the pages. Kent's words echo in my memory. *I got you home without a fight, just like I promised him.*

I jam my fingers against Father's keyboard, using the password in the folder Adelle supplied to log in. On the desktop screen is a photo of Mom with Father and me at about eight during a trip to the coast. He came home for a long weekend, and we celebrated a big deal he'd closed.

He's spent his recent days reliving a picture I've cherished too, like he wanted to turn back time as much as I sometimes wished I could. Tears spring to my eyes. I swipe them away and search his correspondence and records for anything more about Kent. Several chummy photos of them together along with pictures of Kent with me after Peter's release on bail.

Another file is an investigator's report that goes beyond a regular HR background check, including his military service record and interviews with fellow soldiers and neighbors in various places he's lived. Few people had glowing things to say, and one called him a gold brick.

The records go on and on. Some positive, some negative.

I start to see a pattern. Father wasn't satisfied and was either vetting him for a meaningful assignment or investigating him because he didn't trust him. Or based on what Kent said, maybe Father was checking him out as a prospective son-in-law.

I make my way through Father's desk, pulling out drawers past the pens and pencils, paperclips, and dust bunnies. At the very back of the center drawer is a stack of papers and greeting cards, rubber banded together. I'd guess, they're things Father thought were worth saving—Father's Day cards, birthday cards, two have Mom's handwriting on the envelope, a few from me to Father, including those I've mailed since moving from Wyoming. Halfway through the stack, I slip out a letter handwritten in blue ink on copier paper.

> Dear Ed,
> Thank you for your words about my feelings for Ellen. When she comes home, we'll see if she still has feelings for me. I learned what a truly great man is from you.
> Kent

The handwriting is small, not blocky like the note. I reach for the letters. About ten more praising Father but with no more mentions of me until there's only one left. I read.

> Ed,
> Sorry things didn't work out with my mom. We still had fun though, didn't we? I know you won't want to hear this, but let's go get Ellen. Let me do what I know how to do.

Kent

A huge part of me wants to believe it's not possible that Father knowingly arranged all of this, but a more significant part is almost certain Kent is that brazen and Father was so blinded by his desire to cheat Max's family out of their land that he was ready to do anything, go to all means necessary to own it. Add his dying and desire to have me come home, and maybe it equated to murder.

A chill grows from my insides, seeping out until I shiver.

Adelle pings me with an instant message. *Per your father's wishes, I've attached the speech you will give at his service.*

Abruptly outraged, I choke out a laugh.

I'm unsure how useful it is to hate a dead father, but an uncontrollable bitterness overcomes me, surpassing my sorrow.

He wants me to give a speech. Fine. I indulge my most ravenous fantasies over what I might say. It's like a poison spreading through me, making my skin tingle. I click the file Adelle sent and digitally drop it on Father's computer to access all the documents. His eulogy is first. He wants to be buried in New York.

A fist of anger pounds in my head. After all these years, he's not going to be buried by Mom.

I continue reading, getting more frenzied and angrier.

The summary sheet is on the following page. Mom's name. The text for their new joint headstone.

He planned to have someone exhume her body and move her to New York.

I slam my palms against the monitor.

It slides off the desk and crashes to the floor.

CHAPTER 20

MAX

"You're sure about this?" I ask.

Ellen reaches the far wall of her apartment, lined with towering custom-built bookshelves, and turns around. When she passes me, she lifts her shoulders and lets them fall. "I guess."

In a little more pain than yesterday, with aches that will not quit, I sit on the couch and watch her pace. Her posture is stiff, and her expression stressed. She's faced with a choice. Move her mom's body or bury her dad where he doesn't want to be buried. It's easy to understand her uncertainty.

"They hardly lived together, so maybe they don't need to be buried together," she says.

"But legally . . ." I let the thought go before finishing.

She pins me with a look and stops before me, gesturing with her hands as she talks. "Legally, my father had no right to demand my mom's grave be moved on a whim. He should have considered this years ago. She's buried with her whole family in a historic cemetery that meant something to her. His plot is all about the city. They would be surrounded by strangers. It's his last attempt to control her choices, and I won't be part of it."

She paces again then stops. "And, legally, consideration of the deceased's wishes regarding the burial place is instrumental in a court's decision. There's a good chance someone would stop us from moving my mom even if we tried to follow his instructions, which we aren't going to do."

We've both spent the last half hour attempting to understand how cases like this work, what steps are required, and when it's allowed. The answers are complicated, but ultimately the choice seems to rest with Ellen since she's the closest relative endowed with her dad's power of attorney.

Times exist when someone's final wishes and detailed plans make things harder for their family, and Ellen faces a complex question. Is it more important to honor the wishes of her dead father or maintain the wishes of her dead mother?

On her next pass, she throws up her hands and stops. "I'm so furious that I don't even want to go to his funeral."

Now would be a terrible time to point out that she's supposed to read the pre-written eulogy. Instead, I say, "Come here."

She sinks onto the couch and wedges herself into my side, where the chest tube used to be. "This whole thing is a disaster. I mean, could my father have come up with a more fucked-up scenario?"

I inhale her familiar amber shampoo.

Keeping her cheek against my chest, her voice gets animated while her body relaxes. "Seriously, I don't think he could have. I think he was probably laughing to himself when he wrote this out. He knew exactly how mad it would make me and did it all purposefully."

"That's . . . sick. Sad. I'm not sure of the word I'm looking for.

You think it's a game, or do you think he honestly expected your mom would want to be with him wherever he ended up?"

"Pff." She lets a breath out through her lips. "I don't know. Maybe it was a bit of both."

"So if your mom was alive and your dad was gone first, what would she have decided, knowing he wanted to be buried here?"

She pulls back a reasonable distance and wraps one hand behind her neck, leaning forward as she closes her eyes and shakes her head. "I don't know. I always thought they were both going to be buried in Virginia. He bought a family plot and buried her parents there. His spot is right next to hers. That was always their plan."

"How angry do you think he would be about being buried down there if he were still around to complain about it?"

She lifts one shoulder. "He'd get over it. He loved my mom enough to keep all her stuff, even though he hated it."

"So think about it this way. Do you think he'd rather be buried alone or with her down there?"

"I know he'd rather be with her, and I'm angry enough with him at this point that I refuse to disturb my mom's grave so that he can hurt someone I love. I won't do it. I don't care what his attorneys say. I don't care what anyone says. He's either alone or with her down there."

"So he's with her down there."

And that's how Ed Jasper's funeral plans get turned entirely on their head. Is it right? Is it wrong? It seems she's thinking the same thing because she looks at me with glassy eyes. "I'll read his eulogy word for word, and we won't tell anyone he's not getting exactly what he wanted."

She'll make peace with it all at some point. Maybe.

She rests her head against the sofa's back.

I pull her foot into my lap and stare down at her high-heeled shoe then up her legs to the hem of her skirt. I could get used to being around her dressed up, but I'm not so sure about living in the city. I'll do it for her, but I'm not sure how happy she'd be here, either, in the long run.

She rubs her temple, pulls herself upright, settles her feet on the floor, and stands. She's been fidgeting and worrying.

"Want to go for a walk?" I can handle something short.

She focuses on her purse, pulls out a scrap of paper, and walks back to the couch. "I need to show you this, but I was so upset about my mom that I forgot about it. Actually, I tried not to think about it."

It's a wrinkled paper scrap with someone's poor handwriting scrawled in large letters.

YOU'VE CAUSED THIS.

My chest tightens against my broken ribs, and I fight the pain to hold my voice even. "When did you find this?"

"This morning."

"And you held onto it?"

"I think it's about my father or something of his." Her sweet voice tremors.

"What do you think it's about?"

"I don't know. It could be from Kent." The hair on the back of my neck prickles. I go from hot to cold, from short-fused to smoldering.

Shoulda killed that guy.

"I'll brief security and ensure they watch for him," she says.

Still, the note seems threatening but pretty vague. Ed was coercing Abner and who knows how many other wealthy men.

"Why do you think it's from Kent?" I ask.

"I'm not sure who else could have left it. Or why they would have. I dug through Father's correspondence and after everything Kent seems more suspect than anyone else."

"But how could he have gotten into the building to leave a note?"

"I don't know. Maybe someone on our security team is

helping him. Otherwise, I don't think he could have. We canceled all his access cards."

I reach for my phone. Kent's location is still shown via her phone—an apartment building in New Jersey. "We'll go talk to the security team together. We'll file a police report about the note to go with your restraining order."

We discuss the threat with the head of her dad's security team and the responding police officer. She shows him the notes with Kent's handwriting for comparison. I show them my phone and ask if they've tried to locate him. We give them her number again so they can do whatever they need to do to find him.

Heightened staff levels are posted within the building. Kent's photo is circulated. His location remains unchanged. All the while, I'm thinking that if he shows up I will teach him a lesson he won't forget.

In the coming days, we hear nothing about Kent from the police or security. Ellen keeps saying the note was probably a fluke. No one is sure what to make of it.

She's focused on her dad's service and keeps parts of his wishes intact while still planning to bury him with her mom in Virginia.

Ed lies in repose for 28 hours at the chapel he'd selected. Adelle creates a list including dignitaries worldwide to accommodate all wishing to be admitted. Over 2,000 people show up to pay their respects, less than half of those asking to be included. For all the bad her father was, he was a man of reputation and power. Music is played. Reporters and photographers show up en masse. Flags at several financial institutions are set at half-staff.

The two days offer some time for me to reconnect with things back home. I've talked to Carter a few times, catching up on what's happening in our lives, but we still haven't managed to say the things that need saying.

Ellen is occupied in her dad's suite upstairs. I stay plastered to her couch and call Carter. While I wait for him to pick up, I stare at the harbor map displayed on her TV and think through what must be said.

When he answers, I ask if he has time and privacy for a meaningful conversation. When he says yes, I say, "There's something I've been needing to say about . . . everything. Our whole relationship, going back to the night I called you for help with Cody."

"Huh. Okay." Horse nickers carry in the background. Probably the right place for him to be since he's always comfortable in that environment.

I say, "No words can convey how wrong I've felt about how things went down. I never intended for you to take the blame or go to jail. I'm sorry for not doing a better job of telling you what I needed when it came to dealing with what I'd done."

"I think you did try to tell me," he replies with dry humor. "I just thought you were an idiot."

"Maybe I was, but I didn't need you to step in and take my choice away. It didn't help me as much as you hoped. It did a lot of damage to you too."

"I know. I've also thought about it too, and I'm sorry."

Carter apologizing is about as rare as a unicorn.

And he goes on. "Christa tells me stuff like this too. I should have talked to you instead of trying to fix it for you."

Light with a sense of hope, I say, "I need you to trust me."

"I want you to trust me too."

"I do trust you when you're not trying to orchestrate my life."

"I won't circumvent you, okay?" He's upbeat.

"Just talk to me, and I'll talk to you. I'll trust that you'll be honest and that what you're doing comes from a good place, even if we disagree. And I'll consider what you're saying, if you'll do the same for me."

"So? What's it mean in reality?" he asks.

"It means I'm not sure when I'm coming home. I'm asking you to look after the ranch so I can do what I want to do."

"So I get to be in charge of the ranch, but you still own it." By the end, his tone is flat.

And I want to make up for all that's gone on and give us a real chance, like Ellen and I discussed. "What if we go 50/50 and trust that we can work things out?"

"Not 51/49, so you can outvote me?" Because he would have insisted on that if our positions were switched, but I'm not like that.

I'm 100% or nothing at all. "We'd just fight. This way, we deal with it until we agree or nothing gets done."

"Sounds . . ." He lets the thought trail off.

"Like I'm an idiot?" I ask, only half in jest. This is a huge step. Is it right? Time will tell.

A moment later, his voice is strained with emotion. "Like you're fucking brilliant. I love you. You know that, right?"

"I love you too." And I mean it the way I always have. "You saved my life and kept me out of jail. I've never questioned whether you loved me."

"Only whether I trusted you." He chokes out a laugh. "All I ever wanted is for people to trust me, and maybe I've made that impossible."

The bright intensity of his words radiates behind my eyes, making them hot. Days ago, we were at each other's jugulars. Still, this is a moment we've been headed toward for years. "Bottom line, I always trusted you. Now we have to prove it to each other."

"Alright." His voice is solemn as an oath. We share more than blood.

"How'd you know where to find me?" I ask.

"I went all over the ranch, asked people. Then I started

thinking about how shitty you probably felt about everything going on. I went to Echo Canyon and smelled smoke."

"Thank you," I say, but I'm really looking for more words. "Only you would have done that after everything we've been through."

"I don't think so," he says. "I think you'd have gone looking for me the same way, probably in the same place."

"You're probably right," I admit, shifting the scales balancing inside me.

We talk about the ranch for a few minutes. I explain that Ellen plans to squash the strip-mining permit at Echo Canyon. He fills me in on Davis's claim that he's related to the family by some previously unknown link, a brother related to our grandfather, which is bewildering and probably untrue, then switches to discussing Dick's investigation into the fires.

Carter says, "Dick's still talking like it could have been Sam all along, but I think it's only because of that article about his dad. Dick's probably wrong. I mean, you know I've never liked Sam, so I wouldn't mind seeing him blamed, but that article may be the inspiration behind the fires. I also think it's the first false clue."

"I was thinking you'd found that article and framed him."

"You never even asked me if I set the fires."

"And you would have answered me?"

"I didn't start the fires, and I would have told you that, but you wouldn't have believed me."

"But you would have been furious because I'd asked."

"Reasonably so."

I draw a big breath and blow it out. "You had an alibi anyway."

"An alibi? Is that what they call it when you're putting your ass on the line fighting fires."

"You were with Davis."

"No, I was with the fire department."

"But Davis said you were with him."

"Right there was your first clue. Missing it was your first step away from the truth."

"Maybe." I shift on the couch and groan. "My ribs hurt."

"You still trying to figure out who was shooting at you?"

"I just need to find the guy now." Putting my phone on speaker, I navigate to the tracking app. Kent's location no longer shows up. Maybe Ellen's battery died. I refresh the app and then rub my eyes to be sure I see clearly.

Still nothing.

Maybe the police have already located him. I press the heel of my hand into my breastbone as alarm pounds a beat against my temples.

Carter drags my attention back to the call. "By the way, I'm headed up for the funeral."

"Good." My voice is shaky.

We end the call, and I launch off the couch into the bedroom where I paw through shopping bags of clothes Ellen ordered and dress appropriately for the first time since falling down the canyon.

God's truth, I will figure out how to neutralize the threat Kent represents.

Maybe I'll find him and call the police. I feel better. Calmer. At peace with having a plan. I navigate the building and try various things to find Kent based on the location of Ellen's phone. Her dad's IT and security staff have exciting ideas, but the result is the same. Kent's location is no longer shown. One guy keeps repeating that he doesn't think the note was from Kent. He says it's too vague and the handwriting doesn't match. Another one suggests we send it to a handwriting expert, so we gather samples and send them off to be analyzed.

Sitting at the kitchen island in her apartment with my head in my hands, I'm unsure what to think.

"You okay?" Ellen asks. Somehow, I missed the sound of the door.

I exhale and consider how to answer.

Her brow draws up in the middle, and she runs a timid hand down my arm like I'm on the verge of disability.

"You're still going?" she asks.

We're supposed to go out to dinner with Babs and my former sous chef and longtime friend Sandy.

"Yeah." I should be excited about the dinner. I haven't seen Sandy since I sold my restaurant and she moved. I still can't muster the focus to care as much as I should.

I gut my way through the meal in nicer clothes, explaining how I ended up in the hospital, smiling and talking when it seems necessary, but all the time I'm supercharged with tension, ready to snap with the need to do something about Kent. He's still out there, and despite the security detail Ellen has posted around the establishment, we have no way of knowing when he might show up. We don't even know if we can trust her security team, and the police seem as hopelessly overworked here as they are in Wyoming. No one's taking this seriously enough.

On the way back to her apartment, Ellen reaches across the backseat of the car as her driver whisks us through nighttime traffic.

"Sorry for . . . you know . . ." I lift my hand helplessly.

"Letting Kent distract you from enjoying an exquisite dinner planned by your best friend you haven't seen in a year?" Ellen guesses, filling in the blank for me. She has an uncanny knack for knowing what I need to say even when I can't figure out quite how to say it.

"Yeah," I reply and settle my hand on hers, tracing my ring on her finger. "I'll call Sandy and apologize."

"You should do that." She shrugs. "But, you know, I'm worried about Kent too. Still, we can't let him take over our lives."

"You're right." I can't help it though. I have an issue with any guy who wants to mess with her.

"How do you put up with me?" I ask.

She smirks. "I've got a thing for surly guys who walk around growling to keep people away from me."

I smile at her despite the worry and pull her into my side.

She tilts her face up, the corners of her mouth lifted.

"Have you ever had sex in a limo?" she asks.

"I haven't, but we could try it." I trace a finger along the square edge of her neckline. Her inhale makes her chest move into my touch. "I'm always up for whatever will make you happy," I admit, and she has a thing about coming onto me in the car.

With my palm around her slender neck, I drag her toward me. Her fingers wrap into the hair at my collar. Her warm mouth tastes a million times better than the French chocolate and cherry liqueur of our dessert.

I'd been too busy watching for Kent to enjoy it.

He might know the driver. He might meet us in the parking garage or be waiting in her apartment. I don't know what tactic to take because I'd like to find Kent and inflict a bit of the pain he's created for us, but I can't have what I want. I try to shake the thought away.

She breaks our kiss, murmuring, "You're worried about something?"

"Do you know the driver?" I ask.

"I don't." She lounges against the leather seat, sexy as a forbidden delicacy and playful as a fairy sprite. "He can't hear us through the glass," she says.

We've done what we can, but the note bothers me. Kent may have someone helping him from inside of her dad's security. No one can locate him.

Ellen lets out a disapproving titter.

I move toward her.

She rises and comes toward me, resting her knee between my thighs as she grabs my collar with both hands.

I crane my neck up at her.

"We have 15 minutes if traffic is slow," she says, dropping

her mouth to mine, hungry and insistent. She's a little tipsy from seeing friends and letting loose, laughing with them while I brooded over things out of my control. I want to savor her excitement, dominating my senses—the salty taste of her neck. The scent of her skin is musky and sultry and tempting as ever. The sparkly black sheath dress, the thigh-high pantyhose, and the garter she paraded around in while I stared like a golden retriever waiting for his chance at a table scrap. She planned this. She also licked the last bit of chocolate off her spoon at dinner and stared at me like she knew I wanted to lick it off her naked.

The car slows abruptly and turns right down a ramp, sending the tires squealing against concrete. We startle away from each other. She draws back, sitting against the seat, breathing hard, and giving me an appreciative grin.

"You said we had 15 minutes," I accuse.

She pouts. "You wouldn't have played along if I told you we only had two minutes."

"You're probably right."

"It was fun," she says.

I trace the line of her lower lip. "You're fun."

She tilts her head, planting a kiss on my cheek. "Please stop being so grumpy."

"I'll try."

The following two days carry on this way, us distracting ourselves with the need to have each other close, me barely managing to put on a face of calm. Ellen is worried about me and dealing with her dad's funeral.

I'm not entirely the man she needs me to be, but I'm powerless to be anyone else no matter how hard I try.

The following day, we drive to the cemetery for the service in Ellen's G-class Mercedes.

My pistol is tucked into the passenger door side pocket.

If Kent shows up at the funeral . . . I tell myself the gun is for protection. Her security team will be there. We'll call the police and figure out what to do calmly. I make a fist, clenching my hand, trying to convince myself whatever happens will be fine. Kent has probably moved on to tormenting someone else. The records security dug up indicate he's been a bit of a mercenary. Still, we've put precautions in place. Nothing bad will happen to Ellen.

She tells a story from the driver's seat about a trip they all took to Brazil when she was 15. Her mother was volunteering for a rain forest conservation charity while her father was finagling his way into a copper mining deal. Of course, her mother was vehemently opposed. After returning home, her mom sent a check to the charity to offset whatever profit she expected him to make on the mine. Her dad said nothing, and the founders said the substantial donation would ensure their efforts were funded for a decade or more.

I've asked her how her parents fell in love since they seem like opposites. She always says they genuinely loved each other, offering examples to prove her point, leaving me labeling Ed as one of those guys who always came through at the last minute, making it hard to stay truly angry, while her mom forgave and forgot, then did what she pleased whenever her husband wasn't around.

Her parents' conflicting goals and the resulting sparring frequently left Ellen relying on her grandparents for care or reading alone while trying not to become a source of disagreement between her parents. Each of them had unique ideas about what she should be doing instead of anything she chose to do. They eventually shipped her off to boarding school, where she fell in love with a guy who robbed her. It's no wonder that she was so scared to trust when she came to Wyoming.

She moves on to a story about her granddad on her mom's side. He's the one she talks about the most whenever it comes to happy parts of her childhood. He loved working with his hands and farming. He was a stone-mason when he was young, constructing brick buildings and even a few dams at nearby reservoirs. She'd watch him work for hours, and he'd give her little jobs to do for him. Maybe it was jealousy that made Ed destroy the oven Ellen's grandfather built for her mom. Either way, Ellen arrived in Wyoming with the heady goal of building a replica of the oven using rocks she found on her property.

She says, "My grandpa never liked my father."

"Your dad never liked me," I reply, too exhausted with her dad to pretend I have something better to say about him.

"I guess he didn't." Tension sharpens her tone.

I deserve her frustration, because while I've been listening, maybe I haven't really heard her as well as I should have. She's upset, and I could have done a better job at understanding what's really going on in her mind and heart.

But I'm edgy about Kent, angry that I haven't already neutralized the threat he poses, and hurt because Ellen's dad tried to kill me. She's paying for my emotional turmoil during a time when she needs it like a mis-prescribed root canal.

With the radio down to near nothing, tire and engine noise carry in the wake of everything that's tried to pull us apart in the last week. I want to reach out and stroke a finger down her arm. I should apologize, but I don't want to talk about Kent or dwell on what's happening within me. I'm not sure I can apologize for speaking the truth about how her dad must have felt about me. I don't say anything.

CHAPTER 21

ELLEN

I GRIP the soft leather steering wheel and turn my car toward the cemetery where my entire family is buried.

Max sits beside me in a dark suit with this brooding mood coming off him in everything he doesn't say. He's staring out the windshield like he doesn't want to be here. I get it. He's on his way to the funeral of a man who may have tried to have him murdered. The only reason he's here is because I'm here. He loves me so much that he's willing to pay respects to a man who hated him and had it out for his family.

I twine my fingers with his and drag his hand onto the console with mine.

Around the next bend, the cemetery comes into view. Beyond all doubt, Father will be the most famous person ever buried here. He would hate it.

No one needs to know he's buried here. Not his staff. Not anyone, except for Adelle since she'll record the eulogy. She'll help me keep up appearances like this is happening beside his headstone at the plot in New York.

She's not thrilled with the idea, but we've planned it down to where I'll stand while she records me. It will be fine.

I made the right choice, calling off security and insisting on driving ourselves.

Max sighs heavily and rests his head against the passenger window. I need to tell him they won't be here and explain why I asked them not to come.

With every passing breath, my pulse picks up pace. I pull down the main road toward the small brick chapel with a tin roof and say nothing.

Three cars are parked nearby. One is Adelle's rental since she's standing outside. Then there's a black sedan and, in the distance, a white truck—two too many cars.

Still, those people are probably here visiting other graves. Everything will be okay. I ease my grip on the wheel.

The grounds don't sport an ornate gateway, shady tree cover, or an iconic skyline view, but there's history here and family—serenity—along with untidy winter lawn care and barren patches of soil in the grass. Father would describe the bald mountain as slick-faced. He'd gripe about the rounded stones, listed out of plumb through the years, but my grandparents on both sides and even Father's sister are buried here.

A green tent has been erected near their graves with Father's closed casket on a stand, ready to lower it into the ground.

Last time I was here, I bawled my eyes out at Mom's grave. I purse my lips and inhale through my nose. Then I blink a few times. I might cry, but no heat builds behind my eyes.

"Where are the guys from security?" Max asks.

I don't want a security entourage making me uncomfortable like they did during Mom's service. I need this small moment before I dive back into that life.

"Have you heard from them?" he asks.

I park along the curb and turn toward him with hot eyes. Shame burns my throat. I should have talked to him about this, but he would have insisted we bring the security team. I didn't want to argue with him.

"Flynn, where are they?"

"I'm exhausted with the stiff formality and just want to go home," I admit.

"But—"

"I'm falling apart, about to bury my father, hoping I've done the right thing on a million decisions I've made in the last week, and you're going to start in about where are the guys from security?"

"Fuck." Max leans his head against the window for a long moment then sits up and looks at me.

"Kent won't be here. I took precautions."

"You're so worried about your dad's wishes and how everything's going to look to the press that you're not thinking straight."

"We don't know if the note was from Kent. And if it was, who helped Kent put the note in Father's office? Can we trust anyone?"

He looks at me with a determined set of his mouth and a creased brow. He doesn't say it, but he's asking, *What if I can't keep you safe?*

"It's not your job to save me all the time." I try to say it gently, but his face stiffens and turns red.

"Something could happen to me at any moment, and I refuse to live the rest of my life with a staff watching," I add.

He closes his eyes, shakes his head, opens his eyes, and draws a big breath. "Well then, if that's how you feel, maybe we need to go home and stop acting like we're trying to live up to the expectations of a man who had no real regard for his daughter."

"Is this what we're doing?" I ask, almost yelling. I quiet my voice. "You're ready to admit how you feel about my father at his funeral?"

"I don't mean—"

"Don't worry about it. I get it. I don't blame you for being upset, but my father has to be buried, and I've made the decisions I've made. I'll handle it."

He holds out his good hand but stops short of touching me.

I unbuckle my seat belt and reach for the door handle. I can do this entirely on my own.

I start to cry harder than I've cried since Mom's funeral.

I'm once again in Virginia, going against Father's wishes. I'm at odds with Max because I'm so stressed that I'm losing sight of what's important. I'm trying to run a bakery remotely. I'm pregnant and attempting to fix corruption within a global company.

Perhaps I'm having a hard time coping, or it's my hormones, but still I could use a small amount of kindness from him—of all people. The one person I trust. A little reassurance that anything I'm doing is suitable for the situation.

"Is it too much to ask that you see it from my perspective?" I ask.

"No, of course not. I understand what you're saying. I get it, Flynn. You're a private person and you're hurting, but—"

"Please don't lecture me right now. I can't handle it."

He rubs his forehead and says, "Okay, but . . . Okay. Fine."

He opens the door and steps out of the car, scouring the cemetery. I'm sure he's looking for Kent. He doesn't think I'm making sense, but he's not either. I need him to stop focusing on Kent and see what's happening to me.

I'm not even sure what's happening to me.

CHAPTER 22

MAX

WHAT JUST HAPPENED? I stare after Ellen, who is halfway across the grass to the tent. Her shoulders shake as she tries not to cry. But a dull heat is blooming at the base of my skull, and I try to calm down and accept my part in causing our argument.

I need to apologize for what I said about her dad. True or not, it was terrible timing. But genuine fear roots my boots to the grass. I scan the cemetery for the millionth time, and try again to cool the sensation of heat flooding my blood, making my face hot.

Maybe I am being paranoid. She said she took precautions. I should have asked what they were, but it's more than that. *She should have told me.*

Carter approaches, dressed in all black from Stetson to boots.

He extends a hand for a shake. He drove hours to be here, paying his respects to Ed—a man who was wrecking our family a little at a time.

She lifts her palms. An "of course, he's here" expression raises her eyebrows. We talked about Carter coming, but maybe she thought he was coming to the public part of the services up in New York.

He's watching me.

I shake his hand and attempt an explanation. "I didn't know how few people were invited to this part of the service." I had no clue she was planning to have only three people here or that she was dis-inviting the pricey security force at her disposal.

"Want me to go?" my brother asks.

"She was already upset with me." I scrape a hand through my hair. Ellen's dark dress, her curves, and her flat stomach. She'll look angelic with a baby bump.

"Want to talk about it?" Carter asks.

He's still got the long knife on his belt.

Holy shit! I left my pistol in the passenger door of Ellen's car.

I start away from Carter, toward the gun, then imagine that she probably locked the doors and stop. I don't want to argue with her about this more right now. She's about to bury her dad.

The cemetery is practically empty—four cars, including Ellen's Mercedes and Carter's pickup. Even the graveyard staff has vacated the area for the time being. The funeral director is possibly inside the chapel waiting for everyone to leave so he can cue the crew to lower the casket and finish refilling the hole.

Maybe it's for the best that I left it. I should take a page from her book and stop worrying.

I walk toward the grave with Carter keeping pace beside me.

The whole thing is a lot different than I imagined it would be and greatly removed from how we handle burials on the ranch with a massive gathering and enough food for a small army.

Ellen steps behind the podium, her eyes still wet. She's on the ragged edge of grief, struggling to handle her emotions, giving me back what I gave her on the drive over here. She's hormonal. Her dad has died. Kent has stalked her, and her dad tried to kill me.

Maybe she needs me to give her a bit of grace. Or maybe she needs me to stop being so absorbed with the idea that I'll let her down if I'm not hyper-vigilant. I've lost too many people and have almost died. I don't want to lose her or our baby.

A terrifying vulnerability exists whenever you have something you fear losing with the force of your entire soul, and it's made worse because Kent presents a genuine and definable threat I haven't managed to neutralize.

I follow Carter toward his pickup as Ellen visits with Adelle. We talk about stuff at home, and he starts to ask me about Ellen, but I cut him off. He mentions his plans for next season's planting. I nod and agree and tell him he should do whatever he wants.

Adelle stands a few feet away from Ellen, holding a recorder, and gives a countdown with one hand.

In a heartfelt voice, Ellen speaks of her dad's accomplishments. Her voice cracks as she acknowledges the special bond that existed with her father. She explains how she always wanted to live up to what he'd asked of her but also knew whatever she did he would still love her. She's not reading anything. If it's a prepared speech, she's practiced it long and hard. She mentions some of his successes and shares memories of the good times she spent with her parents. Finally, she talks about his values and how his last wish was to leave her with wisdom and a chance to continue his legacy. It's a stunning tribute to her dad and is one of the best I've ever seen. I'm unsure if she rewrote it, but I think she must have.

When she's finished, she leaves the podium to exchange a hug with her dad's secretary.

It'd be hard to imagine she was upset with me when she started, except she's not looking at me like she might have otherwise. I excuse myself from Carter and walk up to her just like nothing's happened.

She won't look me in the eye and steps away.

"Flynn," I say her middle name and wait for her to look at me. "I'm sorry that I hurt you. Please don't be angry."

She shakes her head. "I'm not angry. I'm sorry too. I should have told you, but I knew you'd be upset."

Adelle arrives at her side to say goodbye. They walk toward the road. Adelle gets in her car and drives out slowly, waiting a long time at the stop sign before she turns. She's probably sorting out directions. This place is rural.

I should head back over to find Ellen.

"Hey," Carter's voice is urgent.

"What?"

"Who's that guy?" He points toward Ellen. She stands beside her car with Kent.

My body seems to go bottomless for a second before I can breathe.

Then I'm running, more like staggering across the lawn toward them. They're focused on each other. They don't seem to have noticed me. He's not holding onto her. It's more like they're engrossed in a tense conversation. Maybe he's trying to get her into the driver's side of the car. She could be trying to convince him she needs more time with her father before they leave.

Breathing hard, I try to be silent while interpreting their body language. The car is in the way. It's hard to know exactly what's happening.

Kent puts his hand on her arm. Ellen's posture goes taut. I step forward. He has a handgun.

Ellen minutely shakes her head. Be careful. I freeze. Carter slipped away without a word. Weaponless, I continue despite Ellen's warning.

Every fraction I move seems like it will be the first one he sees.

I'm almost at the passenger's side but can't get the gun without opening the door.

His face is red, and he's speaking very quietly.

He wants her to retract the things she said. He wants the restraining order canceled and thinks it will impact his ability to get another job. Fury builds from the pounding in my ears.

"Maybe you don't need another job in security if you're going to act this way?" Ellen says.

He leers forward and bares his teeth. My limbs go rigid. He jerks her into him. She twists away and yelps. I take two steps closer. Ellen shakes her head at me, her eyes bulged.

I return the gesture, but I have no intention of waiting. I take three fast steps, aiming to come around behind Kent. An eerie whistle screams through the air.

A sound I know so well. A hissing force of air screaming around a thin strip of leather.

The rapid back-and-forth movement of a whip handle causes the tip to move supersonically.

The sound alone, slightly louder and more ominous than a mosquito very close to an ear, is enough to move a herd of cows.

And here's my brother covering my back. He lets go with a chilling cowboy shriek, an eerie and low yell, roiling and raw. It seems to come from everywhere at once. And suddenly Kent is looking at him.

Then all hell breaks loose. It takes seconds. Carter wraps the whip's fall around Kent's wrist and jerks. Ellen springs around the front of the car, stopping near the bumper. I grab the handgun from her passenger door and point it at Kent. Carter's whip is still around his wrist but lacking tension. Kent's gun is pointing at Carter's mid-chest.

I raise my good hand and aim. It's close enough that my Sig's .38 round will kill him. Conscience and cowardice campaign as my finger compresses the trigger.

Air moves right before the muted powder explosion of a

small caliber cartridge. I follow the sound toward Ellen, standing with a palm pistol raised.

Kent yells, a strangled fist of pain coming from his throat. Carter sends a wave through his whip, freeing it gracefully. Kent staggers toward Ellen. A round hole blooms red at his right knee.

He fixes his gun on her. One-handed, I aim for Kent, mid-chest, and pull the trigger.

CHAPTER 23

ELLEN

WE SHOULD HAVE ALREADY CALLED the police. I reach for my phone, planning to dial 911. My breath comes out vibrating. My hand shakes so badly I can't work the screen. Blood spatters are speckled over my shoes in tiny droplets of red against the shiny black leather.

Kent is slumped to the grass. He takes a slow, gurgling breath. His chest cavity expands, and the air goes straight out the wound hole in a grotesque and horrible reversal of how breathing should work. He inhales again, and his blue eyes meet mine, and I squeeze mine shut, blocking out the truth of what we've done.

He's deranged, but he's a person. His mother lives in Florida. He tried to kill Max. He probably would have killed me. Red covers the inside of my eyelids. It won't go away even after I reopen my eyes. Max is at Kent's side, trying to close the wound, but it doesn't help. Kent's body is still. Max's fingers are on Kent's throat, seeking a pulse for what seems like an hour but must be less than a minute. Then he looks up at his brother with shining eyes.

"I've got a truck," Carter says.

Max shakes his head and blinks. "We're gonna call it in."

Carter raises both shoulders and then steps back. He's a felon with two strikes on his record after going to jail for his brother and for what he did to me.

"You think they're going to blame you?" I ask.

"You should go," Max says roughly as he stands, wiping his hands on his slacks and leaving them streaked with blood.

Expressions convey unspoken sentiments. No. Yes. It's a silent battle of wills. The brothers had this conversation after Max beat up the drunk driver who killed their parents, and Carter's attempt to help didn't work out well. Max was defending me, but is it even legal for Max to carry his gun in Virginia? Is mine legal? I have no idea. I never planned on using it.

"Max was defending me," I argue.

Carter snorts. "Even if he was defending himself, it can be ruled that excessive force was used or that the threat of death wasn't truly imminent." He shifts to Max and says, "You'll be charged with manslaughter, maybe something more. They'll ask why you had the gun and why there was no security here if you were so worried about this guy showing up. They'll want you to explain why you didn't try other things before you shot him in the chest."

Max opens his mouth then closes it and shakes his head.

"If you call this in, you're going on trial for killing a guy who almost killed you. You'll probably spend some time in jail." Carter pulls out his keys.

Max reaches for them then stops.

I step forward and hold up my hands, then ignore his tight jaw. "You're not driving around with a body in the back of Carter's truck."

They exchange a look. Lift their chins. *What are we going to do about her?*

Carter went to jail for two years after Max beat up the man who killed their parents. Is Carter right that Max could go to jail for shooting Kent even though Kent was aiming a gun at me? I could go on trial for shooting Kent in the knee. We're going to have a baby. I can't let Max or Carter pay for my decision to call off security. I'm going to deal with this, no matter how awful it is. Our best chance is to act now. Handle this ourselves somehow. Isn't it? We could make what just happened go away before anyone else finds out.

Only three cars remain in the historic and rural cemetery in the middle of nowhere: mine, Carter's, and the black sedan, which must be Kent's. Still, someone must be inside the chapel. If they heard the shot, they'll be coming out soon.

But everything is so still.

No one appears at the chapel door.

No cars pass on the road outside the chainlink fence.

Father's grave sits with the casket on the stand. My decisions led us here, and I can't run from this. I need to be the one to act.

I speak words that will haunt me. "We're going to bury Kent with my father."

They both look at me then at each other.

Max frowns. His hand, sleeve, and one knee of his slacks are covered in Kent's blood, but he has a suitcase in the car. "You want to . . ."

"You're fucking crazy," Carter says.

I give him a demented stare that's only half as insane as I feel. "Kent tried to kill Max. He might have killed me or you. My father helped Kent, and now he's helping us."

The gravity of what we've done and the terror of being caught combine into a black hole of panic. My knees could be made of putty, but I stay by Max and pray the grave workers don't arrive until we're gone. Sweat builds at my neck and back. Still, my arms tremble like I'm freezing.

"I'm sorry for putting us in this situation," I say, regretting every decision that led me to this moment.

CHAPTER 24

MAX

I EXHALE SLOWLY and bring my good hand to the back of my neck. My palm slides against the skin, now slick with Kent's blood.

We're a tragic group. A pregnant woman, a man willing to sacrifice everything for his younger brother for the second time in his life, and me—the guy who already allowed him to do it once before.

They're telling me they love me enough to keep a secret from which we'd never walk away.

And I'll love them both until my dying day.

Tiny specks of blood dot Ellen's black shoes and the back of one of her hands. She's still holding the pistol. Carter remains standing far enough away to have remained clean, except for the braced expression tightening his face.

We're working against a clock. Someone may have heard us. The graveyard is empty, but Kent's car remains on the opposite side of the grass. Hell, someone could be inside. Who knows where the funeral director is?

The cemetery remains eerily, chillingly quiet.

None of us speaks or moves. They're waiting for me to say something, making each moment seem longer than the last. My breath is loud against every tight inhale.

Three may keep a secret, if two of them are dead.

For some infuriating reason, this Ben Franklin quote comes to mind. All the years I spent seeking insights into life and solutions for an insurmountable problem *would* come back with the quotes I used to love.

I can barely even look at Kent or bear the weight of the gun heavy in my waistband. The iron scent of his blood is embedded in my nose.

I finally look at Carter. He holds my gaze, then he drops his focus to the road beyond.

Meeting Ellen's red-rimmed eyes, I say, "It's an idea, Flynn, and I understand what you're saying. I wouldn't have thought of it, and it'd be better than driving around with Kent in the back of a truck, but getting caught trying to hide a body or at any time afterward would be much worse than if we face the police here and now, at the graveyard."

"Sure," Ellen says, brushing stray hair back from her face and leaving a tiny streak of blood on her cheek. She blinks hard. "It was probably the worst idea I ever had."

Carter's looking at me.

"I need you both to trust me right now," I say in the steadiest voice I can summon. "We're going to tell them everything that happened and face whatever comes next."

"Okay," she says, on a watery sigh.

"Then somebody better call it in," Carter says.

I dial and spell it all out to the operator, every mistake I've made along the way, every aspect of the circumstances that could land me in jail.

Maybe I've been waiting for a moment like this all my life, and here I am, about to face the consequences of a temper I still haven't quite managed to control.

CHAPTER 25

ELLEN

I TURN AWAY, blinking the sight from my eyes along with the wetness that drips down my cheeks. We moved away from Kent's body and have clustered near Father's grave, where we can see anyone who might come without having to remain prisoner to a crime scene. In the distance, a patrol car slows and then turns.

"Max," I whisper and pull him toward me. "They're coming."

Max turns toward the casket. He's taken the brunt of all of this and tried to save Kent. His appearance is damning. I stand by his side, shielding him from view. The car pulls up behind my SUV, each revolution of the wheels threatening to give me a heart attack.

They step out of the car.

"Fuck," Max says.

"But . . ." I start to ask, *Do you think they will understand us?* He shakes his head to stop me from speaking. Carter tosses a coat over Max's shoulders.

My black funeral dress and four thousand-dollar shoes are sickening reminders of how wrong I was to suggest that we could bury another body at Father's funeral. My teeth chatter until I clench my jaw so tight the pressure rings in my ears, and I'm so dizzy I can't stand.

Max squeezes my shoulder. He says something, but it's distant and cloudy beyond the roaring in my ears. I can't make out his words. I lay my head on Father's casket and steady myself until my knees are so weak I let myself sink to the grass.

I'm not sure how long I stay that way—a while. The cemetery is quiet, and the sun slips down the sky. The air goes from chilling to frigid.

Two figures come slowly toward me, steps creeping the distance. A twenty-something man in an officer's cap and tan pants walks beside another man wearing a dark suit, engrossed in conversation in a tone that carries. It's an innocent, friendly sort of talking about what he wants to eat and how he wishes he had a wife to cook him a decent meal. His accent is the lilt that comes with living in these mountains.

"Excuse me," he calls, "can we ask you a few questions?"

Behind them in the distance are a white van and about ten squad cars. Crime scene tape surrounds the area and a crew of people in plain clothes are at work near my car.

I'm alone and on the ground. I hurry to stand and straighten my skirt. Then I draw my hands back, expecting to find blood and finding none. I'm freezing. It's so cold that my nose and hands are numb. I start to shiver. Max and Carter are just coming out of the chapel and rushing toward me.

"Are you okay, miss?" the young officer asks. Up close, I'm sure I've never seen him before.

His face, which seemed young and innocent while they were

approaching, now seems worldly and wise. The other man has gray hair at his temples, a thin man. He may be the minister I saw on their website while deciding the funeral arrangements.

I can't trust my voice. I try not to stare at the casket, rolled sod, or disturbed earth. My eyes ping-pong. Nothing is safe.

Max comes to my side. His arm is around my waist, holding me up. He's clean and smells woodsy. His everyday aftershave. It makes it a little easier to breathe.

"Mind if I ask you a few questions?" the officer asks.

"Please go ahead." I nod.

The officer steps in closer, waiting for something.

I can't believe we killed someone. My heart beats faster. A knot tightens in my stomach. Everything happened so fast. I can't think. Do the police know I suggested that we put Kent in the casket with Father? My heart slams into action, fierce pounding against my breastbone and ribs.

Max squeezes my arm and says, "That's Detective Montgomery. He needs you to talk to him privately."

"I've never been part of an investigation like this before," I say.

No one replies. A wave of dizziness rises within me as I wait for someone to say something that makes everything alright again.

"It's an important process," the detective says. "Would you come into the chapel with me?"

"Of course." The words sound foreign, as if spoken by someone else.

We walk side by side across the grass and up the concrete steps. He holds open the door, saying nothing.

A table with four chairs is set up in the back of the room. Four more people wait inside. Three women and one additional man all focused on me.

A modest cross adorned with candles on tall stands is showcased above the pulpit as the reality of this situation washes over me. Polished golden-colored pews arranged in rows, high ceilings, and stained-glass windows. It's a place meant for worship, penance, and forgiveness, and here we are.

Detective Montgomery says, "Have a seat," and motions me into a folding chair that puts the audience at my back. I should have looked at them closer or at least asked who they are. Only, what does that matter now?

I sit ramrod straight across from him and clench my hands between my knees.

He settles a recorder on the table between us, clicks it on, and says the case information, my name, the time and date. Then he addresses me in the soothing voice someone might use when talking to a frightened child. "It's my job to work the crime scene, pursue the truth, and respect the dead." He recites my Miranda warnings, letting me know they want to ask me questions, that I'm protected from self-incrimination and am not being arrested.

"Can you tell me about Mr. Goodwin?" he asks.

My ears buzz. The burden to prove Max isn't a criminal lies with the three of us. Add a realtime murder trial to our troubles. I just need to tell these officers what happened.

Are they doing the entire investigation now? Or is this a precursor? Whatever I say could hurt Max.

"Umm . . ." A mumble is the only sound I can manage. I finally ask, "Did Max answer your questions?"

"He did."

I know better than to do this. Father always said never to talk to anyone investigating anything without a lawyer present, ever, and certainly not in circumstances like this.

"Without an attorney?" I ask.

"Yes, he did. But you *can* call someone if you'd like. We'd have to take you to the station while we wait. It's up to you."

Max said to trust him. I trust Max.

"I'll talk," I offer, despite my fear.

Detective Montgomery draws his sleeves down and folds his

hands on the table between us. "Start with when you first saw Mr. Goodwin."

I tell him the entire story, and he asks questions like this is just a normal conversation. I start with my request that Kent help me investigate the arsons back home, covering my conversations with Father, my desire to find Max, Kent's kiss at the airport, how my keycard wouldn't work while he was harassing me in Father's residence, the restraining order, learning that Kent was the one who tried to kill Max, the note in Father's office, Kent's appearance at the cemetery, and how upset he was about the restraining order.

I think it's clear by the end that I was truly afraid for my life, Carter's, and Max's.

"Why didn't you have security present?"

The void inside me turns glacial with fear and regret as I try to find words but find none that explain what I was thinking.

"Focus on the circumstances that led you to make that decision," he prods.

It is easier if I concentrate on the facts rather than what's going on with me emotionally. I explain Father's desire to exhume Mom's body so they could both be buried in New York and how I chose to bury him here. The officer nods, but that's not what I need to say.

I clasp my hands on the table and will my feet to be still. "I get very anxious whenever my security staff is around. I know there's no real threat or danger, and it sounds silly, even a bit crazy. They're there to protect me, but Kent kissed me when I didn't want him to. He held me in my father's residence against my will. I'm terrified of letting anyone on our staff that close. They all seem like they could be working with him or be on his team. I have no reason to trust them. I'm sure it's irrational." My voice cracks. "Even considering having them close triggered buzzing in my ears. It was disrupting my focus during the day. It's strained my relationship with Max." I barely manage to keep a sob inside. "I hate that I can't control it."

"You've been through a great deal," the detective says. His gentle voice seems to say he understands. "Can you tell me what happened when Kent arrived at the cemetery?" he asks.

I explain how Carter showed up with his whip, how things unfolded as the shots were fired, and how Max attempted to save Kent, all of it—everything except the conversation about hiding Kent's body.

"What are you remembering now?" the officer asks. Maybe he's read something on my face.

I focus on my hands then look up at him and blink. Should I tell him this truth, too? I don't know.

My heart beats into my ears, making me wonder if they can all hear it.

He prods, "It's something—"

I think, no, I won't tell him. We all have thoughts, and we didn't act on them. Instead of shining a light on our darkest moment, I dive into more details about when Kent first arrived at the cemetery and say, "He came up behind me after my father's secretary pulled out. I was watching her leave, facing the street, and he pressed a gun into the small of my back. Then he grabbed my right arm and turned me to face him." I pause and draw in a breath. "He wanted me to drive us to a trailhead about ten miles away. It's a place I went with him years ago. There's a small cabin there, and I said no. I wasn't going to get in the car. He was furious that I refused and became more threatening. He compared how I'd treated him to how I'd treated a man he'd protected me from years ago. He said I'd betrayed him *and* my father and that if I wasn't willing to tell the truth about my feelings for him, I didn't deserve even to be alive. He wanted me to lie to the police and have the restraining order revoked."

"Do you have any injuries or marks from the struggle?"

"He was squeezing me hard, but I'm not sure." I pull up my sleeve and find a raised purplish bruise on my wrist. I roll the sleeve farther, revealing two more, a spot near the elbow and another just below my shoulder.

"So what happens now?" I rearrange my dress.

He focuses past me, on the other people who've remained in the room, silently listening, casting judgment, I guess. He doesn't say anything for a long moment.

"I can't guarantee what the DA will do," he finally says.

"But we've all been cooperative," I insist.

"You have. Ms. Jasper, I'd like to give you my card. In case you have questions, you're welcome to call me. Otherwise, someone will be in touch."

"So, we're free to go?" I ask, my voice almost shaking.

"We may have more questions, but yes." He stands and waits for me to do the same.

I keep my steps as steady as I can but still stumble against the stairs. Max comes to my side and slides his arm around my waist.

"You changed clothes," I say.

"Yeah, inside the church," he whispers, seeming so mournful his voice doesn't quite work.

Carter waits near his truck, a man who once scared me but no longer does.

Kent's body is gone, along with several of the cars, the van, and the crime scene tape. But I can still see where each of us stood during what might have been the last moments of any one of our lives.

Max and I climb into my car, leaving officers at work in the cemetery as others pull out behind us. I imagine how horrid I'd have felt if we'd buried this secret. I'd be living my life expecting every siren was meant for me. There's still a lot to be worked out with the investigators, and we'll likely have to come back to Virginia to sort it the rest of the way out. Still, we can leave now.

I drive away and into the night, down a narrow country road and onto a highway and past city lights, while Carter's truck lingers behind us. I glance at Max. He's staring straight ahead, hardly blinking.

I open my mouth to speak then close it and stare out at the road. A sob tears free as a gasp.

Max puts a gentle hand on my shoulder.

"I keep imagining how I would feel if we hadn't called the police," I admit.

He runs a hand from my shoulder to cheek and down again, caressing. "We did the right thing." Still, the strain around his eyes says he's trying to make me feel better despite his worries.

I blink and stare and try to imagine how they managed to keep themselves together. "I was totally out of it."

"It was a terrible situation."

"I can't believe I suggested burying him with my father. I don't know what I was thinking."

He shakes his head and draws a breath, then exhales saying, "None of us were thinking clearly."

"How did Kent find us?"

"I don't know." His eyes flash, and his mouth forms a grim line.

His jaw tightens. My skin heats.

"Did they find my phone?" I ask.

"I think they kept it as evidence, along with the guns," he says in a dull monotone.

"I'm so sorry for . . ." I want to say that I'm sorry for everything, but that would be trite in light of all that's happened. I can't quite pinpoint what he's most upset about now. "Are you . . . I know you're not okay, but you're angry with me, aren't you?"

"I don't want to be."

"But you are, and I understand. I should have told you that security wouldn't be there."

"I'm just . . ." He groans and turns away, staring out the passenger window at the dark forest and fences whizzing by. "We should talk about it when we're both less raw about what just happened."

"Sure. Okay." Sickness rises in my stomach.

The vein at this temple throbs.

"We're both going to think about it anyway. You should just say whatever's on your mind. We can talk about it and—"

He breaks out with a mirthless laugh. "You want to talk about it now?"

"Yeah. Let's talk about it. I don't think it will help to put it off."

"Okay." His eyes widen as his face turns a little red. He finally says, "You have the whole world ready to help you, and you made a really stupid decision. You knew I'd be upset, and you didn't tell me, and it's really bothering me, Flynn. You can't do stuff like this. How can I trust you if you're going to not tell me things that matter this much?"

"You can't."

"That's right. I can't."

"I'm sorry."

He presses his palms to his face, turning toward the window then drawing them down and staring out. He refocuses on me and asks, "Are you truly sorry, or only sorry that it turned out Kent was there?"

Rain slicks the road ahead and drizzles against the windshield.

"You're right that I was mostly sorry about how it all worked out," I say so mournfully that my voice is a broken whisper.

"You don't trust me either," he says.

"I do, though. More than anyone."

He gives me a tight smile. "To a point, that's true. But you don't trust me to understand what you're worried about. Maybe you're afraid of talking to me."

I draw a steadying breath and say, "I was hoping to avoid an argument. I betrayed your trust, and I can't lose you over this, but I don't know how to fix what I've done. It's so much worse than I ever could have imagined. I can't keep downplaying the mistake I made or defending my choices."

He doesn't say anything, but he stood by me, defended me,

and put his own life entirely in turmoil. His brother risked his life for both of us. They're an entirely different group of people than the people who raised me. Passionate, loyal, and earnest.

"I watched my parents manipulate each other to the point that they lived entirely separate lives while still claiming to love each other," I add.

The car is quiet enough that I can hear each of our breathing.

I keep talking. "I have no excuse. If you didn't love me as much as you do, you might have just left me there and let me face Kent all by myself. That's probably what I deserved."

Max shifts his weight against the seat.

"What happened when you first saw him?" he asks in a low tone.

I tell him everything I told the officers.

A sigh escapes his lips. He turns to face me. "I wish I'd been right there with you."

"You *were* there. I probably wouldn't be here if it weren't for you and Carter."

"The minister was inside. He might have come out and helped."

"He was inside?"

"Watching everything. He told them what happened."

"You think it's going to be okay?" I ask, wanting to have him tell me that *we're* going to be okay.

"I hope so," he says, staring out the windshield.

My nose gets stuffy. I sniff and say, "I promise, no matter what comes next, I will always trust you enough to argue with you. I won't ever do anything like this again." My voice cracks.

He takes a measured breath. Our eyes lock for a long moment, and he says, "I believe you."

And in that moment, I know it's okay. We're going to be okay.

"Thank you. I don't know how I'd survive if you didn't."

He wipes a tear off my cheek with his thumb. "You're going to have to forgive yourself too."

A little sob escapes and I tuck my chin, forcing his hand away. He rests it on my shoulder.

I look up at him, blinking hard and asking, "What if they file charges against you?"

"I think if they were going to arrest me they wouldn't have let us leave."

Some of the tension eases inside me, going from a tight ball to a loose knot.

As the miles whiz by outside the windows, we hardly talk.

Kent's blood remains on Max's cast. He rubs it with two fingers then gets a wipe from the console and scrubs.

Finally, I say, "He must have been tracking Father's phone too. Or maybe your phone. He had access to some tricky technology when we were in Wyoming, monitoring your internet searches or creating a pretty good fake. Maybe he was stalking you too."

"Possibly. Or he could have been tracking your car," Max says.

"I had it checked before we left."

"That was good thinking." He gives me a little smile.

"But it doesn't make me feel better. I keep trying to figure out what we could have done differently. I shouldn't have been so preoccupied with appearances. You're right that I put my father's image ahead of our safety. If we'd allowed the service to be more public, or if I'd had security join us, none of this would have happened."

"Please don't do that to yourself. Not about this."

"I can't help it." I concentrate on the road, trying to calm down while keeping the car between the reflective paint stripes.

"You didn't do this, Flynn. You don't know what would have happened. *I* pulled the trigger that killed Kent. I've been thinking about killing him since he tried to kill me, and I've been trying to convince myself that retaliation wasn't the right choice."

I release a puff of pent-up air and emotion then rest a hand on his bicep above the cast. "You didn't retaliate."

"But Carter was right. I could have shot Kent in the knee or something, like you did. I could have made a different choice that wouldn't have left us considering hiding his body." His smoky eyes fall to half-closed resignation.

"Sure. I guess, but Kent clearly seemed to think he could push me around, and eventually I would bow down and let him make all my decisions. He said that if I wasn't willing to tell the truth about my feelings for him, I didn't deserve even to be alive. He was ready to take what he wanted from me at gunpoint. He was going to hurt me and probably kill me."

I rub my wrist, exposing the raised purplish bruise.

"Fuck that prick," Max says. His anger awakens something inside me, a raw sort of pride that we're still alive.

"I'm not sure what would have happened if you weren't there."

"I'm not sure what would have happened if Carter wasn't there," Max says.

"I had no idea Carter was that good with his whip."

"He can put on a pretty good show when he wants."

I try to come up with a sound that compares to Carter's yell and instead end up pretending to be Bruce Willis in *Die Hard*, and saying, "Yippee-ki-yay."

Max's lips turn up, then he does it, this chilling cowboy shriek that makes the hair on my arms rise.

"You're definitely brothers. I'm glad you're getting along, and I'm glad he was there," I admit.

"He's planning to drive straight through to make it home in time for Logan's Christmas presentation at school tomorrow night."

"He could have flown."

Max rubs the back of his neck. "He hates commercial flights and having his truck worked out decently."

That's very true. Logistically, it would be good to leave my car on the East Coast. "We could fly him home on one of Father's jets. Then we could drive his truck the rest of the way home and stop off, taking it slower. I'm not sure I can keep driving, and you shouldn't push yourself either." He's still on several prescriptions. I'm not sure how he's still upright.

"Want to call Carter and offer to fly him home?" Max asks.

I shrug half-heartedly. "Last time I phoned, he said you'd threatened to kill him if I even said hello."

"That's true." His mouth twists.

"I figured it was."

"I wouldn't have killed him for saying hello," he says.

"I know."

"I'll never make a threat that flippantly again, especially not to Carter." He rubs the back of his neck. "If you're okay with it, we could talk to him and figure out what to do."

"Sounds good," I agree. We've already talked about how he's reconciled with Carter. I hope things between all of us are going to be much better.

Max dials Carter, and we agree to stop at the charter airport in Roanoke and exchange cars.

While we're on the way there, I start to consider how badly this could go legally.

I call Mr. Elias, the attorney who helped me with the restraining order against Kent. I lay it all out for him, explaining that we spoke to the police without legal counsel present.

I close with, "We were cooperative, but the detective said he couldn't guarantee what the DA might do."

"I wish you'd called us," Mr. Elias says.

"Sure. I understand. We were trying to be forthright."

"I've represented two women who went to prison in different cases because they assumed that as they were innocent it would be fine to speak to the police without representation. It wasn't. Their male partners lawyered up and pinned the crimes they had committed on the women. Neither could prove their innocence, and both went to jail. One of them spent more than a decade in prison."

A chill pricks over my scalp, so powerful I reach for the heater knob. I exchange a glance with Max.

"I'm the one who put Max in the worst possible situation imaginable. If anything, I'd rather be the one going on trial."

Mr. Elias makes a non-committal sniff, like a verbal shrug. I tighten my grip on the steering wheel and glare at the wet road.

"Any idea how long it might take before we find out for sure?" Max asks, reaching out to trace a finger over my finger.

"We'll get started on it and let Ms. Jasper know what we find out."

"But they let us go. They know we're heading to Wyoming," I mention.

"That's encouraging but inconclusive. The DA has to be very organized, filing papers for charges with the court, arranging what needs to be arranged."

CHAPTER 26

MAX

I'M behind the wheel of my brother's truck, while he's on a flight home, and Ellen's beside me with her head lolled toward the window. I can't get the thoughts out of my head. Kent holding onto her. The bruise on her wrist. She shook her head to stop me from trying to help her. Her face after she shot him. Familiar ulcer pain blooms in my ribcage.

It's the middle of the night, and the road ahead is a maze of lights and shadows.

If I wreck Carter's truck, he'll be pissed.

Restricted by my arm but having given up on the sling, I ease my grip on the steering wheel and breathe. We need a hotel room, somewhere to shower and sleep. We mapped our way to a spot pretty close up the highway.

Carter's words from earlier come rolling back. He was about

to get on the jet and stopped at the bottom of the stairs. He apologized for judging Ellen and for burning Maker's down and scaring her, but he didn't say it to her. She's probably still as anxious about him as ever. I don't know how she feels. It isn't straightforward. Her dad tried to break us up at minimum, and maybe he wanted to kill me. I drive the icy roads, work out words, and when she sits up a few minutes later, I ask, "What do you think about me reconciling with Carter?"

She pulls her dark hair into a bun. "We could have Christmas with them if you want."

"You want to?"

"They're the only family we have left." Her words are a low fire, warming me on the inside.

We talk about many things as we drive, settling back into a comfortable routine and orchestrating what's coming next. I have no restaurant, half a ranch, and no career. I'm unmoored from my life, have taken someone else's, and will be a dad in about eight months.

Ellen is taking off on a new and demanding endeavor, attempting to fix the things she's felt were wrong in her past. Her father is dead, and she's pregnant.

"How do you feel about taking the helm of Cross Mountain Capital?" I ask dryly. We've talked about this. I know the answer, but I want to hear her thoughts.

"If I can get in front of the issues . . . Um . . . It's going to be hard to face it all. I can't fix the forged reports without confronting the pollution head-on. The fraud will become public. The shareholders are going to mutiny. Father's name will get dragged through the financial news. His legacy will never recover, but I might stop having nightmares."

She draws her dress up, brings her foot onto the seat, and wraps her arms around her knee. "The backlash could make Cross Mountain uninsurable, and remediation costs will wipe out a significant portion of our working capital reserves. If there's a panic and minority shareholders pull out all at once, it could bankrupt the company, so needless to say it's going to be super fun." Her voice rises at the end. "Or maybe I mean it's going to be a superfund?"

"That was funny," I say, knowing she meant it as a joke.

Her eyes are glassy. "Yeah, I guess. I want to try to make it all better than it is, but I'm not sure I can."

"What if you walk away, let the worst sites become superfund sites, and let the insurance company clean them up?"

"They'd come after Father's estate for negligence. The mines will either be shuttered, or new companies will buy them out and potentially continue the same cycle. It's better to face this, convince the shareholders that we can manage the fallout, and offer them an even brighter future."

"You can do it if anyone can."

"Mm . . ." She purses her lips. "Maybe, but I'm going to miss my days at the bakery and all the customers and their gossip."

"I'll miss it too."

"I know, and I'm sorry. What do you want to do?"

"I'm not sure. I don't have a career anymore," I admit.

"You could work with me at Father's company and help me determine the next steps. It might be strange initially, but we're a good team. You'd make things a lot more bearable. Eventually, we might be able to recruit a proper chairperson then go back home and raise our family."

"I think you know I'm not a board meeting guy, but I'll always be wherever you want me."

"I know." She nuzzles her cheek into my arm. I trace a finger up her neck, twining into her hair until she relaxes against me.

At the west of Louisville, we stop for the night. The motel is right off the highway and has a vacancy sign that's only partially illuminated, but it's someplace to stop. Neither of us is in a mood to be particular.

We drag our luggage into the lobby and check in, getting an old-fashioned key with a plastic tag that has to be returned in the morning. She holds it in one hand as we walk down the hall.

The key sticks in the worn round knob, one more obstacle at the end of a very long day, but eventually the teeth align, the handle turns, and the door creaks open.

A bright fluorescent light bulb in a lamp beside the bed leaves a circular shadow on the low popcorn ceiling. We set our bags near the door and let it close us inside.

"At least it's not dark," Ellen says, but the air is as frigid as a meat locker.

"It's colder than it is outside." I turn the dial thermostat, and the ancient wall-mounted radiator clanks then knocks to life. We might have been better off sleeping in the truck.

She stands beside me in the cramped area between the bathroom and the bed with a dented mattress and polyester covers fitted over the corners.

"Sorry I didn't read the reviews," she says.

None of it matters. We're together and alive.

"It's fine," I say, turning toward her, studying the slope of her nose, the way her lower lip is drawn up, clutched between her teeth. She's cold and scared and terrible at making reservations.

I want to have her up close. I want to press my skin against her skin and remind myself that I didn't die in a canyon while wishing to tell her how much I loved her. She didn't die at the end of a psycho's gun while trying to save me from danger. I want to flip the bird to a world that seems to have had it out for us almost since we got together.

I reach out, catching a tendril of her hair and a whiff of her amber shampoo. The strands slide against my still tender fingers —fragile and precious. I get this strange feeling in my chest, the same one I've gotten to know as familiar when she's around but that always seems just as new as the first time I saw her. There's sorrow in her eyes but also curiosity and a bit of heat. I pull her into my arms, and I like how it feels, so I cup her face and bring my mouth to hers. Kissing her softly, tasting the coffee on her lips, feeling the warm softness, and loving her fingers looped into my belt and the way she pulls me in. My heart hammers against my breastbone underneath my long-sleeved t-shirt and coat, making me hot on the inside.

"I could warm you up," I whisper.

Her head tilts back, her lips parted, waiting for me to rejoin our kiss.

It feels genuinely like a time to whisper, to wait for her to tell me if this makes sense. I can kill a man and drive for hours and end up in a mediocre hotel room and still want her as much as I would at home in our bed on a night when we lounge around watching movies or planning the next steps of our lives.

"Do you want this?" I ask.

"Can you?" Her breath is warm against my mouth. Considering my injuries, maybe she expects me to say no. Perhaps I should.

I drag my coat and shirt off, wrap my casted arm around her waist, resting my fingers on her ass as my good hand skims hip to breast. She presses flush against me, so close I can't feel anything except her. I whisper in her ear, "I still can't believe we're having a baby."

"Me neither." Her smile is the sweetest thing I have ever known.

I lean in, closing the distance between us and tracing my fingers down her jaw.

She moans, a contented sound supercharging my already potent desire, then she brings her lips to mine, slanting her mouth and levering up less than usual since she's still in heels. She runs her hand around my neck, under my collar, splaying her fingers in my hair.

"The woman of my dreams," I murmur against her ear. She gingerly runs her fingers over my torso and waist, careful and afraid. I kiss her harder, sinking my tongue into her mouth, feeling the electric slide of her warmth, a pleasurable tingle of craving, and becoming invigorated by a perception of only her. I adjust my grip against her nape and angle my mouth down, finding the perfect pleasure of exploration and rhythm. I'm fed by her surrender and trust.

She turns her back, begging me to lower the zipper. I draw it down, wanting her naked. I slide my hands under her dress around her ribcage and breasts to her budded nipples then trace from her belly button down to the lace of her panties. She trembles under my touch, then strips the dress over her head and turns in my arms, pressing against me with all her skin and a lacy black bra. She's warmer than my chest. Still in her high-heeled shoes, she runs her hands up my shoulders to my neck and draws me in. I take all she's giving, tasting her mouth.

She breaks away and whispers, "I'm still freezing."

We grope toward the shower, into the dark bathroom, and reach the sink. Not separating, she flicks on the light, revealing skimpy towels, and a fiberglass tub with a shower curtain and grab bars. I lean with her as she turns the water on. We break away long enough to strip off our clothes. My boots and socks come off, bare feet meet the cold tile, and I hiss before I drag off my jeans.

She stands naked before me, shivering as she removes her shoes and pantyhose.

Her pink tongue traces her bottom lip, and I kiss her again. I'm already hard against her stomach, ready to lift her onto the counter and fuck her.

"Flynn," I say her name and pull her in, cocooning her in my arms, trying to warm her up.

"Mmmhhm." She gives me this little moan.

I grip her more urgently, pull her into me, kiss her harder. She arches her back, sparking every cell in my body. I beg her closer, wrapping my hand around her nape and angling down, quivering with need. She yields to my pressure, moving even closer, rubbing the inside of her silky thigh against my outer leg. A surge of excitement drives my hips closer. A shiver skates over me. She gasps into my mouth. I realize I've lost my breath and break away. She pants at my neck. Steam fills the bathroom.

She nudges me into the tub and drags the curtain closed, hooks raking against the bar until it feels like we've entered a new place, safer and warmer.

Hot water prickles my skin, drenching us in comfort as we move toward each other. I reach out, past the curtain, fumble for the tray of bottles on the counter, bring a bar of soap inside, and unwrap the paper. Its slipperiness in my hands becomes exotic against her soft skin. She takes the soap and reaches behind me with a silky hand, lather sliding down my back and legs as my fingertips trace the dips and valleys that make her familiar and tantalizing.

Washing ourselves of the raw frigidity of terror, despite the cast, scrubbing my hands and her hands.

I pull her into me, wrapping her in my arms, loving the way she fits in my embrace and into my life.

We stay together in the shower until the hot water runs out. Her warm breath remains against my chest. I dip my head to meet her lips, gently tasting her mouth.

She shuts off the shower. I grab fresh towels and smooth them against her skin, blotting her wet face as she looks at me tenderly.

We peel back the bedspread, meet freezing sheets, and snuggle together under the covers so close we could be a single body. We fall asleep holding each other, trying to believe that doing the best we can means it will all be okay.

Light streams into the motel room from the gap around the blackout curtains. The room is freezing again.

Ellen's naked and asleep, taking up two-thirds of the bed, a sweet and hopeful portrait. Her hair is a mess on the pillow, hanging halfway off one side. Her feet are across the bottom diagonally. The comforter and sheets are wrapped around her legs and ass, leaving me stretching and groggy with one corner of the covers.

I lumber out of bed, mess with the thermostat until the radiator starts again, and climb back into bed. I want nothing more than to lie on this motel mattress in this still-drafty room with Ellen in my arms. I roll onto my side and draw her back with me, onto me. She settles into our everyday routine, resting her head on my shoulder, her leg over my legs. I extract the covers, pull them over us then wrap my arm around her and try to fall back asleep. I relax against the lumpy pillow with her steady breaths leading me. It's so good to be surrounded by her soft curves. Her cuddled into my side. Both of us safe from whatever the world wants.

We stay that way, until she stirs and sits up. The covers fall away, and thankfully the room is finally warm.

"You let me sleep," she says, yawning.

"We both needed it."

"You've been awake for hours, haven't you?"

"Meh. Not really."

"You're lying."

"I liked having you snore on me." I smack her on the ass.

"Now you're being honest." She gives me a sweet peck on the cheek.

CHAPTER 27

ELLEN

THE MILES GO BY EASILY, in the relaxed comfort of having time together that we've been needing for a while. We talk about the baby, when we'll be headed to the doctor, and when I want to go back to New York.

"We'll have to stay for a few months," I say, testing the idea aloud for the first time.

Max rubs his chin thoughtfully. I love everything about his face, from his full bottom lip to his cut jaw and arrogant nose.

"What are you saying?" he asks.

"I don't want to raise our baby there," I eke out.

"No?" He anchors his attention on my face.

I shake my head and lift one shoulder. "I've been thinking of promoting someone from within the company who we can trust to act as CEO. Of course, I'd retain an oversight position as the majority shareholder, but I wouldn't have to be there all the time. Then I could bake, and we could live the way we want."

A small grin steals across his lips.

"This is a total surprise," he admits, the fingers of his casted arm seeking mine and closing around them.

"You don't always know everything I'm thinking," I joke, trying to ease the tension.

A laugh breaks from his chest. "Most of the time, I do."

"Maybe, but I *always* know what you're thinking. Like how you've always wanted a chance to run the ranch with your brother, and now you'll finally have one."

"That's true, and I love that this is possible now."

Happiness floats over me.

"But you still don't know everything I'm thinking," he says. An impish smile makes his lips twitch as he ramps off the highway.

"Where are we going?" I ask.

"It's a surprise." He turns right then right again.

I grip the door hard. "Where are we going?"

"I *told* you that it's a surprise." He's so smug. I drag a hand through his soft hair.

"So, maybe I don't always know what you're thinking," I confess. What is he up to?

We meet a forest service road and climb the mountain, cutting through the trees as the sun goes down. He's focused on the narrowing road, slows over a rutted spot, and makes a hard turn as the fire tower comes into view. White twinkle lights are strung between the majestic trees, a wintery mountainside with acres of forest. I've been thinking of coming here since the day I learned about it, before I'd moved to Wyoming. With all its glorious history and incredible views of peaks and lakes, it was formerly used as a lookout post to detect fires. It was purchased by a couple who turned it into a rental, sitting five stories above a forested mountaintop within an epic mountain range.

Beside me in the truck, he's smiling.

"It's so cute." I tug his good arm, which is also the only one holding the wheel.

I quickly release him and instead lean forward and focus out the windshield. When I was young, my grandpa on Mom's side took us to Mount Haveren's lookout tower. It's one of my best girlhood memories. Ever since, I've been fascinated with seeing other similar structures.

I still cherish the first time Max and I ever talked about my desire to come here. We hardly knew each other, but that day we connected and started learning to trust each other.

He parks the truck, and we grab what little luggage we have, then start toward the tower.

Big sky meets pine and spruce at the horizon. Above the tree line, the darkness is lit with panoramic stars, making the Big Dipper readily visible with its seven bright sparks forming a bowl and handle. My city shoes crunch against the paired pine needles blanketing the ground. The frigid air nipping at my face and neck is scented with a perfect holiday backdrop.

Max is still a little slower—although not much. I stop on the upper deck, locate the key, and open the door.

Warm air rushes out. I turn back and whisper, "It's warm."

He closes the door behind us as I stop in the tidy kitchen.

Wide plank floors, an open sitting room lies off the side, with its kitschy forest decor, a vintage concert poster on one wall, a big telescope, and wrap-around windows overlooking a sea of trees and an expansive deck.

I turn to face him. "I love this."

He draws me into his chest then nips at my ear, moving down my neck. His casted arm rests around my waist. I trace past his belt to tease his sexy abs then nuzzle my nose into his dreamy neck, relishing the mountain man scent of his body that's uniquely Max. It makes me want to lick him, so I swipe my tongue near his shirt collar then kiss my way up his neck to his ear.

"You remembered this?" I whisper.

"I remembered what?" He draws my top up and settles his hands above my hips.

"I've been thinking about coming here since that day in the park."

"Me too."

Love makes his eyes soft, while lust makes them dark.

He leans forward and kisses my forehead, the tip of my nose, and my lips.

I move my hands to the back of his neck and kiss him with a passion and frantic surrender.

He moans a hoarse and sexy growl. "You know how much I love you?" he asks.

This is our game. I love it. "Definitely."

"You're so sexy when you look at me like that."

I lick my bottom lip then draw it up between my teeth, imagining him shirtless and hard. My fingers dip between the buttons on his shirt, teasing the sexy muscles below before I tug his belt free of the buckle.

A gritty groan escapes him.

"You were supposed to make me say your name, but then you didn't come home," I complain, adding in a playful pout.

"I plan to make good on that promise." He draws my lower lip into his mouth and kisses me like I've never been kissed before.

"Do it now," I say with a laugh.

We fumble through the fire tower to the bedroom. He tugs me onto the mattress then hovers over me, kissing me as we pull each other's clothes off, losing our shirts and then almost everything else. He pauses, lingering over the lacy underwear I put on to tease him. He's looking extremely gorgeous and focused as he strips them off.

Leaning forward, he takes my breast in his hand, lowering his mouth and nipping then capturing my nipple as his legs tangle with mine. The friction of our bare skin and ragged breaths against the buzzing intensity of the past days is pain and pleasure together. I like it and lift my feet, hooking my calves around his pelvis, positioning my hips as he arches his back, pressing against me. I roll my hips up, enjoying the feel of the silky stiffness. He adjusts upward so his chest is closer to mine. His cock slips lower. The tip teases my pulsing core.

He's inside me, just the head and the heat. He raises using his abs, his hand capturing my breast, the veins on his neck visible. He shuts his eyes. His breath, controlled and shaky. His arms, straining. I want more of him, but he's bare, and we never usually do that.

But now we're pregnant, and it seems like a moment to savor. He's concentrating so hard. He feels it, too throbbing against me. He rotates his hips but doesn't push in farther. I move, working to release the firey heat of my need for him.

"Slow," he murmurs into my hair. He releases a small breathless gasp and then presses in a bit deeper. Stopping himself, he says, "I love you."

"I love you too," I say. He's all I ever wanted. I try to swallow, but my throat tightens against the emotion, trapping the words.

He makes a rumbling, growly noise in his throat but then sighs and relaxes, bringing himself lower on top of me, framing me with his elbows and holding himself up.

He inhales sharply, probably still hurting.

I push up and murmur in his ear. "Move onto your back."

"You just want to make me say your name," he says, adorably grumpy.

"We can't both win," I reply, waiting for him to move.

With a grunt, he rises onto one side and flips over, giving me a full view of his impossible body. It's like being with a natural bodybuilder. The stuff he does at the ranch, combined with the exercises he's always loved, make him both real and fantastic, with lusty, piercing eyes that seem to beg me to let him have a moment to collect himself.

"You're so competitive," I tease, settling my knees over his pelvis and setting my mouth on his nipple. I wiggle against his straining cock while licking until his budding peak stands up stiff, enjoying the warm hardness of his body, the way he flexes against me, in mock protest. I flick him with my tongue, playfully biting, blowing, slowing us down like he wanted, and smothering him until neither of us can stand it. We're hot and panting.

I sit up and ask without words if it's okay to move now.

He says nothing, just watches me like he can't quite believe we're here, and I know what he's thinking. It's a miracle, really. My chest catches on my breath, knotting until tears threaten. He sits forward, lifting with one arm, his hips coming tight against mine, and he takes hungry possession of my mouth.

I bend my knees and tilt my hips. He tilts and pushes in, and I'm so wet that we're instantly flush.

His quivering breaths meet mine as we kiss. Fusing. Reuniting. My breaths escape in tiny pants. He pulls back, almost out. I lower my hips as he slides back in, our mouths still tangled.

"Mine," he says, breaking away, placing slow kisses from my ear to my collarbone. He pauses his lips, heavenly whispers of breath rasping against my neck, his hips rhythmic and hitting me in precisely the right spot. "You're mine," he says again.

"Yes, Max, sweetheart," I say, breathless as I start to come, not even caring that he's won our game because he follows me over the edge with my name on his lips and a flush on his cheekbones.

When I open my eyes again, Max is still sleeping beside me. Dawn light streams through the windows of our private oasis in a forest of trees. It feels like a protective bubble, sheltering us from the last few days.

He stretches beside me, tousled and relaxed, not fully awake. His toned body tangled in the sheets. His gray eyes flit open. The corners of his lips turn up as he draws me into his side. I nuzzle into him and kiss the stubble on his jaw.

I can't let anything happen to him. I tug my ear then rub the side of my face.

"Relax," he says, stroking his less injured hand down my neck to my shoulder and arm.

Tension is coiled in between my shoulders.

"We should probably get up," I offer with a weak smile.

"Probably." Awareness and acceptance combine in the slight downturn of his mouth.

I slip from under the blankets, grab my phone, and wince against the bright screen as I pad across the room toward the bathroom while looking for an update from Mr. Elias. Finding none, I message Gena, explaining I'm considering listing most of Father's homes for sale and asking her to get me their current condition and information on anyone presently leasing or residing at any of them. In a roundabout way, I will learn if Kent's mother is actually at Father's St. Augustine house. I'm unsure what we'll do if she's there, but knowing will help us make a plan.

I message Adelle next, wishing her a Merry Christmas. Considering how much Father worked, it might be the first holiday she's had truly to herself in years. Adelle has been around long enough to know the history of my less flattering moments, like that time I let Peter back into my life instead of pressing charges when Father insisted we should have. It's a wonder she hasn't said more during the moments we've spent alone. She probably doubts my ability to step into Father's role, but she's always been entirely professional and private, keeping her opinions to herself.

Maybe I won't be able to do it. A shiver goes over me, and I turn the handle to make the water hotter before I step inside. I must do it, or I'll forever wonder what would have happened if I'd had the backbone.

Max joins me in the bathroom, shaving while I shower. I shift slightly so I can see a little more of him. As if he can feel me thinking about him, he peeks past the curtain and smiles. I bask in it, entranced, as I remind myself we're going to get married. I reach out and loop him in by the wrist, bringing his hand up so I can kiss his hurt fingers.

He wraps his palm around my cheek and presses his lips to my forehead.

Life has been fragmented these last few days, but we're together again and we both cherish it.

Still, we made a bit of a plan, and both of us need to get back. I promised Laura she wouldn't have to keep handling the bakery mostly on her own, and a team in New York will be waiting for our return after the holidays, working toward finding the right people to sort through the fallout of Father's mines. Max needs to get back too. He's still got a lot to sort out with the fires, and he needs to reconnect with Carter.

We hit the road and, along the way, decide it will be fun to celebrate with Carter's family rather than doing it alone, so Max makes arrangements, and we head there. We stop to buy gifts and food to contribute to the celebration and play Christmas music as we drive. Slowly, it seems like a surreal version of the holiday has arrived. I usually would talk to Father. Even when things were strained between us, he sent gifts.

I check my phone and find updates on Babs's holiday plans and Gena's response with the requested information. I told Max about the mystery of Kent's mother while we were getting ready this morning. Now, I fill him in on this latest news.

"Kent's mother is at my father's St. Augustine house."

His mouth pinches into a thoughtful frown. "What if they were dating?"

An icy tingle radiates from my stomach. "I guess it's possible, but I'm not sure I want to know."

"Maybe there's no closure to be found in worrying about it."

"You're right about that, I'm sure, but it's hard not to consider every possibility."

"It is a compelling drama, the billionaire dating his security guard's mother." He rests his fingers on the bottom of the steering wheel and turns toward me.

"I've even wondered if Father might have been involved with Adelle," I admit. "He wrote her into his will as the alternate in case I didn't accept what he'd done."

"I saw that," Max replies. Returning his focus to the road, he adds, "She probably knew Kent pretty well too."

I straighten my jeans with long nervous strokes. Then rub my hands together, my palms suddenly damp.

"Do you think Adelle might have been helping Kent?" I ask. My next breath snags on something inside my chest. I draw in a gulp of air. "What I mean is that I told her everything about the service. She might have told him that it would only be the two of us there. They might have planned to kill us both at once."

"He'd get away with trying to kill me, and she'd inherit the company."

"I hadn't fully considered that angle, but yeah. Plus, as it is, she might look bad when the corruption at the mines comes to light. She and Kent were both facing changes. Maybe they were desperate."

"Let's tell Mr. Elias and see what he thinks," Max suggests.

So we do. I fill the attorney in on the theory, which he indicates could add another dimension to the investigation. Once I'm off the phone, I turn back to Max, twisting his ring on my finger.

"I've been thinking about my father's role in all this," I begin. "Maybe he was sucked in by Kent the same way Peter tricked me. It was a con. Kent wanted Father's money and power. He was hoping to get it by winning his favor. My father might have suspected something, but he didn't want to believe that the person he was enjoying spending time with was only there because he was hoping to rob him."

"Possibly," Max says, but he sounds doubtful. "And if that's the case, it's very tragic."

"Yeah, I agree, but at the same time, he was using Kent to

make everything go according to his master plan too. If he tried to have you killed . . ." I say, struggling. "If he did that, then I hate him for trying to take you away from me and for hurting you. I can't quite figure out how I should feel about it—my past, the things I've done in the last few days. I've been really struggling about what to do with every decision I've made. I've done a terrible job of letting you in on that."

I reach up and run my fingers down Max's cheek to his neck. When he looks at me, I say, "I'm still so sorry for being awful at the funeral."

"I plan to take full advantage of your remorse." His playful eyes widen, his full lips parted. There's no mistaking the heat in his words or the way he's shifting the conversation away from mistakes we have agreed to put behind us.

We stop again for an overnight stay in Nebraska and return to western Wyoming early on Christmas day. For the rest of the ride home, we spend our time on us, stopping at restaurants with good reviews and singing Christmas songs as the endless prairie gives way to the mountains of home.

CHAPTER 28

MAX

Davis's text comes through as we turn off the county road toward the ranch.

I'd like to discuss the malfeasance that was discovered.

It might be the first time anyone has used the word malfeasance in a text. Beside me, Ellen's frowning. I hand her the phone so she can read it and then take the main road while trying to distract myself from an itch under the cast on my broken arm.

I need to go in for a checkup, and they will ask me what happened. Jamie and the other hospital staff will be curious to know what went on with Kent after I left the hospital so abruptly. I guess it's quite a story. Although I'd rather forget some parts, other aspects are definitely among the best moments of my life.

I wind the truck through the ranch's central hub. It's peaceful and devoid of staff due to Christmas celebrations, the slowness of winter, and the time of day putting us squarely between any required chores.

Sharp concrete and splintered wood remain in the place of the horse barn, among fresh snow. The horses never did a thing wrong. It must have been terrifying for all of them. The heat and sound. I rake a hand through my hair then lean over the wheel, blinking away the horror and trying to move past it. Carter's taking things on at the ranch, resuming his old role as farm foreman, and trying to get the building back together before the end of April, which will be a relief.

Davis's text retakes its place, doing a slow lap through my mind. Malfeasance is when someone is intentionally doing something illegal or wrong. So, now, someone is stealing from us?

I grip the steering wheel harder than necessary. He might have called. Instead, he sends me this strangely concerning message on Christmas when he knows I've been out of the state. It must be significant, yet something about it is off.

Turning to Ellen, I ask, "Will you text Carter and let him know we're stopping at Davis's?"

She does then sets the phone in the cupholder.

Beyond the main arena is a row of bunkhouses and a cluster of original homes. Built of low-slung adobe and Spanish tile roofing, they're in the same style as the main house. Davis's place is beyond that cluster on the rise, surrounded by a low fence and mature trees. Built to be impressive, it's a smaller version of the main house intended as a reward and status symbol for the farm manager. We lived in it with our parents before they died, and Carter coveted it after he'd gotten out of jail and was forced to prove himself to Pops. He had nothing of his own.

But maybe that isn't enough for Davis.

Or maybe I'm letting my annoyance lead me astray.

According to Dick, almost any of the day money cowboys

could have started the barn burning not to mention the forty other employees around the ranch, plus all the people who could have come in off the street. Why assume this fire is tied to the other fires? Maybe it's coincidental or a copycat.

We don't maintain a secure perimeter. Locals stop by constantly. But Carter mentioned Davis referring to some previously unknown tie to our family—a brother related to Pops. The fire started right after those real estate agents started poking around the ranch. Davis is one person aware of the goings on.

I park near the low fence and turn to Ellen. "This should only take a minute."

Her frown deepens. Davis's tidy house has rockers lined up on the porch, and fresh paint shines on the front door. He has Crick and Waylon living with him and working on the ranch, a little wild, but they're teenagers. I heard his wife left a few years ago.

He's probably learned someone is taking a bit of alfalfa on the side, stealing our hay cube mix, breeding plans, or stock to start their venture. He thinks it's critical because he's seeing things based on a smaller picture of the whole. If someone is doing one of those things, it's urgent but also something he could explain over the phone.

I pause with my hand on the door handle and return my focus to Ellen. "Everything's going to be okay."

"I know." She offers a tight smile.

I haven't been inside the farm foreman's house since Davis has lived there and might have had him come to the main house for a talk, but this is a chance to learn more about him without being obvious, to extend courtesy, and let him know he's got my attention.

I leave Ellen in the truck and then head for the house, where I rap on the front door and wait.

Footsteps carry from inside. Davis draws the door in and steps back. His standard jeans and collared shirt are replaced with track pants, a black thermal, and a hatless head, with feathered blond hair. His watery brown eyes blink too frequently, taking in my arm in a cast, my face still slightly bruised. At least I'm finally wearing real clothes.

He says, "You're still on your ass?"

"It's not so bad. Wanted to talk about your text."

He steps out onto the porch and pulls the door mostly closed. I gaze through the crack. His fireplace wouldn't seem as warm and compelling if I weren't starting to freeze through my coat, jeans, and leather boots. I wait for him to speak. Around us, the day goes silent, sucking fresh air out of the surrounding winter landscape and stopping the breeze and the ice from melting, drawing sound toward us like an open microphone.

Given a chance for a long conversation about our operations, Carter will suggest firing Davis, who breaks my thoughts with, "I may not understand the finer points of your family's inner workings, but I know ranching."

We stare at each other in the wake of that statement laden with potential reactions, laced with replies. The pause grows heavy, bearing the weight of his perusal and the words I consider saying and don't say. In the silence, snowflakes land on snow, impactful and delicate on the tile roof and frozen ground.

I ask, "You mentioned malfeasance. Are you saying someone is stealing from us, or what exactly are you trying to say?"

"What if Carter and Christa are back at it again? I'm just thinking . . . You know, they could have . . ."

"You keep saying that." If he says it one more time, it's going to be all I can do not to hit him.

"I know this is a strange thing to say. I wanted to talk in person. You had these real estate people stopping in."

"You think my brother's trying to scare me into not selling the ranch?"

"Well . . . I'm not saying . . . I'm just thinking. Things are haywire. Three real estate people came by taking pictures." His mouth works for a long moment before he asks, "To be clear, we are letting Carter take charge?"

I start to say *I am* putting Carter in charge, but instead I say, "My brother has half-ownership and full authority to act as he sees fit in running things."

"Sure," Davis replies. "Maybe explain to me why."

"Why not?"

Davis blinks. "Hear that?"

"What?" I ask—my brow wrinkles.

"Ten thousand head of cattle that aren't there."

I don't know why he's suggesting we ever have an enormous feedlot near the houses. God's truth, he is an enigma—a man who has been loyal to our family and yet also annoying and condescending as fuck.

He says, "Don't be embarrassed. It's easy to be fooled."

"What are you even talking about?" I ask.

Davis widens his stance and puts his hands on his hips. An old-fashioned gunfighter ready to duel it out. "In the last week, Carter has changed every aspect of our operations. He's not my brother. Nothing like Charles Corbett. He's not anything close to the men who ran this ranch. He has no idea what he's taking on. I can't believe you're letting him."

"So this is the conversation you want to have on Christmas." Insulting Carter while offering an explanation about his "brother," imagining himself related to our grandfather because they worked together. I guess I should be mad, but somehow it seems so stupid and pointless in comparison to everything that's gone on in the last few days. Maybe my temper is finally cooling off.

Davis rubs his head. "What other conversation is there? Currently, I have no job at West Creek."

His words draw an ironic urge to laugh because he considers this malfeasance. "Did Carter fire you?"

"It's wrong for him to step in and do things . . . force me out of a job I've had for years. You just gave me a raise." Davis's voice comes out loud and tense.

The door shifts an instant before Waylon pulls it back far enough to peek his head out and ask, "Daddy, you okay?"

Davis holds out a staying hand. "Go back inside."

I get this eerie sense from that wording and his tone, reminding me of the few times I've spent around Davis's boys while they're together—a little unrestrained and bold.

I've missed something stupid-simple, and it's about to bite me.

Everything fades into the background as Waylon emerges from behind the front door holding a sawed-off shotgun.

CHAPTER 29

CARTER

It's Christmas, the first I will spend with my brother in years. My son is beside me, convinced that for his uncle to be happy about being here, we need fancier food than the steaks and potatoes I can cook. I have no other plan.

My phone chirps with a message from Max: *We're stopping at Davis's.*

Huh. Okay. I shove the phone back in my pocket and refocus on Logan, who shuts the refrigerator and stares at me with sad eyes.

Christa's busy with her parents in the great room, and we gave Kay the week off to spend time with her son's family in Missoula.

So I walk into the pantry with Logan following. Institutional-sized cans of green beans share a shelf with endless jars of things

Kay has canned. Can we make what's here into something five-star enough for Max?

Choke me. But all right. If it makes my son and brother happy, I'll try. I grab a box of noodles and a jar of Kay's chili. Logan shakes his head and puts the noodles back. Still, Max's message bugs me. Why would he stop at Davis's now?

I replace the chili on the shelf and nudge Logan's shoulder. "Want to go for a ride?"

He looks up at me with one brow raised. My kid, I swear, he's a bigger joker than I was. Still, I grin at him.

We stop in to let Christa know. Then we head for her old truck. Of course, I let Logan drive because it's our ranch, and he's finally tall enough to reach the pedals. He loves it, and I love watching him do the stuff I used to do.

But as we turn away from the main house toward the ranch's central hub, a sheriff's squad car approaches on the driveway, a meandering road leading to the public road.

Logan looks at me, his mouth a firm line, hands knuckled on the steering wheel, and posture erect—probably afraid he'll get a ticket before he's eight.

I lift my chin. "Pull to the shoulder and put it in park."

A little more timid than before, he does as instructed. We watch the car approach.

It's Norm, a deputy sheriff I grew up with.

"Stay put," I tell Logan and hop out to meet Norm.

He rolls down his window and smacks his gum with an open mouth. The guy loves sunflower seeds but can't eat them in his car because of the mess, so he chews bubblegum instead.

Last time Norm was here, he was arresting me, and I didn't go easily. We killed a guy back in Virginia, maybe they've decided they have more questions. I want to ask, *What brings you by?* Instead, I say, "How've you been?"

He gives the window jamb a light tap. "God knows I could be better."

"Here to pick me up again?" It sounds light and easy.

His brow creases. "I hate how that went down for you and Christa."

"It's fine." A Christa reply if I ever heard one.

"I've been trying to do something about it ever since." He chews, working his jaw muscles double-time. Maybe I should be thanking him for her "lost" journal, but maybe I'm wrong. I don't think he'd be comfortable with that, even if it's due.

Still, I say, "Getting the case thrown out sure was a stroke of luck."

One corner of his mouth raises.

"Sure owe somebody something for that," I say.

He meets my eye and lowers his chin.

"What brings you on Christmas?"

Norm lets out a slow sigh. "Some news, and there's a squad coming up behind me with a warrant."

CHAPTER 30

ELLEN

A SLENDER, tall teenager with shaggy blond hair holds a stubby black shoulder gun.

My heart slams into action. Davis steps toward Max.

I strain forward in the truck staring through the angle between the windshield and the driver's door while attempting to hear over the engine and through the partially unrolled window.

Frigid air wafts into the truck, but I turn the heater down to quiet the fan.

Davis's voice is loud enough that odd words carry, but it's impossible to know what Max is saying. He's facing away from me.

He widens his footing. I'd love to have my pistol now. Still, I shot Kent in the knee, and that ended up with him dead.

I reach for the key to kill the engine's rumbling but stop with my hand near the radio.

I ease the door open.

Max says, "What the hell?"

The young man lifts the gun.

Max takes one step back. I step forward. My stomach is hollow, and the pressure is expanding—I can't breathe. He may pull the trigger. But he moves the gun up, up, up.

He leans it against his shoulder and steps back through the door into the house, vanishing.

The boy might be just beyond the wood or peering through the small glass windows about head height.

I step back and inhale against tight lungs. I may worsen the situation. If I wait, I risk allowing it to worsen on its own. I lean against the rear bumper.

Behind me is the sound of an engine louder than the engine of our truck. At a distance and coming closer, making me turn to the road behind.

A squad car comes into view, lights off, followed by an old pickup and four more cars.

They pull to a painstakingly slow stop. It seems they're double and triple checking things in their cars, preparing to make an iron-clad case. This happens when you consider burying a body in your father's casket. Sometimes, they realize maybe you're guilty after all, and they come after you in another state, or at least that's what's happening to us now.

CHAPTER 31

MAX

EVERY PATROL CAR owned by Pultney County law enforcement may have descended on the ranch this Christmas. Logan's driving Christa's old truck in the second position. Nine cars come up the road behind him. No lights or sirens, but their sheer number is a message.

"Holy smoke." I take a big breath and refocus on Davis. He's got angry kids inside, me pissed off on his porch, and the law barreling up the snow-covered driveway.

He's blinking triple-time and fixed in place by fear or indecision. Never was one to act when it counted. I don't bother telling him not to move before heading toward the approaching officers.

My feet want to kickstart an exit.

Ellen's lips are pursed into a tight line. She's asking what I'm asking. Why are they here? Why now?

I skim her fingers in a light touch, trying to tell her it will be okay. Attempting to appear surer than I am, I head for the lead squad car.

Norm gets out, dressed characteristically in a beige uniform bulky from the ballistic vest underneath, clad with a duty belt and pistol. His hair is gray at the temples, like the job has become more than he can manage.

Carter exits Christa's old truck and comes to my side, leaving Logan frozen statuesque with a stern look.

Around us, officers are pulling out guns and checking ammo clips and grips.

Norm motions us forward, rolling a white paper in his hand, fidgeting.

I plaster a neutral expression on my face and approach. "Must be bad to get you all out here on Christmas."

He rolls the paper into a tube and then straightens it. "We're hoping to get home just as soon as possible."

Carter's annoyed. "Mind finally telling me what's going on?"

"We're here to search the house and arrest Waylon Davis on probable cause for arson at your horse barn."

"What's the evidence?" I ask, still tripping mentally.

"Two witnesses and video surveillance identified a photo of Waylon Davis as the person moving the Davis's horses out of the barn right before the fire started. We noted a threatening post on social media, making the situation urgent. That's all I can say for now."

I step forward, catching Norm's focus and stopping Carter's retort before he gets the first word out. "Waylon's inside. Last I saw, he was holding a sawed-off 20-gauge."

Carter says, "I can't fucking believe it. Waylon? He's just a kid. No way he did this alone."

Norm shakes his head and purses his lips like he wants to say more but won't.

Carter's vehement and gesturing with his hands but is speaking in a low growl. "Davis did this. He lit all the fires with his kid's help and framed Christa. He fucking hates me."

"We're also about to arrest the other two Davises related to the arsons last year," Norm adds.

"You're arresting all of them?" I ask. Even Crick? I want to get all the details, but now isn't the time.

"That's what I said," Norm replies.

Guess I owe Carter another apology and Christa too, but I glance back at the porch. Davis remains where I left him, but how much preparation is happening inside the house? Ellen's leaned against the truck's rear bumper, watching everything with the attentiveness of a general planning a retreat.

"Let us do our job, okay?" Without waiting for a reply, Norm joins the officers huddled around Sheriff Hughley.

Once Norm's out of earshot, Carter mutters, "Because that went so well last time."

He's right, of course. Still, I say, "Maybe it'll be better this time."

Carter gives me a wry grin. "Always the optimist."

I guess that's true in some ways, but I'm still having difficulty seeing how this could go well.

The officers talk low, discussing their approach and not wanting to be overheard.

I motion Ellen toward us. When she's close, I explain what's going on.

She asks, "What about the kid inside with the shotgun?"

"I told them."

She nods and grabs my hand tight. I squeeze back.

Norm makes eye contact with Carter then walks past, leading the men straight up the porch.

They announce themselves as representatives of the Pultney County Sheriff's Office then hand Davis the warrant.

We're too far away to hear what's said. Davis's head tilts. He moves toward the door.

Waylon comes out, a younger version of his father with longer hair and a pissed sneer.

The nearest officer moves in behind and pulls his hands together. He struggles, and the supporting officers cluster closer and get him into restraints without much trouble. He's not strong enough or determined enough to put up a real fight.

They start marching him toward the stairs.

Waylon shrieks, "Well, I ain't hurt nobody."

Carter's face goes slack for a split second before it goes glacier frigid.

I reach for his arm and almost catch him, but it's useless. Even if I tried, it took this whole force to arrest him when they came here before. He didn't go without a fight. Trying to stop him now would go about as well as standing in front of a freight train.

He storms up the porch steps and shoves the officers back.

They're grabbing him, but he's still in Waylon's face yelling, "You fucking punk. Didn't hurt anybody? Did you just say that?"

Waylon lifts his chin, defiant. "Didn't do no more hurt than what's been due and comin'."

Carter's whole frame jolts with the force it takes to keep himself from beating the life out of a boy in handcuffs. "You will shut your fucking mouth, or I will teach you a life lesson your daddy missed."

Davis doesn't move.

But Waylon lurches forward. "My daddy's shit for brains, and there ain't no lesson you can teach me I ain't already figured."

"You're somethin', aren't you?"

Waylon smiles. "All my life, I've listened to him bitch about how dumb you all are while he's makin' me do shit I don't want to do. All we've got to show is a house that ain't ours, a mama who left us, a few good horses, and whatever else we could get."

Carter shakes his head, then gazes at the farm foreman's

house, a place that means a lot to him and our family.

Finally, he steps toward Davis.

A surge of officers follows him.

Ellen puts her hand on my arm. I try to explain without words, but my feet are already moving. Carter's not going to jail for pummeling Davis no matter how much he may want to teach him a lesson that can't be forgotten.

There's a unique joy in the quiet stillness of a family gathered around a Christmas tree. Logan's gifts are opened, and everyone else is fed, tired, and at ease, headed home or preparing to spend a few hours lingering in each other's company. I'm back at the ranch with my brother. Logan is putting together a Lego fort that's proving to be as complex as the engine in my truck. More of his presents, still in packages, are strewn across the floor, scattered around the massive Christmas tree in the same place we once played. Ellen sits beside me on the leather couch with her hand on her belly and our baby on the way.

I imagine my parents might have felt this way years ago, content that life was leading them toward a happy future. The tree still seems the same as it did back then. Huge and cut from the property. We made the clothespin ornaments when we were kids. Mom strung the beaded garland out of acorns we hand-painted. It took about three months to finish because we hated sitting still when the fun was all outside.

Ellen's almost smiling as she watches Logan, her expression soft. She's happy, and another piece of my life feels right.

Carter struts into the house from the patio, owning the place the way he's always been meant to. Christa holds his hand and lifts her chin, placing a soft kiss on his lips. They stop at the hearth near the domed-mouth fireplace to strip off their insulated coats and fur-topped boots.

She holds her hands out to the fire, warming them after being outside and saying their final goodbyes to her parents, aunt, and cousin.

At every family get-together since I've been grown, I've been the one who never entirely belonged. It would still be that way if it weren't for Ellen. I lean down and whisper in her ear, "I love being here with you."

She gives me a small smile and then nestles into my side. Easy contentment settles over me with my fingers splayed against her waist. Her eyes flash to mine then shift to the engagement ring on her hand.

"You didn't even tell me you're getting married." One corner of Carter's mouth lifts—a question and a statement.

"We haven't decided when," I hedge.

She shifts against me, sitting up straighter and focusing on Carter. "You burned my house down and deleted my messages off his phone to break us up." Stress makes her tone a little higher than I'd like. I want to hold her to me, shield her, but she's strong and determined to speak her mind.

Carter blanches—a man cornered between his desire to fix a wrong and avoid making it worse by saying the wrong thing. He looks to Christa for advice. She lifts one shoulder like, "You know what to do."

He raises his eyebrows, shakes his head, and stares at the tree like he's deep in thought.

"You also saved my life and Max's. You're about to be my brother-in-law," Ellen adds.

He apologized to *me* for what he did to her, but he never said it to Ellen. They don't exactly talk. Some of that's my fault for threatening him. It's Christmas, and we were having such an excellent time.

But I know Ellen. She's not trying to stab him with the pointy end of an ice pick. She wants to smooth the path toward healing. She's forcing them to talk, no matter how hard it is.

"I'm honestly ashamed of how all that went," Carter admits. "I'm sorry for hurting you and scaring you. I'd change it if I could, even if it meant Maker's was sold." That's a massive concession from my brother. I hold his gaze.

"You think we can put it behind us?" she asks.

His lips quirk into a half-smile. "I'm alright with it if you are."

"I think we should start over as a family and get to know each other."

"So you're getting married?" Christa asks.

"We are," I say, smiling at my fiancée. I squeeze Ellen's hand as I look into her eyes to be sure she's okay with all this silently asking, "Should we tell them?"

Her eyebrows raise along with one shoulder. She tilts her head and gives me a little nod.

"We're having a baby," I say as the smile inside of me breaks out.

"Holy shit." Carter hoots. "I'm going to need all the details on this."

"Yeah, yeah." I grin. "I also need to tell you something else."

"What now?" He's half laughing, half serious.

What I'm about to say weighs on me, but it's the right thing, at least for now. "I'm moving to New York for a few months," I admit.

"Holy shit," Carter says, his tone a lot less amused. "Watch out, big city."

"Yeah." I crack a grin despite the way my shoulders bunch. At least it's not forever.

Logan walks over, carrying a big box wrapped in green and white paper. He hands it to Ellen. It's a sweet gesture cued by Christa that neither of us expected, thoughtfully welcoming despite our last-minute plans to join them for Christmas.

Carter takes the cue and grabs a couple of other boxes wrapped in colorful paper, bringing one to me and setting a small box in Christa's hands before turning back and pointing an index finger at me.

"Watch out for him," he says to Ellen. "Once he gets an idea, he can be impossible."

"And you're not?"

"You refuse to pull your head out of your ass," he jabs.

"You keep talking to me anyway."

"You never stop listening."

"I guess I don't."

"Still, what a disaster," Christa says. "I feel like I can finally breathe again for the first time in months."

It's a moment we could all tell her how sorry we are, how wrong it must have felt to be accused. I can't quite find the words.

"I've been trying to figure out how my journal became evidence," she adds.

"I've written many things I never meant for anyone else to see," Ellen admits.

Christa offers a bitter smile as her eyes get glassy.

Ellen adds, "I mean . . . I can imagine this will sound strange —or like it's too late, but since we don't know each other very well, I never had a chance to talk to you. But I watched you with Logan. It seemed crazy that you'd have lit the Bowmans' house on fire. I thought they must have gotten something wrong while investigating or that maybe Carter did it, but that didn't make sense either, since he clearly loves you. I can't imagine how hard it must have been for both of you."

"It was hard," Christa says, blandly. "I was investigating the arsons. Everything in my journal was written after the fires. It was so infuriating that they planned to use that against me when I was actually doing their job."

"She was pretty detailed about it. That's just how Christa is." Carter strokes a hand down her back. "Your sunglasses suddenly make a little more sense too," he adds. "Those boys have been in and out of our house since they were kids."

"I don't want to talk about it on Christmas," Christa says, plucking at the bow of the gift in her lap. "I still can't believe they were involved."

We draw a collective breath.

"Why do you think Davis did it?" Ellen asks. It's the question we've all been thinking but not speaking about while Christa's family was here.

Carter leans back against the fireplace, a boot box half-opened on his lap. He crosses one socked foot over his opposite knee. "I guess he was that determined to force me off the ranch."

"Maybe he thought Nonna would give him everything," I speculate. "Davis was constantly in favor with her and Pops. She was upset with us, threatening to do something drastic. He might have seen himself as the best option for West Creek. Maybe he thought she felt that way too."

"Fuck that guy," Carter says.

I smirk because it's exactly how I feel. Each time it seemed like Carter was getting close to assuming a chance he'd always wanted, Davis did something to make him seem untrustworthy. And sometimes Carter did that to himself by doing things that proved Davis's points.

"You think he had something to do with her fall?" Carter asks.

"I don't know." I'm also a little leery of casting judgment without all the information. Davis and his sons are currently attending the holiday festivities in the county jail, and I feel a little conflicted about Crick.

"Maybe we'll never know," he says.

"I've got a forensic accountant showing up on Monday to dig through our books," I add since he should know.

"What a disaster."

"Yeah," I agree, and we don't even know all the facts yet, but the most critical questions have been answered. My brother didn't light the Bowmans' house on fire, and neither did Christa.

"And Waylon?" Christa asks. "I still can't believe it. He loves the horses. He was crying when it seemed we might not be able to get to the last row of stables before the roof caught."

"He's just a dumb kid." Carter strokes her back and then

pulls her to his side. "If Waylon hadn't set the last fire on his own, no one would have known it was them. They might have never been caught."

"Waylon is dumb," Logan says.

Everyone looks at him.

Christa says, "Great point, Moon, but don't call people names. Remember?"

"Uh-huh." The boy returns to his Legos, but it's a reminder that small ears are still listening.

"It's so scary," Ellen says to Christa. "I can't even imagine how hard it would have been being accused wrongly, and the uncertainty . . . You're stronger than me."

"It was terrifying. I was dreading going to court. If they could put me on trial for something so awful and take months with paperwork, what did they have? You know? I was constantly asking myself, 'Who will believe me?' It's made me reconsider my entire life. I'm honestly thinking about starting a foundation for the wrongly accused."

"We probably should," Ellen agrees.

Christa chuckles, but it's a pained effort. As Carter and I drift into a conversation about the ranch, she changes the subject, talking to Ellen about the baby instead. It's like we have family again, and I guess we always did. It's just that families are complex. We know each other's secrets and remember them at their best and worst. Sometimes, the best we can do is to understand that we share more than blood. No rotten chasm has hollowed out our center. We love each other because of our past, which binds us.

When we leave the ranch just before midnight, Ellen embraces Christa and awkwardly hugs my brother—a one-armed squeeze. I shut her inside the cab, and Carter pulls me aside before I get in the truck. "When everything went to hell, she stood by you without flinching. She'll make a great Corbett."

And I know he's right.

CHAPTER 32

ELLEN

A FEW DAYS after the new year, I'm back in Father's building, alternating between sitting in on board meetings, interviewing staff to form a remediation team, and sifting through the aftermath of Father's life.

Max is sitting beside me at the long conference table with a laptop open in front of him. In faded jeans and a flannel shirt open at the collar, exposing the undershirt below, he's a portrait of his everyday self and the kind of man who isn't likely to change what he's wearing just because everyone around him is doing something different. A glass wall shelters us from the bustling cluster of cubicles, chock full of the most experienced environmental experts on the company's payroll. We've both been studying the mining records, attempting to make sense of

Father's record-keeping system entirely on our own. I want to have a handle on the fallout before facing it publicly.

But nothing makes sense.

It's not surprising that Father changed how he treated the fraudulent reports. He probably altered his process because he knew I'd asked Gena to restore my access to his systems after he'd disowned me. What is surprising is that everything seems to be fully compliant. He always used a coding system, tracking which records went with which site. Now, I'm unsure what's going on.

"Are you thinking our only choice is to retest all the mines?" Max asks, pushing his hands against the table to roll out the chair he's been in for the last couple of hours.

"We could, or we might go out there." I point beyond the glass. "We could talk to the people working for the company," I offer.

"You want to?" he asks, focusing on me.

My knee shakes under the table, but I give him a little smile. "I've learned something about keeping secrets and trying to hide from what scares me."

He cocks his head to one side and gives me this soft look that pulls at my heart.

"I can't do it without you," I say, meaning it. "People will say I should have done something before now. They'll say it's my fault. I've let people get hurt by trying to protect my father and myself."

Most of me would like to hide in my bakery and pretend I can run away from this.

Even walking away and letting Adelle take the reins, as Max and I have guessed she might have wanted to do, seems better than walking out of the glass room we're in and admitting everything that's terrifying me.

They'll crucify me.

I'm hit by a physical reaction so strong I get dizzy then break into sweat followed by chills.

Max pulls me into his arms, holding me close. "It's going to be okay, Flynn."

And I want so badly to believe he's right.

It's like he knows how scared I am, because he wraps me up close. I listen to his heartbeat and feel a little better.

"You're being real quiet," he says.

"I'm scared."

"You're going to be scared, but you'll keep going. You'll do the right thing even when no one praises you. You'll do your best, and you'll do it because, eventually, things *will* change. You'll do it because you love yourself enough to stop pretending other peoples' opinions matter more than yours."

"Right." I choke on the word.

"You'll do it because every mistake gives you a little more experience and one more chance to do the next thing a little bit better than you did the last. And you'll do it because if you don't, you will lose yourself to fear."

"Right," I say again, leaning into him as if we could get any closer. "But maybe I'll do it because you believe in me so much that I can't let you down."

"You won't." He's so sure that I start to believe it.

I draw a shaky breath and tilt my chin up as I blink back the heat in my eyes and nose, and then I pull away from him and walk out of the conference room. On my instructions, the department head calls her direct reports for a meeting.

Missing a few due to extended holiday breaks, 22 people stare at me while I explain all the things that terrify me the most. Father taught me that half the battle is about fooling people into thinking you still have the reins, and in a strange way I believe that's as true now as ever. I hold my voice steady and speak as if I trust them not to turn on me when really I'm not entirely sure I wouldn't turn on me were our positions switched.

No one interrupts as I spell out the details of Father's charade, admitting things that reveal my guilt and may eventually incriminate me.

When Ms. Abercrombie, president of our environmental compliance department, suggests I give her a chance to speak, I bob my head in agreement and take a clumsy step backward before Max puts a steadying hand on my hand and pulls me into the seat beside him.

She's in her sixties, with glasses on her nose, short gray hair, dark-blue slacks, and a silk blouse patterned in a Christmasy tartan plaid.

She starts with, "What I want to say first is that it's courageous of Ms. Jasper to bring these concerns to our attention. It seems she's following in her father's footsteps and asking that we step up our compliance efforts. While this will create additional work during the new quarter, I understand the nature of her objective and believe we need leadership willing to address the environmental concerns of our operations head-on, and that's what's happening here. So, I'd like to thank Ms. Jasper for calling us together and having this talk."

Those listening draw in a collective breath and seem to hold it.

She continues, "We all know the importance of accurate record-keeping, and each of you is responsible for some part of that process. I want you all to take what's been said today very seriously. Let's work together and determine the implications of this new information. Report back to—" She stops herself short and turns to me with a question on her brow.

I say, "Please report to Ms. Abercrombie with your findings. She'll brief a team with whatever information you share."

A murmur carries through the room as chairs squeak through the awkward silence.

Ms. Abercrombie dismisses the meeting with instructions to keep this information confidential, limited to those in the room, and to have preliminary reports back by three o'clock, giving them a few hours. She places one hand on the table, crouches near my side, and asks, "Who's on the team?"

"Let's keep it small, just you, me, and Max."

She nods, but a grim expression settles into the lines on her face. She stands and smooths her slacks.

"Thank you," I say, then add, "It's not that I don't want to bring everything into the open eventually. It's simply that I'd like to see what we're up against first."

"Your father came down here unexpectedly one day and conversed with us. The message was similar to this one."

"So he spoke to you about the pollution?"

"Frequently. He'd stop in and complain that he couldn't smoke. He started sneaking candies off one of the intern's desks. Red licorice was his favorite, and after that meeting I had some for him daily. He'd sit in that chair where you're sitting now and talk to us about how we could make things more efficient while eliminating the pollution, completely containing anything we couldn't fully eliminate."

"But why?" I ask. "And when?"

"About a year ago."

I push the chair back, stand, then stop short. It's the kind of moment for which there is no answer. Why didn't he tell me?

Ms. Abercrombie takes a tentative step toward the door.

I thank her, then turn to Max, who remains beside me with a little smile tugging up one corner of his mouth.

"Are you thinking what I'm thinking?" he asks.

"That we should head downstairs and cook something to forget what's going on?" I ask.

"That your dad may have left you something truly worth saving," he says.

My phone pings. I check it and find an internal message from Gena. The press frenzy following Kent's death has been nothing short of traumatic. Combine that with the meeting we just had, and the fallout could be scandalous.

I'm expecting another expert to suggest this is the beginning of the end of things here at Cross Mountain Capital. I wouldn't be surprised if half of those streaming out of the room are headed to their desks to write their resignation letters and pack up family photos.

Except Gena's message says Mr. Elias is downstairs in my office, asking for an impromptu discussion.

I show Max the screen. He nods and stands, stoic as ever.

My stomach becomes increasingly unsettled as we take the elevator toward my office.

Mr. Elias stands beside Gena's desk, engrossed in a conversation about her two boys.

"That's your cue," Gena says as soon as we're in sight. She's always been incredibly efficient.

I lead the way into my office and sit against the top of my desk, gripping the edges with either hand.

Max settles onto one wingback chair while Mr. Elias takes the stiff, modern couch directly in front.

"So, what's happening?" I ask.

Mr. Elias hesitates.

I suck in two shallow breaths through my nose before I realize I won't be able to breathe right until he speaks.

"The matter with Mr. Goodwin has been tendered to the DA, and he's refused the case," Mr. Elias says.

"That's it?" I ask on a whooshing exhale.

"There's a lot more to it than that. The investigators gathered evidence. They spoke to witnesses. They presented a case. That's a lot. It's no small thing and it would have been much worse if the funeral director hadn't corroborated your individual testimonies."

"What about Adelle?" I ask. The police found several similar notes in the file cabinet beside Adelle's desk, and at first I thought it might have been a long-game tactic. Perhaps she was working with Kent and wanted to make me fearful enough that I'd tuck and run back to Wyoming, but the handwriting expert said she didn't write them. Adelle said the notes were innocent, part of a strange game Father used to play, leaving clues for people and taunting them. She's also denied being involved with Kent's arrival at Father's funeral.

"Unofficially, I heard that mentioning Adelle didn't help us," Mr. Elias admits. "She didn't say much, and since there's no evidence that she's involved, I suspect it only extended things a few more days."

"Oh. Well . . . thank you," I say sheepishly. Father may have been fixing his mines, and he may have also been playing games with his longtime secretary.

I shake the thoughts away. My mind is not a safe space.

Mr. Elias takes his feet and moves toward the door. "You've been well served. It could have gone much worse." The way he holds my gaze seems to say, "I hope you've learned a lesson about incriminating yourself."

A pit opens in my stomach. They're arguably some of the most qualified legal minds in the nation, and I have no doubt they've done their best for us. Maybe I'll return to his office begging for help again in a few hours. I hope not.

"Thank you," I say again, as a knot catches in my throat.

I turn to Max and find him already heading toward me and just as quickly gathering me into his arms.

"I think it's all going to be okay," he says, planting a sweet kiss near my ear.

———

Max may be right about everything.

A weight lifts off of my chest along with the idea that Mr. Elias doesn't expect anyone to file charges. And I'm starting to believe Father may have tried to fix things before he died.

I spend the hours after leaving our discussion with Mr. Elias sifting through the contents of Father's residence. Max is downstairs in my apartment, reconnecting with the forensic accountant and digging into their financial records.

It's not that I need to empty Father's apartment for practical reasons. Still, emotionally, I need to know what Father was thinking, and being active is better than staring at reports that seem convincingly accurate or worrying about what the environmental team will say about the mines.

I want to feel right about the little glow I still feel for my father, and I haven't felt that in a long time.

I'm back to the same question rattling around in my head since I returned to New York. How much did Father direct Kent's choices?

Even though Max says it would be okay to let it go, and I have genuinely tried, I haven't been able to sleep hardly at all in the days since this started.

Little reminders Father wrote to himself dot the surfaces around his home. They're just like those I leave around the bakery, my apartment, and my car. A sticky note stuck on his mirror is about doctor's appointments. Tucked into his nightstand drawer are pages of scrawled fears about losing his independence if he were to let the illness progress.

I sit on his old bed. The headboard is one Mom bought from an artist years ago. He hated it but kept it regardless. They were always making little concessions to remain together and I guess that was part of how they showed each other love. I lean against the pillows and read.

On one page, he outlines worries about what it would do to me if he left me with a mess to clean up. Based on the dates, he's known he was sick since before I left for Wyoming.

He learned just before he tore down Mom's old home. Maybe his emotional state back then was partly responsible for how things fell apart between us.

Going through his possessions now that he's gone is painful. All of this happened so quickly, and it comes back to Kent. He came to get me and tried to kill Max.

Could Kent have done something to Father? Part of me wants to blame everything on Kent. It's probably irrational, the product of a daughter who wishes her father wasn't a criminal even when she knows he has done terrible deeds.

Still, Kent managed to trap me inside Father's residence. Two holes mark the plaster near the entry where the keycard reader used to be. Following my instructions, someone removed it while we were in Wyoming, but why did Father let anyone put it inside his home?

Pushing the stack of notes back into Father's nightstand, I scoot off his bed and stand, stretching for a minute. I'm finally learning his real secrets, and Father was far more complex than I even realized.

Maybe I'll head down and see security. I step into the elevator as a confused daughter on her way toward finding answers.

The same security expert who helped us with the hand-writing analysis may know something about the keypad. As I'm entering the basement offices, Max stands in the small room. He's talking to three men on Father's security team about college football, the bowl game match-ups, and the schedule.

"I could get us all tickets," one guy says to Max.

"Maybe we'll still be in town," he replies at the exact moment I push the door far enough open that he has to move back. He catches sight of me, and his face lights up.

"You're still hanging around down here?" I ask, lifting my chin to study his expression.

"These guys are great," he says. "Have you met all of them?"

"Not yet," I admit.

He introduces them as Eric, originally from Boston; Rick from Michigan; and James from the Bronx.

"Nice to meet you all," I say with a smile.

He's down here getting to know them, and I love him so much for it. We're going to need people we can trust to help us, and I never want him to feel like he has to do it all by himself again.

"What are you doing down here?" he asks.

"I was thinking about the keycard reader on Father's door," I offer while trying not to feel embarrassed about how he's managed to befriend people while I've been too afraid to do it myself.

A small crease forms between Max's brows. "You guys know anything about it?" he asks.

"Oh yeah," they all say in unison.

"So my father allowed it?"

"He insisted on it," James says. "We tried to talk him out of it, but only he had the keys to enter or exit his residence."

"Why?"

"We don't know." They genuinely seem clueless.

"When you're in a job like this and someone asks you for something, you don't ask why they want it," Eric says, filling the silence.

Father must have been truly afraid or maybe paranoid, and a lifetime of living with secrets finally made him that way. Or perhaps someone was leaving him notes that made him afraid they were onto him. Or perhaps it was Kent or Adelle. Or both. Who knows?

I tilt my head at Max. He raises his eyebrows.

Would keeping a secret have eventually made us that vulnerable and afraid?

I don't even want to know.

We head upstairs and go into a meeting with Ms. Abercrombie, who confirms that Father started correcting things with all the mines after I left.

The reporting they produce is aligned with the mines. She insists that they would know if anything was amiss. Even as part of me is screaming that they didn't know before, I start to believe this was Father's way of trying to fix what was broken between us, or maybe it genuinely was his conscience that finally got the better of him.

I want a little more closure about what happened between Father and Kent but expect I'll never get it.

"Let's go home," Max says, tugging at my hand as we head out of the small conference room adjacent to Ms. Abercrombie's office.

"Let's do it," I agree. We start down the long hall toward the elevators.

"They're having a second New Year's party at Berty's Saloon," he says. "The first one was so crowded the fire marshal stopped it halfway through."

"Really?" I ask, scrunching my nose. That place wouldn't even hire me when I moved to Wyoming.

"You want to go?" he asks with an evil grin.

I've never set foot in that place.

"Maybe you should open a bar," I offer. "Then I'll go to all the parties."

"Maybe," he says, then runs his thumb over the ring on my finger as he holds my hand.

Within a few hours, we're flying back home.

I rest on the bed in the master suite and tuck into his side as he watches a cooking show on the built-in flat screen. He's making notes on his phone.

"Are you thinking about opening a bar?" I ask.

"I'm thinking about buying Sterling's back from the new owners," he admits.

"You should."

He settles in beside me, staring up at the ceiling.

"What?" I ask.

He turns toward me with a little smile. "Any chance I'll be getting my baker back?"

My heart does a little flip. "I'm ready to be your baker," I offer.

"I love that," Max says. He gives me a long look, then tugs me into his shoulder so my back is against his chest, whispering into my hair. "Honestly, Flynn. A few things are more important to me than owning a restaurant."

I start to draw away from him to read his expression, but he holds me close and squeezes my waist.

"Buying Sterling's back or opening a bar or anything like that would take too much of my time."

"Okay," I say softly. "You've been conflicted about everything since your grandmother passed away and left you in charge of the ranch. I get it. Having Father bequeath me his company, I can relate to where you're coming from. Maybe you need to take some time and think about it."

He turns, readjusting so we face each other, then says, "I want to build our life the way we want it."

A smile grows inside me and breaks across my face. "Okay."

"I could build you that plantation-style house you've always wanted. We might pick a spot out at the ranch and put it there. That'll take some time. I want to be around a lot with our baby, and you'll need help at the bakery. I can fill in or help us find the right people to take on whatever needs to be done. Carter will want me around the ranch."

"Okay," I repeat as joy bubbles up inside me.

"I think I'm about to have everything I've ever wanted," he says.

CHAPTER 33

MAX

IN EARLY FEBRUARY, I stand in a small chapel in my hometown where my parents were married.

Despite all we've been through, life is better than it's ever been.

My arm is out of the cast. We're sorting out what happened with Davis and his sons, pending a new arson trial scheduled for May. A forensic accountant has spent hours combing through our records, and Davis was responsible for a fair amount of malfeasance after Pops died. Nonna and I weren't up for the challenge or as invested as we should have been, and Davis saw an opening.

A ranch like West Creek needs an owner with passion and brains, and Carter has that in spades. He would have fired Davis from a job that kept becoming more lucrative.

Carter stands beside me. Half the county has shown up on short notice, putting on a show in their best duds and coming through with food, cake, and flowers, overflowing into the foyer and propping the doors open for air despite the frigid weather.

While I have to admit I've made a mess of it at times, trusting the wrong people, I'm alright with having been wrong. I've finally agreed with Carter that I might actually be the luckiest one—his little brother, the golden boy. I never really appreciated what I had until it was coming apart around me.

Babs comes into view at the end of the aisle as maid of honor and sends us a knowing grin.

I seek a glimpse of Ellen without seeing her.

Carter leans toward me. Amusement raises the corners of his mouth. "Never thought I'd see this day."

He's a wise-ass, but I wouldn't change him either. I nudge him with my elbow. "Keep it up."

"We'll be brawling on the floor before she gets out here."

I smirk. "Christa and Ellen will be trying to pull us apart."

We're both trying not to laugh as the local band plays the opening notes of "Here Comes the Bride" with instruments and original vocals.

Babs starts down the aisle wearing a floor-length magenta dress. It's a shade lighter than her hair.

Ellen comes into view wearing an elegant white gown with a sleek waist and a low-cut bodice. The crowd focuses entirely on her. White flowers grace her hair. My breath stalls. She wanted this now because of the baby, and we both wanted it because we spent so long worrying we might never have this chance.

She walks alone.

With her father gone, there's a void beside her and inside her.

But everything about the moment is right.

When she reaches the altar, the same minister who married Carter and Christa starts his part in his rodeo announcer voice.

Ellen grins at me and raises her eyebrows.

I grin back because this is the family she's signing up for.

Her hazel eyes sparkle, and I'll be forever awed that this is what she wants when she could have so much more.

We each say, "All I'm worth is this vow I make to you, to stand by your side just like you have remained beside me."

The minister blesses our marriage with, "You may now kiss the bride."

Nobody needs to tell me twice.

***

Wondering what the Davises were thinking when they started all the homestead fires?

Read on for a bonus scene, with Crick Davis, a young cowboy in a world of hurt! Who does he call when he's trying to find his way out?

Looking for more West Creek Ranch stories?

Keep an eye out for ALL THAT GLITTERS, a West Creek Ranch Stand-Alone. A swoon-worthy friends to lovers story, featuring Abner, Skyler, and Andrew. I hope you will enjoy reading about these childhood friends as much as I loved writing about them.

***

If you want news about the West Creek Ranch series and more free bonuses, you can join my newsletter at: https://subscribepage.io/XW6lGf

Or follow me on Amazon at: https://amazon.com/author/sage-evans

Linktr.ee

BONUS SCENE

CRICK

The round-bellied officer who drove me here nudges a chair away from the desk-size table in the center of the room using his dusty boot. "Have a seat."

I stand stock-still. Following stupid instructions is precisely what got me into this mess.

"Take a seat," he says, crossing his arms as he leans against the wall. It's a closet-sized space with scuffed white walls and a single door with mirror glass. Two cameras in domes are mounted on the ceiling. They probably have microphones everywhere recording everything.

The officer coughs a little hoarsely then snorts and blows his nose.

He's the same guy who talked to Waylon last year after he tried to break into the bank by crashing his old truck into the brick wall. But nobody knew that's what Waylon was doing. He managed to lie his way out, just like Daddy will skate through this.

I sit in the chair. The cold metal comes through my jeans and cotton shirt. I tense my abs to keep my knee from shaking the table and let my hands hang limp at my sides.

The interrogation room door swings open.

A woman walks in—not much more than a girl—in her twenties with short brown hair, dark pants, and a tan shirt. She smiles at me, a little like she wants something. My leg gets more jittery.

The officer remains leaning against the wall.

The lady sits across from me at the table, sets her yellow pad in front of her, and says, "Christopher Davis, I'm Detective Delmonico. I've been assigned to your case."

"Pleased to meet you, ma'am. You can call me Crick." There's a reason they call me Crick, short for Cricket. I've always hated being still. I cross my ankles over each other under the chair.

"Okay, Crick," she says my name like it's embarrassing. "You have the right to remain silent. That means you do not have to say anything." Somewhere along the way, she switches to a teacher's tone.

I nod. My goal here is to tell them as little as I can so they'll put me in a cell and leave me alone. Then I can figure out what to do next.

"Anything you say can be used against you in court. You have the right to get help from a lawyer right now. If you cannot pay a lawyer, the court will get you one for free. Do you want a lawyer to be here with you while you talk to me?"

"I guess I'm alright."

"You have the right to have one or both of your parents here. Do you want your mother, father, or the person who takes care of you here while you talk to me?"

"I reckon I'll be better off on my own."

"Is there anyone you'd like to call?"

"Doubt anyone would help me now."

"You have the right to stop this interview at any time. Do you want to talk to me?"

"I don't have a choice, do I?"

"You don't have to say anything. I can ask you questions, and you can choose not to answer or ask me to stop at any time."

"Okay."

"Can you explain what I've said in your own words?"

"I don't have to say anything if I don't want to, and I can stop talking, but I can't leave, can I?"

"I'm afraid not. If you want to talk to me, please sign this form. It's a juvenile Miranda acknowledgment and rights waiver covering our discussion."

I sign my name at the bottom, and she retrieves the paper and the pen.

"What's your favorite winter activity?" she asks.

"Can we not talk about things you don't want to know?"

"Sure. I do want to know you though, Crick. I appreciate you being honest about not wanting to talk about your everyday life. It's important that you're truthful during this interview."

"Okay. So ask me something."

"Why light the horse barn on fire?"

"Ask Waylon," I reply. That stupid shit was all him.

I try to keep my unconcerned expression in place as she thinks up the next question.

"I want to know what you think," she says.

"Not sure what to think."

"Tell me about your father."

I give my standard reply, flat and monotone. "My bosshole is an arrogant, condescending knob, but I'm suffering through the next eight months because I would be no one without him. But you're not supposed to know that. Don't let on."

"You want to stay here?" She sounds unamused.

"This primary-colored kindergarten jail is fine." The truth is, I'd love to go live with my mother. When Mama left us, she waved. She looked back and waved again, and she smiled. That made me laugh because I thought she was coming back. Then she honked twice and left for good.

A trickle starts running down my nose. I lift my hand to wipe it away but stop short and sniff.

"So you're a *smart* guy?" she asks.

"Might not be the smartest one."

"You get good grades though. Do you want to go to college?"

"Don't worry about that."

"Why don't you just talk to me? You know why you're here. Tell me what happened."

Perhaps I say a stupid thing or two, which is entirely predictable. I'm more like Mama than Daddy. Every once in a while, I get myself into trouble because of this.

"Why target the Bowmans?" the officer asks next.

"I don't know." I'm a high school senior. I sell a little pot that I grow myself. I didn't target anybody. All I did was rewire a heater and set it up in a greenhouse.

"You have two choices." She draws a line down the middle of the page, then she writes something. She turns the paper around and points at the words as she talks. "We can make a case against you for lighting the Bowmans's home on fire. You will remain in detention unless you can make bail. It may take a year or more."

"Wait a minute. That's all wrong."

"What's wrong?" she asks.

"Just that. What you said isn't quite right." I didn't light anybody's home on fire.

She moves her pencil over to the second column. "Option two, you cooperate, talk to us, offer a plea, serve your sentence, and move on with your life."

"You want me to do what, exactly?" I ask.

She slides out a single yellow page, Waylon's handwriting scrawled across it. "This is your brother's statement. Waylon says you handled the Bowmans."

Now . . . that's not exactly what happened.

My heart hammers. I bite down a cuss. I would cuss if a lady wasn't present. I can't go on trial the way Christa's been on trial.

I skim Waylon's messy handwriting upside down and catch enough words to see that Waylon's told the truth about everything except what he did. Before I get it all read, Ms. Delmonico slides it under her notepad.

"Are you ready to cooperate?" she asks.

"What did Waylon say about Daddy?" I ask. It was Daddy's plan to begin with. He took it a little personal how much Carter hated the homesteaders—he was giggin' mad every time Carter griped about other people buying their land while he was busting his ass to make the place into a showcase, all while we were working just as hard and getting a lot less for it. Daddy never thought much of Carter at all, and Daddy said Mrs. Corbett didn't think much of Carter either.

"I need to hear your version of the events," Detective Delmonico says.

All I did was set up a heater in a greenhouse at the Masseys' then went with Waylon to the Bowmans' while Daddy started two other fires. All Waylon was supposed to do was catch the Bowmans's woodshed, but he decided lighting their house would be a lot more fun. And if I say my brother is lying, how will they know who's telling the truth?

"Maybe I'd better make that phone call," I finally say, unsure who I'll call.

Do you want to know who Crick calls? Do you have any guesses? I'd love to hear from you. I'm seriously considering writing Crick's story, and your thoughts will go a long way toward this next project. There's a survey on my website's extras page. https://sageevans.com/extras/

Let me know what you'd like to see coming your way next!

Did you enjoy reading this book?

If so, I'd appreciate it very much if you wrote an honest review.

Anywhere you post the review will help spread the word about this book's release. But I will appreciate an Amazon review. Here's the direct link: https://a.co/d/9sS4tjc

Thanks! I really appreciate it!

Sage

ACKNOWLEDGMENTS

This book wouldn't be what it is without the early readers, critique partners, and editors who helped me build it into something more. A few of you read my various attempts at writing the beginning. Thank you for sticking with me through that process. I couldn't have made it half this good without your help.

Thank you to Caroline Leavitt, a critically acclaimed novelist and a fantastic manuscript editor who helped me bring this story together with her direct criticism and encouragement.

Thank you to Kelly Siskind. You have been a fantastic ally and are still one of my favorite authors.

Thank you to my husband for supporting me patiently and believing in me through all the ups and downs of publishing.

I am awed by the readers who have picked up my books and taken a chance on a new author. I will be forever grateful to those of you who left the first reviews and helped spread the word about the West Creek Ranch Series books.

Thank you so much to everyone who reads, reviews, buys, borrows, lends, and posts about my books. You will always be the reason I write.

A NOTE ABOUT THE AUTHOR

Sage Evans lives in a tiny Colorado town—so small there is no stoplight. Everyone knows everyone, and if she's not running with her dogs, shoveling snow, or mowing a lawn, she's buried in a book or restoring classic cars and attending hot rod shows with her very own small-town hero hotty.

Sign up for Sage's newsletter at www.sageevans.com for freebies and insider news. And connect with her on Instagram and Facebook (@sageevansromance).

https://subscribepage.io/XW6lGf

https://amazon.com/author/sage-evans

https://www.bookbub.com/profile/sage-evans

linktr.ee/sageevansromance

www.ingramcontent.com/pod-product-compliance
Lightning Source LLC
Chambersburg PA
CBHW061234310726
48971CB00007B/2054